P9-DCC-762

Praise for the Bestselling
Tea Shop Mysteries
by Laura Childs

Featured Selection of the Mystery Book Club
"Highly recommended" by The Ladies' Tea Guild

"You'll be starved by the end and ready to try out the recipes in the back of the book . . . Enjoy!"
—*The Charlotte Observer*

"A page-turner." —*St. Paul Pioneer Press*

"Tea lovers, mystery lovers, [this] is for you. Just the right blend of cozy fun and clever plotting."
—Susan Wittig Albert, national bestselling author of *Spanish Dagger*

"Delightful" —*Tea: A Magazine*

"The luscious descriptions of Lowcountry cuisine will make your mouth water." —*Publishers Weekly*

"Engages the audience from the start . . . The right combination between tidbits on tea and an amateur-sleuth cozy."
—*Midwest Book Review . . .*

continued. . .

DRAGONWELL DEAD

Tea Shop Mystery #8

LAURA CHILDS

BERKLEY PRIME CRIME, NEW YORK

THE BERKLEY PUBLISHING GROUP
Published by the Penguin Group
Penguin Group (USA) Inc.
375 Hudson Street, New York, New York 10014, USA
Penguin Group (Canada), 90 Eglinton Avenue East, Suite 700, Toronto, Ontario M4P 2Y3, Canada
(a division of Pearson Penguin Canada Inc.)
Penguin Books Ltd., 80 Strand, London WC2R 0RL, England
Penguin Group Ireland, 25 St. Stephen's Green, Dublin 2, Ireland (a division of Penguin Books Ltd.)
Penguin Group (Australia), 250 Camberwell Road, Camberwell, Victoria 3124, Australia
(a division of Pearson Australia Group Pty. Ltd.)
Penguin Books India Pvt. Ltd., 11 Community Centre, Panchsheel Park, New Delhi—110 017, India
Penguin Group (NZ), 67 Apollo Drive, Rosedale, North Shore 0632, New Zealand
(a division of Pearson New Zealand Ltd.)
Penguin Books (South Africa) (Pty.) Ltd., 24 Sturdee Avenue, Rosebank, Johannesburg 2196,
South Africa

Penguin Books Ltd., Registered Offices: 80 Strand, London WC2R 0RL, England

This is a work of fiction. Names, characters, places, and incidents either are the product of the author's imagination or are used fictitiously, and any resemblance to actual persons, living or dead, business establishments, events, or locales is entirely coincidental. The publisher does not have any control over and does not assume any responsibility for author or third-party websites or their content.

PUBLISHER'S NOTE: The recipes contained in this book are to be followed exactly as written. The publisher is not responsible for your specific health or allergy needs that may require medical supervision. The publisher is not responsible for any adverse reactions to the recipes contained in this book.

DRAGONWELL DEAD

A Berkley Prime Crime Book / published by arrangement with the author

PRINTING HISTORY
Berkley Prime Crime hardcover edition / March 2007
Berkley Prime Crime mass-market edition / March 2008

Copyright © 2007 by Gerry Schmitt & Associates, Inc.
Cover art by Stephanie Henderson.
Cover design by Lesley Worrell.

ISBN: 978-0-425-22045-0

BERKLEY® PRIME CRIME
Berkley Prime Crime Books are published by The Berkley Publishing Group,
a division of Penguin Group (USA) Inc.,
375 Hudson Street, New York, New York 10014.
The name BERKLEY PRIME CRIME and the BERKLEY PRIME CRIME design
are trademarks belonging to Penguin Group (USA) Inc.

PRINTED IN THE UNITED STATES OF AMERICA

10 9 8 7 6 5 4

Most Berkley Books are available at special quantity discounts for bulk purchases for sales, promotions, premiums, fund-raising, or educational use. Special books, or book excerpts, can also be created to fit specific needs.

For details, write: Special Markets, The Berkley Publishing Group, 375 Hudson Street, New York, New York 10014.

This book is dedicated to Tickle Bee.

ACKNOWLEDGMENTS

Many thanks to Sam, Samantha, Bob, and Jennie. And to the many booksellers and tea shops who have not only carried my mysteries but recommended them. This whole crazy process—writing, marketing, selling—is so very much a contact sport.

1

❧

Theodosia Browning stared at the fluttering green wall in front of her and frowned. She'd taken what she thought was the correct turn and still hit a dead end!

Biting her lower lip, Theodosia pushed back a swirl of thick auburn hair and considered the English hedge maze that surrounded her. It certainly hadn't *looked* difficult when she and Drayton had wandered in on a lark some twenty minutes earlier. Yet here she was, confounded by this twelve-foot-high ivy maze that twisted and turned in all directions and held them unwilling captives on the grounds of Carthage Place Plantation.

Birds twittered overhead, an insect droned in her ear. And Theodosia could distinctly hear the laughter of guests floating above her. Pushing up the sleeves of her cream-colored cashmere sweater, Theodosia's broad, intelligent face, with its peaches-and-cream complexion and intense blue eyes, settled into a perplexed yet slightly bemused look. Here she was, stuck in a puzzle maze when hundreds of guests wandered about freely so very close by.

"Any luck?" asked Drayton as he came panting up behind her. Drayton, who was sixtyish and dapper, had tagged along with Theodosia today, happy to partake in the annual Plantation Ramble out here on Ashley River Road. This was the spring weekend when a half dozen privately owned plantations threw open their doors to the public and invited local church and civic groups onto their grounds to host teas, flower shows, and rare plant auctions. This was also the weekend the camellias, jasmine, magnolias, and almost every other species of South Carolina flora and fauna were in full and glorious bloom.

"Another wrong turn," Theodosia told Drayton. "Sorry."

"Not your fault," said Drayton, tilting his patrician gray head back to survey their leafy prison. "I thought it would be child's play to wander through this old labyrinth." He paused, as though pondering his words. "Obviously I was wrong."

"What time is the rare plant auction?" Theodosia asked him.

"Three o'clock sharp," said Drayton. He glanced at the ancient Patek Philippe that graced his wrist and grimaced. "Which means I have barely ten minutes to figure out some sort of escape route. If I miss a chance to bid on a Cockleshell Orchid or even a Machu Picchu, I'll never forgive myself!"

"I got you into this," said Theodosia, trying to keep her game face on. "So I'm going to get you out."

"And how do you propose to do that?" asked Drayton, curiosity evident in his voice. After all, he hadn't figured a way out either.

Theodosia lifted her chin and let the warm afternoon sun caress her face. "We're going to follow the basic tenets of any seasoned explorer," she told Drayton.

"Which is?" he asked, cocking his head sideways.

"Navigate by the sun."

"Ahh . . ." said Drayton.

"And," said Theodosia, holding up an index finger, "I propose we use your watch as a compass."

"Like they did in Civil War times!" said Drayton excitedly. "Well, aren't you the clever one." He pushed up his shirtsleeve, anxious to give Theodosia's suggestion a try. "Since we know the sun is in the southwestern quadrant of the sky, we'll say southwest is somewhere between eleven and twelve." Drayton made a couple mumbled calculations. "So west is at one o'clock . . ."

"And east is at seven," finished Theodosia.

Drayton's face split into an eager grin. "I should have figured this out myself."

Two dozen twists and turns later, they came upon a black wrought-iron grate set into the green turf.

"We passed this before," said Theodosia.

"Indeed we did," agreed Drayton. "I remember hearing the faint sound of running water."

Theodosia leaned forward and peered down into the grate, but could see only darkness. "Must be an old well or cistern," she mused as a low gurgling echoed in her ears.

"There used to be thousands of acres of rice fields around here," said Drayton as they stepped around the grate. "With a very complicated series of rice dikes. So this is probably part of the old drainage system. After all, the Ashley River is just a mile or so over."

"Had to be part of it," said Theodosia. Back in the middle 1800s this entire area had served as the world's leading producer of rice. Fine Carolina gold, as it was called, was sent out on clipper ships to countries all across the globe.

They rounded the next turn and stopped in their tracks.

"Well, I'll be," exclaimed Drayton, a slow smile spreading across his lined face.

"Success," breathed Theodosia.

Not quite ten feet away was the entrance—or, in this case, exit—to the maze. A wrought-iron arch looped above a most welcome six-foot-wide gap in the hedge of ivy. The ornate scrollwork of the arch made it a companion piece, almost, to the grate they had inspected earlier.

"Good work," Drayton told Theodosia, as he consulted his watch a final time. "And we made it with two minutes to spare."

"Better hurry," Theodosia urged as Drayton hustled off. Just down the hill she saw that a large wooden stage had been erected specifically for this event. And crowds of eager bidders were jostling about, surveying plant-covered tables even as they jockeyed for a position on the semicircle of folding chairs that spread out around the stage.

"Where on earth did *you* run off to?" demanded the imperious voice of Delaine Dish. Attired in a flouncy white eyelet dress and large straw hat, Delaine stood poised behind a whitewashed tea stand that was festively strung with white twinkle lights and floral garlands.

"Long story," Theodosia told her friend tiredly as she slipped into the booth.

"Here," said Delaine, holding out a tall, frosty glass garnished with a fresh sprig of mint. "Your tea is quite excellent, but we're woefully short on pitchers." Consternation showed in Delaine's violet eyes and on her flawless heart-shaped face.

Theodosia accepted the glass of sweet tea and took a sip. It was excellent, of course. Drayton, as master tea blender and clever visionary of all things tea at the Indigo Tea Shop, had invented this sweet tea recipe on the spur of the moment. In this particular instance, Drayton had combined delicately flavored Dragonwell green tea from China's Chekiang Province with fresh-squeezed lemon juice and locally grown honey. And each glass served today was accented with the customer's choice of fresh mint leaves, sprigs of lemon balm, or small stems of edible flowers.

"So you've been busy?" asked Theodosia. Probably, she decided, Delaine had been kept hopping. The day was warm, the event well attended, and sweet tea was always a major crowd pleaser.

"You don't know the half of it." Delaine sighed dramatically. "I could *really* use another pair of hands here. And these dinky little pitchers and teapots . . ." She indicated the teapots that sat on the counter, then made a most unbecoming face. "I have to keep *filling* them up."

"I brought the largest ones we had," Theodosia told her. As proprietor of the Indigo Tea Shop in Charleston's historic district, Theodosia was used to scooting around her tea room with an elegant bone china teapot clutched in each hand. Perfect, of course, for refilling customers' dainty cups, but probably not so suitable for the Plantation Ramble where everyone was hot and thirsty and expected a tall, cold glass of tea.

"While you and Drayton have been wandering through these lovely gardens," sniffed Delaine, "I've been working my fingers to the *bone*." She held up her hands and wiggled her fingers as if to confirm her statement. "I've been pretty much stuck here when all I *really* want to do is visit the build-your-own-bouquet stand before all the prettiest flowers are snapped up."

"Sorry," said Theodosia, even though she wasn't all *that* sorry. Earlier today, she and Drayton had given up several hours of their time to help set up this tea stand as a favor to the Broad Street Garden Club. Delaine, as vice president of that club, had decreed that the club maintain a "formidable presence" at today's Plantation Ramble. Of course, Delaine had also volunteered Theodosia and Drayton to prepare the gallons of iced tea, known throughout the Southern states as sweet tea.

Now, the members of the Broad Street Garden Club were nowhere to be found and Delaine was upset that the task of manning the booth had fallen to her.

Delaine's unhappiness suddenly morphed into sweetness and light as two customers approached the booth, eager for tall glasses of sweet tea. "Sweet tea?" she asked pleasantly. "And how about a lovely garnish of edible violets?" She turned toward Theodosia with a proprietary flourish. "Do we have more flowers and herbs?"

"Sure thing," said Theodosia, popping the lid off a plastic container and fishing out a tangle of greenery.

"There you go," said Delaine, as she sent her customers on their way, then gazed off, studying her surroundings. "Isn't Carthage Place Plantation an absolute wonder?" she asked. "Wouldn't you just adore *living* out here?"

"It is beautiful," admitted Theodosia. Even though she loved this lush, wooded country, she herself lived in a cozy upstairs apartment over her tea shop on Church Street, smack-dab in the middle of historic Charleston. With her dog, Earl Grey, as roommate.

Seemingly in a good mood now, Delaine continued to rhapsodize. "Besides the spectacular old plantation house and that adorable English maze, there's also a rose garden, water bog, and english garden. Really, this place is just too Old World and gracious for words!"

Theodosia's eyes traveled about the plantation grounds. They were, as Delaine said, quite lovely and gracious. Spread out from an enormous Georgian-style home with hipped roof and elegant columns was the undulating green of impeccably manicured grounds broken up by numerous flower beds, gardens, and fountains. And today, of course, dozens of food tents and flower stands as well. Past the main house and a half dozen wooden outbuildings, a hardwood forest rose up to form a dramatic backdrop.

"Well, look who's here!" cried Delaine. Grabbing a pair of white gloves that were lying nearby, she quickly pulled them on and waved vigorously. "Hello, Bobby Wayne!" she called delightedly, then cocked her head and did everything but flutter her eyelashes.

"Hey, sweetie!" Bobby Wayne Loveday, round of both face and form, looking natty in a cream-colored summer suit, gave a hearty wave back at her.

"Theo, darling," said Delaine, grabbing for Bobby Wayne's arm and reeling him in possessively. "Do you know Bobby Wayne Loveday? He's the senior partner at Loveday and Luxor. You know, Charleston's most prestigious commodity firm?"

"Of course, I know Bobby Wayne," said Theodosia, favoring him with a warm smile. "We catered a tea awhile back for one of your retiring partners."

"Wonderful to see you again," said Bobby Wayne. A friendly grin lit his broad face as he put an arm around Theodosia's shoulder and gave her a quick squeeze.

"And here's Angie and Mark Congdon, too," squealed Delaine. "Talk about old home week." Delaine's tinkling laughter filled the air. "Isn't this great fun?"

"Actually," explained Bobby Wayne, "I talked them into driving out with us. Mark works at our firm now," he said as an aside to Theodosia. "Has for some time."

"I heard Mark was back in the commodities business," replied Theodosia. "Well, you certainly couldn't find a better, more qualified man."

"Please," said a slightly embarrassed Mark.

"Our firm wholeheartedly agrees," said Bobby Wayne. "We believe that Mark will soon become one of our top-producing brokers."

Mark and his wife, Angie Congdon, had both worked as commodity brokers in Chicago several years ago. But they'd given up those careers and moved to Charleston to run the Featherbed House Bed & Breakfast, just blocks away from Theodosia's tea shop. A few months ago, however, Mark had gotten the itch to jump back into the business. So now Angie was managing the Featherbed House with the help of a new assistant.

"What on earth have you got there?" asked Delaine, gazing at a sparkling object clutched in Angie's hand.

"Oh," said Angie, "we just picked these up at the Graphicus Art Booth. There's a bunch of artists there who are hand-painting stemware in all sorts of fun designs." She held her glass up. "See? I got daisies. And, look, Mark got one with a purple orchid and Bobby Wayne chose a golden leopard pattern. All the proceeds go to support children's art programs," Angie added.

"What a terrific idea," commented Theodosia. "And they're painting stemware right there? At the booth?"

"Using some new kind of acrylic magic markers," said Angie.

"Wish we could get that kind of teamwork going here," commented Delaine.

Angie suddenly picked up on Delaine's unhappiness. "Do you want me to help out?" she asked. "Because I sure will." Besides being a dynamo, Angie was wonderful with people. With her perpetually smiling face and dark hair cut into a no-nonsense bob, she was always ready to jump in and tackle any task.

"Well, maybe," allowed Delaine. "If it gets real busy."

"I think most folks are over at the auction right now," said Mark, glancing about.

"Then let's all of us go over and watch," urged Delaine, turning her focus back to Bobby Wayne. "Besides, Bobby Wayne, you promised to bid on one of those fancy orchids for me."

"A rare flower for my sweet flower," said Bobby Wayne, setting his glass down and putting a hand to Delaine's cheek.

"We're going to leave the stand unattended?" asked Theodosia. *Could we do that? Should we do that?* she wondered. *And why am I always the one to worry about this kind of stuff?*

Delaine pulled her lips into a pout. "Is there a *problem*? Honestly, I've been slogging away at this booth for almost half an hour. I really need a break." She glanced at Angie and Mark. "Just leave your stuff here and let's *go*." She caught Theodosia's eye and raised her eyebrows in a questioning gesture. "Okay?"

"Okay," agreed Theodosia. This wasn't her stand after all. She'd just helped nail it together and donated the sweet tea. And if they left it for a half hour or so it wasn't going to just walk away. "Let's go watch the auction. But I'm positive it's already started."

"Oh, it has," said Bobby Wayne. "I can hear the auctioneer's chatter over the loudspeakers."

"Might not be any seats left," said Theodosia when they got close to the auction stage. The bidding was in full swing and the auctioneer, a tall, lanky man in a pristine white suit, was stirring up the crowd that was seated on folding chairs and benches, as well as all the people who milled about clutching their bidding numbers.

"Look, Drayton's waving at us," said Angie. "I think he might have saved a couple places."

"You ladies go up front with Drayton," urged Mark Congdon. "I want to get a closer look at the orchids on display. I've been wanting to get my hands on a few more for my collection and this could be my chance."

"Hurry up," called Drayton as he motioned Theodosia, Delaine, and Angie to come forward and grab a seat.

"How's it going?" asked Theodosia, sliding in next to him.

"I've already bought a *Dracula bella* and a Debutante, one of the Odontonia hybrids. Don't really need the little beauties, but they're always a delight to have."

"Typical orchid fanatic," Angie said with a laugh. "Mark's the same way. Always on the lookout for the next exotic flower."

"I take it he's got quite a collection?" asked Delaine.

"Let's just say there are more than fifty." Angie laughed again.

"Oh, good heavens," said Drayton, dropping his voice in awe. "Do you see what's coming up next?"

"What?" asked Delaine, squinting at the stage. *"What?"*

"A monkey-face orchid," said Drayton. "Technically a *Platanthera integrilabia.*"

"That's rare?" asked Theodosia. She knew nothing about orchids except that she enjoyed looking at them.

"Extremely rare," replied Drayton. He was jittery now, waiting for the auctioneer in the white suit to start the bidding again.

"This will go high?" asked Delaine, sounding slightly bored.

"Let's hope not," said Drayton, fidgeting in his seat. "Oh, how I'd love to get this one and enter it in next Saturday's Orchid Lights show. If I repotted the monkey-face in my Chinese oxblood pot, there might be a chance to earn a blue ribbon!"

The auctioneer's assistant placed the elegant monkey-face orchid on the podium for all to see. Instantly a buzz ran through the crowd. These were South Carolina plant lovers and they knew their stuff.

"We shall start the bidding at two hundred," announced the auctioneer.

"Dollars?" asked a stunned Delaine.

Drayton's bidding number shot up.

"Do I have two-fifty?" asked the auctioneer, imperiously surveying the crowd.

Five rows back another sign was raised.

"Three hundred?" asked the auctioneer. His sharp, darting eyes surveyed the crowd. "It's got best of show written all over it."

Drayton hesitated for a mere moment, then his sign went up again. "See," he whispered to Theodosia. "Best of show."

An intense murmuring rose in the audience. This was a very rare plant and the bidding was likely to become increasingly heated.

"Do I have three-fifty?" asked the auctioneer. His sharp eyes sought out the bidders at the back of the crowd, then he bobbed his head, pleased. He obviously had three-fifty.

Both Theodosia and Angie swiveled in their seats to see who else was bidding.

"Oh, good heavens," whispered Angie. "Mark's bidding against Drayton."

Theodosia nudged Drayton with her elbow. "Did you hear that?" she asked. "Mark's bidding, too."

"Are you serious?" said Drayton. "Mark is? Well, then . . ." He hesitated for a moment, then set his sign down in his lap. "That settles it," he said, pursing his lips. "I don't want to bid against Mark. Let him have the orchid."

"Do I hear four hundred?" asked the auctioneer, a sly, encouraging note in his voice.

There was a pause, then the auctioneer gave a brisk nod. "Yes, indeed, I have four hundred."

"Someone else is bidding," whispered Theodosia.

"Who?" asked Drayton.

Now Theodosia and Drayton both swiveled in their seats to see if they could determine who was bidding against Mark Congdon.

"Rats," muttered Drayton, catching sight of the other bidder who'd entered the fray. "It's Harlan Noble."

"The rare-book dealer?" asked Theodosia.

"The very one," said Drayton. "Let's hope Mark brought his checkbook."

But in the end, it turned out that Mark Congdon was high bidder. With a rather breathtaking final bid of nine hundred dollars.

"Hmm," said Delaine, as they all rose at the break. "That's a big pile of money for such a dinky little flower."

"But well worth it," Drayton assured her.

"I thought for sure you'd hang in there, Drayton," said a flat voice at his elbow.

"Mr. Noble," said Drayton, turning to look at the man who'd just spoken to him. "One could say the same about you."

"Unfortunately not," said Harlan Noble. And this time he sounded upset.

"I didn't realize you were an orchid hobbyist," said Theodosia, looking at the tall, dark-eyed, slightly beak-nosed man. She only knew Harlan Noble enough to say a distantly polite hello to him. He was a member of the Heritage Society and he might have come into the Indigo Tea Shop a year or so ago, but that was it. All she really knew about him was he owned a rare-book shop over on King Street and he specialized in Southern writers and Civil War literature.

"Orchids aren't just a *hobby*," said Harlan Noble, seeming to spit out his words in anger. "Like ship models or mummified butterflies. Orchids happen to be my absolute passion!" And with that he bolted off into the crowd.

"Well," said a slightly stunned Angie, "I guess it's no secret how Mr. Noble feels. I just hope he's not too put out with Mark."

"Somehow," said Theodosia, "I get the feeling Harlan Noble's more than a little put out."

Mark Congdon, on the other hand, was beaming from ear to ear.

"Look at this," he crowed, holding up his orchid for everyone to see. "An actual monkey-face orchid. You could spend *years* paddling through the swamps and bogs of South Carolina and never stumble across one of these babies."

"It's really that rare?" asked Delaine, looking askance at the pure-white helmet-shaped orchid with delicate lip petals. "Look at Mark's plant," she told Bobby Wayne as he rejoined her. "Hopefully, he'll be able to keep it going."

"Mark's a whiz at orchid cultivation," Angie assured everyone. "I once watched him bring a half dozen pots of bog buttons back from the dead."

"Bog buttons," said Drayton, "now that's something. You *must* be good."

"Are you sorry you didn't keep bidding on the orchid?" asked Theodosia quietly as they headed back toward the sweet tea stand. Drayton had his two orchids tucked safely in a cardboard box, but seemed to be in a pensive mood.

"Yes and no," said Drayton. "The older I get, the less *things* I want or need. I suppose that's called divesting one's self."

"Please don't sound so morbid," said Theodosia. "You're still in your prime."

"Relatively," shrugged Drayton.

"Glasses of sweet tea all around?" asked Delaine, slipping back behind the booth and looking, for all the world, like she enjoyed being there. Of course, Bobby Wayne was still smiling and following her every move and Delaine was relishing each delicious second of his attention.

"Sounds perfect," said Mark as he set his monkey-face orchid on the edge of the counter. "I think I actually started hyperventilating during the final round of bidding."

"I can understand why," said Theodosia as she joined Delaine behind the stand. "Nine hundred dollars is a major investment."

"Nine hundred dollars would buy a lot of *other* things," murmured Delaine as she plopped ice cubes into the fancy stemware her friends had purchased earlier.

"You want me to run and grab more ice?" asked Theodosia, seeing that they were starting to run low. If she was going to tend the booth for the next couple of hours or so, and it looked like she probably was, they'd for sure need more ice.

"Good idea," said Delaine. She poured out the first glass of sweet tea and handed it to Mark. "Congrats," she told him. "I guess."

Theodosia headed off across the lawn in the direction of a flapping white tent. There, the ladies from St. Paul's Church were serving tea sandwiches, homemade pecan pies, and lemonade. And they'd trucked in a huge freezer filled with ice, enough for . . .

A high-pitched gargling sound rose up behind her. And Theodosia paused in her tracks.

Strange, she thought. *Sounds almost as if . . .*

Theodosia spun around just in time to see Mark Congdon's beet-red face contort in agony. Lips rigid, eyes fluttering frantically, he clawed hysterically at his throat. Then his arms flayed out stiffly in front of him as his body was suddenly wracked with a series of violent tremors. Then Mark clamped one arm solidly across his chest as tiny gluts of foam rolled out of his mouth.

"Mark!" screamed Angie, reaching out to him. "Honey, what's . . . ?" She turned to address the horrified onlookers. "I think it's his heart! Mark's having a heart attack!"

"Somebody help him!" screamed Delaine. She threw her hands up in a gesture of supreme panic and the pitcher of sweet tea she'd been holding exploded at her feet.

At that precise moment Mark Congdon let loose a low, agonized wail and jack-knifed forward. Then, just as quickly, he toppled backward, his eyes sliding back in his head, his body shuddering as he gasped desperately for air.

And in the few seconds before Bobby Wayne regained his composure and pulled out his cell phone to dial 911, all Theodosia could focus on was the terrible rapid-fire drumming of Mark's hands and feet as they beat uncontrollably against the green grass of Carthage Place Plantation.

2

༺❦༻

"*Can you believe* it?" fumed Delaine as she sat in the Indigo Tea Shop sipping a cup of English breakfast tea. "That sheriff pulled *me* aside for questioning. How on earth could I have had anything to do with poor Mark Congdon suffering a fatal heart attack!"

"Delaine," said Theodosia, who was trying to calm her friend even as she herself attempted to wrap her arms around the fact that Mark was dead. "Please don't take it personally. The man was just doing his job." Along with the ambulance, Sheriff Ernest T. Billings had arrived on the scene within a few minutes of Mark's collapse. The sheriff, a man Theodosia had met once before, had been competent, caring, and organized, all the things an officer of the law should be.

"We're all upset over Mark's death," said Drayton as he set a Crown Ducal teacup down on the table next to where

Delaine was unhappily perched. "And who among us even realized that Mark had a bad heart?" Drayton gazed at Delaine with a combined look of sadness and intensity. Mark and Angie had been good friends, and yesterday's event had been a terrible shock to him. To all of them.

"Did you know that the doctors even questioned *Angie*?" asked Delaine. "The poor dear had just witnessed her husband convulse in *agony* and suddenly she was on the hot seat!" Delaine dabbed at her eyes even though no tears seemed to mar her flawless makeup.

"I know, I know," responded Theodosia. "But I'm sure they were just trying to ascertain Mark's medical history. The doctors did everything they could. Drayton and I followed the ambulance directly to the hospital in Summerville. We were there when the emergency room doctor pronounced Mark dead upon arrival. He seemed very upset."

"Then you saw poor Angie being *harangued*," said Delaine. "She was just this side of hysterical, but they continued to ask all sorts of impertinent questions."

"I'm sure they didn't mean to be impertinent," said Theodosia, suddenly realizing she had precious little time to get the Indigo Tea Shop ready for their usual Monday morning bustle of customers. It was going to be difficult to carry on this morning, she decided, after Mark's shocking and untimely death.

Drayton adjusted his bow tie, then picked up a linen napkin, shook it out, and refolded it.

"You already did that," Delaine pointed out to him.

He frowned. "You're quite correct. In fact I'm so addled, I haven't even selected today's teas yet."

"What a day," sighed Haley Parker as she came rushing out of the kitchen, carrying a silver tray filled with cut-glass sugar bowls and tiny pitchers of fresh cream. "Our doors open in ten minutes and all we can think about is poor Mark Congdon." Haley paused. She was their head chef and baker extraordinaire, a young woman with enthusiasm to spare, a smiling face, stick-straight long blond hair, and what could be a dangerously caustic wit. Each day Haley whipped up the most amazing scones, muffins, breads, and biscuits. To say nothing of the delicious quiches, chowders, salads, and tea sandwiches that the Indigo Tea Shop served at lunch.

"What exactly was Mark doing when he suffered his heart attack?" asked Haley. "Or myocardial infarction or whatever it was."

"He was sipping a glass of sweet tea," said Drayton. "And celebrating his orchid purchase."

"Do you think the intense cold from the ice could have caused cardiac arrhythmia?" wondered Theodosia.

"Oh, I seriously doubt that," said Delaine. "There wasn't that much ice, remember?"

"Or bradycardia," said Haley, edging over to join them. "That's when the heart beats a little too slowly."

"Maybe," said Drayton. "I suppose we'll have to wait for a final medical report."

Delaine sat there squirming. "Goodness, I could use a cigarette," she murmured. "This is all so upsetting."

"Not very healthy," chided Drayton. "Especially for your heart."

"Are you going to open your shop today?" Theodosia asked Delaine. She decided it might be time to gently oust her friend from the tea shop so they could all get to work.

Delaine glanced at her watch, an elegant Chopard, and sighed. "Oh, I *suppose* so. Although I called earlier and told Janine I'd probably be a tad late this morning. I was planning to stop by the Featherbed House to see how Angie is doing."

"I'm sure she's utterly bereft," said Drayton, who looked fairly bereft himself.

"Poor Angie," said Haley. "She's such a dear soul. And she's been so successful at making a go of the Featherbed House all by herself. I hope Mark's death doesn't put her in a tailspin."

"Being a small business owner is tough work," said Theodosia. She understood firsthand how difficult it was. When she left her marketing job to open the Indigo Tea Shop she'd had to figure out a laundry list of tasks. Like dealing with leases, payroll, quarterly taxes, inventory, and cash flow. And then there was the day-to-day worry of pleasing customers, staging events, and constantly testing and updating menus. Theodosia knew that even though Angie had hired Teddy Vickers as her assistant, keeping the Featherbed House going would still be a difficult task.

As if reading Theodosia's mind, Haley asked, "What about Teddy Vickers? Won't he still be a help?"

"For Angie's sake I hope so," said Delaine as she finally got up and started moving slowly toward the front door. "But Mark was the one with the real business smarts. That's what I've always heard anyway."

"Bye-bye," waved Drayton, hoping to move Delaine along. "See you later."

Once Delaine had made her reluctant exit, Theodosia joined Drayton behind the counter where he fussed about, pulling down colorful tins of tea. "What's on the docket for today?" she asked him.

"I feel the need for a somewhat strong cup of tea," Drayton told her. "So I'm considering serving the Ching Wo black tea from Fujian Province. Oh, and probably a nice oolong, too."

"Which oolong?" asked Theodosia, hoping their customers were also in the mood for a bracing cup of tea. Although Drayton was always happy to brew whatever kind of tea they requested.

"The Ti Kuan Yin," said Drayton.

"Ah, the monkey tea," replied Theodosia. "Love that amber color and earthy flavor." She had hoped to cajole a smile out of Drayton, but no luck.

Haley finished lighting several small tea candles and came over to join them. "I've got sweet potato scones, apple muffins, and raisin spice bars about to come out of the oven," she told them. "So my breakfast breads should be the perfect compliment to your tea choices."

"Thank you, Haley," said Drayton, still looking upset.

"Gosh, Drayton, you look awful," said Haley, who sometimes spoke her mind a little too plainly.

"Exactly what I need this morning," responded Drayton in a cranky tone. "Moral support." He peeled off his dove-gray jacket, hung it on a nearby peg, and carefully rolled up his shirtsleeves so they both corresponded to the millimeter.

"I didn't mean it *that* way," said Haley, backing off.

"Of course you didn't," said Theodosia. "You were just trying to be solicitous, weren't you?"

"I sure was," said Haley, nodding in the affirmative. "Really."

"Then pardon my prickly nature," said Drayton, softening his words a bit. "I just wish there was something we could do to help Angie."

"What if I fixed a nice tea basket for her?" offered Haley. "You know, put in some tins of tea, a dozen scones, some honey, and a jar of Devonshire cream. Maybe include some of that lavender-peppermint tea, too, that's supposed to be such a stress buster. You guys could run it down to Angie's place after lunch. We usually have a bit of a lull then."

"It's a start." Drayton shrugged.

"I think it's a superb idea," said Theodosia as the door to the tea shop flew open and a half dozen eager customers pushed their way in.

Business was as brisk as Drayton's teas this Monday morning. Theodosia and Drayton, clad in long, black Parisian waiter's aprons, found themselves rushing about the tea shop, pouring tea, delivering scones and muffins, bringing extra dollops of Devonshire cream, strawberry jam, and lemon curd to their customers.

At ten o'clock Harlan Noble shuffled into the tea shop and glanced around imperiously.

"Mr. Noble?" said Theodosia, eyebrows slightly raised. He was the last person she expected to see here this morning. Dressed in a black sport coat and black shirt, Harlan Noble looked both stern and austere. A fragment of Edgar Allan Poe's poem "The Raven" suddenly floated into Theodosia's head. Probably, she decided, because Harlan *looked* so much like a raven. Then, shaking her head to clear away that strange thought, Theodosia said, "May I help you?"

Instead of answering, Harlan Noble lifted his chin and gazed past her.

"May I help you?" Theodosia asked, a little more insistently this time. "Are you here to pick up a take-out order? Or perhaps I could show you to a table? We have one left."

Harlan Noble finally focused dark eyes on Theodosia. "I

need to talk with Drayton," he told her. His voice seemed as brusque as his manner.

Theodosia put a hand on Harlan's arm, hoping to impart a little courtesy by osmosis. "Drayton's busy with customers at the moment, but if you'd like to be seated, I'll send him over as soon as he's free."

"I suppose," said Harlan, rather ungraciously.

"Right this way," said Theodosia. She guided him to a small table next to the stone fireplace, normally one of their coziest tables. Today it was elegantly laid out with a cream-colored damask napkin, a flickering tea candle, polished silverware, and a floral cup and saucer.

Just as Theodosia was pouring a cup of Darjeeling for Harlan Noble, Drayton ambled over. "Mr. Noble," he said, an inquisitive look on his face.

Harlan Noble wasted no time. "Drayton," he said, suddenly looking more than a little sheepish. "I wanted to apologize for my harsh words yesterday. Especially in light of what's happened . . ." Harlan's voice trailed off and he shook his head. "Such a tragedy about Mark Congdon."

"Indeed it is," agreed Drayton.

"We're all rather heartsick," added Theodosia, who'd stuck around to see exactly what Harlan Noble had on his agenda.

"Mark was a lovely person. So talented," said Harlan. "We were actually in a book discussion group together . . . Greek classics."

"He will be greatly missed," intoned Drayton.

"What . . . uh . . . do you know what happened to Mark's orchid?" Harlan asked. He'd stumbled over his words, but his eyes glowed clear and bright.

Theodosia stared at Harlan Noble for a few long seconds,

then decided the man was a lout of the first magnitude. Here he was, nosing around on the pretense of feeling bad, but really trying to figure out what happened to Mark's monkey-face orchid!

"I have it," said Drayton, his tone just this side of frosty.

"Good, good," said Harlan, hunching his thin shoulders up, his dark eyes darting between the two of them. "I was just concerned . . ."

Quoth the raven, nevermore, thought Theodosia.

"In fact I'm going to take it to Angie this afternoon," said Drayton. "So you need not concern yourself."

3

❧❧

"*Two entrées today,*" Haley told Theodosia as she darted about her small kitchen, stirring and tasting. "Lavender-infused egg salad on croissants and roast chicken breasts stuffed with root vegetables."

"Wonderful," declared Theodosia. "Honestly, Haley, I don't know how you come up with such inventive recipes."

"Just one of the tricks of the trade," responded Haley, clearly pleased. "Oh, and I'm baking several pans of madeleines as well. You'll be able to take some over to Angie this afternoon."

"I'm sure she'll appreciate your efforts," said Theodosia, knowing that Angie might very well be numb for the next week or so and not have any idea what she's eating or even tasting. Still, Haley's extra efforts were both admirable and heartwarming.

"Madeleines are the new muffins," declared Haley as she

carefully sliced fresh-baked croissants, slathered them with butter, then topped them with dollops of lavender egg salad. "They're a little more futsy to make, what with the shallow pans and the delicate little shell shapes. But in the long run, I think madeleines are incredibly versatile. Because they're such petite cakelike cookies, you can serve them with jelly and Devonshire cream, or top them with chocolate or butterscotch sauce, or just serve two on a plate with a nice scoop of sorbet."

Theodosia leaned against the doorway and listened to Haley's friendly chatter, watched her spin and pirouette from oven to counter, doing her intricate little chef's ballet. As heavy as Theodosia's heart was over Mark Congdon's death, it was reassuring to be in the place she loved most— her beloved Indigo Tea Shop.

Theodosia knew she'd made the smartest move of her life when she'd bid sayonara to her job in marketing and gambled her savings on establishing the Indigo Tea Shop. What had started out as a dusty little diamond in the rough had become one of the most popular spots on Charleston's Church Street. Pegged wooden floors, brick walls, and a beamed ceiling made for a cozy, cottagelike atmosphere. Antique wooden tables and chairs, fine china, and sparkling silver lent an upscale, Old World feel. Antique breakfronts and bookcases, crammed with teacups, tiny spoons, tea cozies, jars of lemon curd, tea books, and packaged teas, lined the walls and completed the picture.

Of course, this was Drayton's domain, too. One wall was floor-to-ceiling wooden shelves lined with shiny tea tins filled with the finest, freshest, and most aromatic teas available. As a master tea taster and tea blender, Drayton demanded perfection. Which was why the Indigo Tea Shop always stocked the best Formosan oolong, first-flush Darjeeling, smoky Lapsang souchong from China, rare Japanese Sencha, and exotic Kenyan teas.

And when the teacups were rattling, the teapots chirping, and customers filled the small shop with their excited hum, Theodosia knew she was clearly at home.

"Say now," said Drayton as he came up behind Theodosia, rousing her from her reverie. "We have some very hungry customers waiting out here."

"Isn't it good, then, that we've got some marvelous luncheons ready to serve," Haley answered blithely.

Drayton peered over his tortoiseshell half-glasses and consulted his order pad. "I require fourteen egg salads and twelve chicken breasts," he told Haley.

"Coming up," sang Haley.

But Drayton wasn't finished. "For now," he told her. "As you probably know, we're expecting two rather large groups in another forty-five minutes. Red-hat ladies, I believe."

"We're amazingly busy for a Monday," commented Haley as she pulled a pan of perfectly golden chicken breasts from the oven and set it atop the stove.

"Can you believe how busy?" asked Dayton, making a wry face. Then he glanced toward Theodosia to hurriedly explain. "Not that I'm *displeased* we're making such a go of things. It's just that . . ."

"I know what you're saying," said Theodosia, nodding. "I feel exactly the same way."

"We all do," said Haley. "We may carry on as usual, but Mark's untimely death is hanging directly over our heads."

"We're still planning to run over and see Angie, aren't

we?" asked Drayton. He watched as Haley carefully placed each plump chicken breast atop a mound of baby field greens, then added a spoonful of honeyed white wine sauce.

"Count on it," said Theodosia.

A stiff breeze off the Atlantic had chased the last wisps of clouds from the azure skies above Charleston. The afternoon sun sparkled down, highlighting the enormous grand and graceful mansions of the historic district. There were Italianate-style homes with low pitched roofs and wide verandas, Victorian-style homes with fanciful turrets and gingerbread trim, and here and there a few of the old shotgun-style homes, too. And everywhere, a riot of foliage. Gnarled live oaks arched over cobblestone streets, dogwood and box ivy lined cobblestone drives, magnolias, pansies, and English daisies exploded with color in every yard.

"I'm so glad we're doing this," said Drayton as he and Theodosia strolled down Murray Street on their way to the Featherbed House.

"Agreed," said Theodosia. "There'll probably be friends and relatives jostling about. So it's the least we can do."

"Help fortify them," added Drayton, trying to put his game face on.

But when Theodosia and Drayton climbed the front stairs of the Featherbed House Bed & Breakfast and let themselves into the spacious lobby with its cypress paneling and twelve-foot-high hand-molded plaster ceiling, the place seemed deserted. Angie's collection of ceramic, plush, and needlepoint geese were the only inhabitants, tucked as they were in cabinets and nestled on couches. An antique grandfather clock ticked loudly in the silent room.

"Nobody's here," said Drayton, looking puzzled.

"Hello," Theodosia called out. "Anybody home?"

"Hold on," said Drayton, listening intently. "Somebody *is* coming. Must be . . . Teddy?"

Theodosia paused, focusing on the sound of approaching footsteps.

Teddy Vickers, Angie's assistant, suddenly loomed in the doorway. He looked both subdued and a little surprised at seeing them.

"Drayton. Theodosia," said Teddy. "Nice to see you even under these sad circumstances." Teddy Vickers was one of those men who was of an indeterminate age. He could have been thirty-three, he could have been forty-five. He was boyish-looking with a crooked grin and a shock of dark blond hair combed to one side. It gave him a distinctly East Coast preppy look, like he might be an assistant headmaster at some exclusive school. Except Teddy worked for Angie.

"We brought tea and sandwiches," said Drayton, holding up a large basket.

"And scones and madeleines," added Theodosia. She winced inwardly, thinking her voice probably sounded overly cheerful. "And Mark's orchid from yesterday." She indicated the little plant she'd tucked carefully in a box and surrounded with tissue paper.

"I thought there'd be more people around," said Drayton. "Friends, relatives . . ." His voice trailed off.

"Guests," said Theodosia, suddenly struck by the emptiness of the normally thriving B and B. Or maybe it was just a sadness that had settled over the old mansion.

Teddy Vickers shook his head. "Angie's sister and a few other relatives will be arriving from Chicago later this afternoon. As for the Featherbed House, it's closed for now. We found space for all our bookings at other nearby B and Bs and won't be accepting any new reservations." He shrugged. "Basically, we've taken the phone off the hook."

"What about current guests?" asked Theodosia. She was a little surprised to hear that the Featherbed House was in the process of shutting down completely.

"We've got two rooms occupied right now," said Teddy, "but once they leave tomorrow morning . . ." He shrugged his thin shoulders and turned his palms upright as if to say *who knows?*

"And how are *you* doing?" asked Drayton.

Teddy sighed loudly. He'd also been at Carthage Place Plantation yesterday and, in the melee following Mark's collapse, had accompanied Angie, Theodosia, Drayton, Delaine, and Bobby Wayne to the hospital.

"Holding up," was Teddy's terse answer. "Although this hasn't been a happy place for quite some time."

Theodosia's brows knit together at this strange comment. "What makes you say that?" she asked.

"The Featherbed House is in dire need of some rather major repairs," said Teddy. "And lately, Mark had been extremely involved with his job. So not a lot of decisions got made."

"I'm sure working at Loveday and Luxor was very stressful for him," said Theodosia. Considering the circumstances, she felt Teddy's words seemed somehow disloyal.

"Lots of competition between brokers, too," added Teddy, dropping his voice. "I got the feeling the place was pretty much a viper's nest."

Really? Theodosia thought to herself. *Viper's nest? First I've ever heard of that.*

Drayton cleared his throat. "Is Angie around? We'd like to say a quick hello and express our condolences."

"I'm sure she'll speak with you," said Teddy Vickers. He waved a hand. "Have a seat and I'll tell Angie you're here."

Theodosia and Drayton made themselves as comfortable as they could in the lobby of the Featherbed House.

"This place is so unnaturally quiet," remarked Drayton.

Theodosia had to agree. Usually the Featherbed House was bustling with guests checking in or checking out, enjoying wine and cheese in the lobby, or lounging on the back patio amid the gardens. And everywhere Theodosia looked—the polished floors, the hand-painted goose mural on the wall, the overstuffed pillows—were reminders of the love and care Angie and Mark had put into the place.

"Theodosia?" came Angie's whispery voice as she walked slowly into the lobby. "Drayton?" Angie Congdon stood there looking pale and thin, as though a stray puff of wind could blow her away.

Theodosia and Drayton rushed to put their arms around her.

"How are you doing, dear lady?" asked Drayton. "Are you holding up?"

"Oh, Angie," cried Theodosia. "I wish there was something we could do to help."

"You're doing it," said Angie, giving them a sad, lopsided smile. "You're here. Both of you. And that means the absolute *world* to me."

"We were afraid we might be intruding," said Drayton. "Even though we brought goodies. And Mark's orchid."

Angie glanced about the lobby, a wistful look on her face.

"As you can see, you're not intruding at all," she said. "In fact, I'm afraid Mark's death has completely knocked me for a loop. There are still people to contact, things to do." She dabbed at her eyes with a hanky. "But I can't seem to manage it. In fact, I spent most of the morning on the phone with the hospital over in Summerville."

"Come," said Drayton, motioning to both women. "Let's sit down and talk."

"Have you received a more definitive cause of death from the cardiologist?" asked Theodosia, once they were all seated on low club chairs around a small wooden table.

Angie gazed at them, a strange, pinched look on her face. "Funny you should ask," she said. "I just got off the phone with Sheriff Billings." She reached in the pocket of her light jacket and pulled out a piece of paper. "He faxed me this report."

Angie held it out, as if willing Theodosia to take it.

Theodosia reached for the piece of paper in Angie's hand and accepted it gently. "May I read it?" she asked.

"Please," said Angie, who seemed to be in a mild state of shock.

Theodosia unfolded the paper and scanned the report. It appeared to be a standard hospital form with most of the pertinent medical facts filled in by hand. The first part of the form was a list of all the symptoms Mark Congdon had presented with. Dilated pupils, respiratory distress, cardiac arrhythmia, convulsions.

The next part listed the lifesaving measures the EMTs and ER personnel had employed. Blood gas analysis, epinephrine, defibrillation, cardiac catheterization.

Theodosia's eyes skipped to the bottom of the report, to

the line that read *Cause of Death*. Her brow furrowed, her heart thumped inside her chest as her eyes focused on the phrase that had been scrawled in: *nonspecific toxin*.

"Good heavens," breathed Theodosia, as her brain suddenly started racing. *A toxin is a poison, right? Sure it is.*

"What?" asked Drayton, upon seeing Theodosia's reaction. "What?"

Wordlessly, Theodosia handed him the paper.

Drayton put on his glasses and quickly scanned the report. "Nonspecific toxin!" he exclaimed when he got to the bottom of the page. "What's *that* supposed to mean?"

Angie swiped at her eyes again with her hanky. "I have no idea. But I've been under the complete impression that Mark either suffered a heart attack or had some kind of brain aneurysm. Those were the two things that fixed in my mind. And the doctors and medical personnel had pretty much confirmed that." She leaned closer toward Drayton. "You know, Mark always pushed himself so hard. Up at five, at the office by seven. Of course, that's what being a commodity broker is all about." Her shoulders slumped, her hands shook. "Now this . . ."

"Good lord," said Drayton, aiming a level gaze at Theodosia. "This medical report changes everything."

But Theodosia's mind had already leapt into overdrive. *If toxin means poison, then poison means murder,* she told herself. "Here, Drayton, let me see that report again."

"I . . . uh . . . couldn't bring myself to read the entire contents of the report," said Angie. "It seemed . . ." Her voice cracked. ". . . so very final."

"You should call the hospital and see if you can get more detailed information," said Theodosia. "This simply isn't acceptable. I'm sure there are more specific lab tests that can be run. Certain . . . uh, what would you call them? Tox screens?"

"I'm not sure I could manage that right now," Angie said. Her voice was a whisper and her shoulders slumped dejectedly. Tears trickled down her pale cheeks. She seemed on the verge of collapse.

"Would you like me to see if I can find out more?" asked Theodosia. Her heart went out to poor Angie Congdon. She'd never seen her friend look so fragile.

"Theo," said Angie, reaching for Theodosia's hand. "Would you really?"

"Of course," said Theodosia. "I'll phone the hospital and . . ."

"She'll take this up with law enforcement, too," volunteered Drayton.

"Bless you," Angie whispered to Theodosia. "You're such a calm, take-charge person." Her eyes drifted toward Drayton. "You, too, Drayton. If the two of you can find it within your hearts to help me, I'd be eternally grateful."

"We'll do whatever we can," promised Drayton even as he threw Theodosia a pleading look. "Won't we?"

"Count on it," said Theodosia, realizing she'd somehow backed herself into a fairly serious investigation.

A murder investigation? Yeah, maybe.

"There's so much to handle all at once," fretted Angie. "Plan a funeral, notify all our friends and relatives. I suppose I'll have to go down to Mark's office and pick up his address book . . ."

"I'll do that," volunteered Theodosia. *In for a penny, in for a pound,* she told herself.

"Would you really?" asked Angie.

"No problem," said Theodosia. "I'll stop by Loveday and Luxor first thing tomorrow."

"And I'll certainly assist with funeral arrangements," said Drayton. "Do you know when . . . uh . . . when Mark's body will be. . . . ?" His voice trailed off.

"No," came Angie's choked voice. "I'm afraid I don't."

4

"*What exactly does* nonspecific toxin mean?" Drayton asked Theodosia as the two of them hurried back down the street, headed for the tea shop.

"It means something got into Mark's system and killed him," said Theodosia. "But the docs don't know exactly what it was."

"Like a poison?" asked Drayton.

Theodosia looked grim. "It's not a pretty thought, but that notion had crossed my mind."

"How ghastly," said Drayton.

They walked along in silence for a while.

"You know," said Theodosia, "there's a possibility someone might have tampered with the sweet tea yesterday."

"You can't be serious," said Drayton, fingering his bow tie nervously. "I brewed that tea myself!"

"Think about it," said Theodosia. "Mark drank a glass of tea, then immediately collapsed."

"But anyone could have drunk that tea," sputtered Drayton. "Others *did* drink that tea."

"Good point," responded Theodosia.

"Delaine was the one who was pouring," murmured Drayton. "You don't think she somehow . . . ?"

"Of course not," said Theodosia. She'd known Delaine for years. The woman was ditsy, yes. But a murderer? Hardly.

"I *suppose* someone could have gotten to that tea," allowed Drayton. "Although there wouldn't be any evidence. Everything got spilled or thrown away yesterday in all the commotion."

"What if there was something wrong with Mark's glass?" said Theodosia. She was suddenly reminded of the painted glasses that Angie, Mark, and Bobby Wayne had purchased at the art booth.

"You think there was a dangerous toxin in the paint?" asked Drayton.

"It's a thought," said Theodosia. At this point she had no idea what happened. "Although lots of other people purchased those glasses, and nothing happened to them."

"Or did someone know which glass belonged to Mark?" asked Drayton. He suddenly stopped in his tracks and stared at her. "The one painted with purple orchids."

"That's an awfully chilling thought," responded Theodosia. "It would mean someone was stalking him, just waiting for some sort of opportunity." She paused. "It would mean Mark's murder was premeditated."

Drayton grimaced. "Good heavens, there had to be six

hundred people at Carthage Place Plantation yesterday. Maybe more. That makes for an enormous pool of suspects."

"Even so," said Theodosia, "we should probably get that glass checked out. There could be trace remnants of the toxin or whatever it was. And fingerprints."

Drayton blinked hard. "I thought Mark dropped it, that the glass got smashed."

"He did," said Theodosia. "And it did. But I scooped the broken pieces into a cardboard box and stuck them in the back of my Jeep."

"And they're still there?" asked Drayton.

Theodosia gave a tight nod.

"So they could be analyzed," mused Drayton.

"Sure," said Theodosia. "If that's what Sheriff Billings thinks we should do."

"Good lord. Please don't tell anyone else that you have those broken pieces," said Drayton.

"No kidding," replied Theodosia. She had no intention of broadcasting the fact that she might possess a possible clue to Mark's untimely death.

"Which means you're going to be having a rather intense phone conversation with Sheriff Ernest T. Billings?" asked Drayton.

"Soon as we get back," replied Theodosia.

"It's terrifying to think someone might have wanted Mark Congdon dead," said Drayton. "Had schemed and planned for it. I wouldn't think he had an enemy in the world."

They walked along in silence for another fifty paces and then Theodosia said, "Do you find it strange that Harlan Noble came sniffing around trying to buy Mark's orchid?"

"It is strange," said Drayton, scratching his head. "Then again, orchid collectors are pretty odd ducks."

"So I've noticed," said Theodosia.

"How's Angie doing?" asked Haley. She was standing at the counter, ringing up a take-out order, when Theodosia and Drayton walked into the Indigo Tea Shop. It was now late afternoon and only two tables were occupied. Sun slanted in the heavy leaded windows giving the interior an Old World, painterly feel. Like background lighting in a fine Rembrandt painting.

Drayton put a finger to his lips. "Some strange things are happening," he said under his breath.

Haley was instantly on alert. "Tell me!"

So they did.

But much to their surprise, Haley immediately pooh-poohed their poison theory.

"I still bet Mark suffered a heart attack," she said.

"Why on earth would you say that?" asked Drayton, "when evidence seems to point to the contrary?"

"That's not quite true," said Haley. "From what you told me, Mark exhibited all the classic symptoms of a heart attack. Then factor in the notion that he was just too nice a guy. He didn't have any enemies."

"We don't know that for sure," said Theodosia.

"Oh, right," said Haley, rolling her eyes. "Some visitor to Charleston didn't like their room at the Featherbed House? Somebody thought the percale sheets were too stiff so they decided to retaliate?"

"He worked for Loveday and Luxor for the past six

months," suggested Theodosia. "Maybe somebody there had it in for him."

"Maybe." Haley shrugged. "But we did a tea for them not too long ago. They all seemed like nice, reasonable people. I bet this whole poison thing is just a tempest in a teapot."

"Interesting choice of words," remarked Drayton.

"Just you wait," said Haley, gesturing for Theodosia to follow as she turned and headed for the kitchen. "I bet everything will turn out kosher."

Theodosia followed Haley through the velvet celadon-green curtains where a sweet, chocolaty aroma suddenly enveloped her. She was still pondering Haley's words and sincerely hoping that Haley was right.

Haley grabbed a tray of elegant-looking chocolate truffles and held them out to Theodosia. Half the candies were drizzled with zigzags of white chocolate, the other half were smothered in rich-looking cocoa powder.

"Of course," said Haley, as Theodosia chose a truffle, "Mark is still dead. And that's a terrible, terrible thing. But murder? I just don't think so." She peered at Theodosia. "What do you think?"

"I hope you're right," said Theodosia, chewing thoughtfully.

"No, I mean about the truffles."

"Oh," said Theodosia, still chewing. "They're absolutely wonderful." She rolled her eyes for emphasis.

"I was thinking of whipping up a few more batches and selling them in the tea shop this week," said Haley. "On a kind of trial basis. You know, see how it goes."

"If they're all this good, we'll be sold out by noon tomorrow," said Theodosia, reaching for another piece.

"Ohhh . . . you like them," cooed Haley.

"What's this about a trial basis?" asked Drayton, stepping into the kitchen.

"Truffles," said Theodosia. "Haley thinks we should expand our repertoire."

"Why not?" said Drayton. He grabbed one, popped it into his mouth. A look of sublime happiness immediately washed across his face. Drayton had a bit of a reputation as a chocoholic. "More than a few tea shops are offering truffles these days," he commented. "And, lord knows, chocolate pairs beautifully with so many different teas. I mean, think about Moroccan mint tea with chocolate. Or black tea with hints of citrus. Or a raspberry tisane. Or a peppermint-flavored tea. Oh, I could go on and on."

"No kidding," said Haley.

"Would you consider serving your truffles at Orchid Lights?" asked Theodosia. Orchid Lights was the combination orchid show and fund-raiser that the Heritage Society was staging this Saturday night. Theodosia had volunteered to do a refreshment table with a small assortment of tea and sweets. Her sort-of boyfriend, Parker Scully, who owned Solstice, a French- and Mediterranean-influenced bistro over on Market Street, was going to handle wine and spirits.

"We could include truffles," said Haley. "If you think people would like them."

"Oh, I definitely think they'd be a hit," said Theodosia.

Drayton reached for another truffle. "You'll be at the meeting tonight?" he asked Theodosia.

She nodded.

"Shouldn't run too long," he told her. "We just need to tie up a few loose ends. You know how Timothy likes to have all the details figured out and everyone accountable."

Timothy was Timothy Neville, the octogenarian director of Charleston's Heritage Society.

"Speaking of loose ends," said Haley. "You did remember that your intern starts work here on Wednesday."

Drayton feigned a puzzled look. "Intern?" he muttered.

"Don't try to weasel out of this," said Haley, taking a stern tone. "This intern thing has been set up for *months*."

Drayton drew himself up to his full height and peered down his aquiline nose at Haley. "What possible use would I have for an intern?"

"The general idea is to use her as a sort of assistant," said Haley. "But remember, it's supposed to be a positive learning experience."

"For who?" asked Drayton.

"For the *intern*," said Haley, holding her ground. This wasn't the first go-round she'd had with Drayton; it certainly wouldn't be the last.

Drayton shook his head, as if scolding an unruly child. "I simply don't require any assistance whatsoever."

"Sure you do," said Haley. "Of course, you do. Half the time you're running around here completely frizzle-frazzled."

"*Frizzle-frazzled?*" Drayton lifted an eyebrow and pursed his lips. His face took on a slight resemblance to a thundercloud. "Although I have no idea what that means, I take serious umbrage to the fact that it's probably an accusation of sorts."

"Okay then," said Haley, deciding to reverse gears and try another approach. "You're overworked. You're a real champ, but you've got way too much to do."

"Haley's right, you know," said Theodosia, who'd been thoroughly enjoying herself watching this somewhat bizarre exchange. It was like watching an unscripted soap opera. Or an episode of reality TV. Everyday dramas and events that got blown out of proportion.

"I beg to differ. Haley is wrong about my needing an intern," declared Drayton in an ominous tone. "Quite wrong."

5

❧

"*You're late,*" called Parker Scully. He lifted one arm in a wave and flashed a welcoming smile at Theodosia as she hurried up the sidewalk toward the main door of the Heritage Society. Earl Grey trotted beside her, tethered by his red leather leash. "Is it *your* fault?" he asked gazing down at Earl Grey.

Earl Grey turned liquid brown eyes on Parker. The dog had picked up a crinkly yellow fast-food wrapper during his walk along the Battery and was now reluctant to relinquish his treasure.

"I almost ran out of time," said Theodosia with a laugh. "Between taking care of business, walking his majesty here, and grabbing my notes for Orchid Lights." She held up the sheaf of papers that was clutched in her hand. "Correction. Make that grabbing my *disorganized* notes."

"And solving a murder mystery?" asked Parker. His

bright blue eyes twinkled, he reached up a hand and casually ran it through a tousle of blond hair.

"Huh?" said Theodosia. She'd talked to Parker on the phone Sunday evening and relayed to him all the events of that utterly horrible day. But she hadn't breathed a word to him about a murder. Or even a mystery. Come to think of it, Mark Congdon's death hadn't yet taken on the status of murder mystery at that time.

"How did you know about . . . uh . . . that?" Theodosia asked.

"Drayton blabbed," said Parker, grinning. "I called your shop a little while ago hoping to get you and your Mr. Conneley picked up the phone. I asked how your friend Angie was doing and one thing just sort of led to another."

"You'll keep it under your hat, won't you?" asked Theodosia. "Everything's kind of in flux right now. We don't even know if there is a . . ." She glanced around nervously. ". . . a toxicology issue."

"You secret's safe with me," Parker assured her. "But what I'm really curious about is, why are you such a lightning rod for this stuff? I mean, somebody in this town drops dead and you're Johnny on the case."

"That's so not true," protested Theodosia.

Parker Scully peered at her. They'd been seeing each other on again and off again for a while now, so he could push the boundaries a little. But Parker chose to retreat. "Okay, I amend my statement. Not everyone warrants your getting involved."

"That's right," Theodosia told him.

"However," continued Parker, "from what I've seen, your investigative skills are rather impressive."

"Oh . . . not really," hedged Theodosia, anxious to change

the subject as they pushed their way through the doors and hurried down the main hallway.

"Yes, they—" began Parker, but Theodosia interrupted him.

"I'm not exactly prepared for this meeting," she said in a loud whisper. "Drayton kind of pulled me in at the last minute."

"You'll be fine," Parker assured her as they rounded a corner and headed down another lengthy corridor lined with fine oil paintings. "Besides, with Timothy Neville at the helm the Heritage Society runs like a finely tuned Swiss watch. Probably all we'll have to do this Saturday evening is show up and serve refreshments."

Easier said than done, thought Theodosia.

"Theodosia?" called a high, papery voice. "Is that you?"

"Hello, Timothy," said Theodosia as she and Parker swung around the doorway into the cypress-paneled board-room. "I brought Earl Grey along, hope you don't mind."

Timothy Neville waved a gnarled hand. "No problem. As long as he doesn't try to usurp my position or lodge an opposing vote. But he *does* have to come over and give a proper hello."

Theodosia unsnapped Earl Grey's leash and the dog padded over to greet Timothy. While most of Charleston, including the board members, employees of the Heritage Society, and donors, were deeply intimidated by Timothy Neville, Earl Grey viewed Timothy as his buddy. To him Timothy Neville wasn't a prominent member of Charleston society whose Huguenot ancestors had helped settle Charleston. Or a domineering old codger who lived in a splendid mansion over on Archdale Street and played first violin in the Charleston Symphony. No, to Earl Grey Timothy Neville was a guy's guy who pulled his ears, gave him hearty pats, and occasionally produced a liver-flavored dog cookie from the pocket of his elegant pleated trousers.

"Ah," said Timothy, removing the lump of soggy, yellow paper from Earl Grey's mouth. "What do we have here? A treasure map? Long lost documents, perhaps?"

Earl Grey settled down happily at Timothy's feet as Theodosia and Parker took their seats at the oval table alongside Drayton. Another half dozen volunteers also sat at the table, talking among themselves.

Timothy wasted no time in calling the meeting to order.

"Good evening and thank you all for coming this evening," intoned Timothy. "I've invited Arthur Roumillat, president of the Charleston Orchid Society to join us. As you well know, his fine organization is partnering with ours to present Orchid Lights."

There was a smattering of applause from everyone seated.

"Yes, yes," said Timothy holding up a hand. "But remember that the main reason for this event is fund-raising. While other museums and nonprofit organizations are struggling, the Heritage Society fully intends to thrive." Timothy favored the group with a thin smile. He wanted to make it crystal clear that under his leadership the Heritage Society was vigorous and highly viable.

"Which means," continued Timothy, "that our two groups will be running concurrent events. During the same time members of the Orchid Society are exhibiting prize specimens on our patio, the Heritage Society will be holding a silent auction in our great hall. Of course, there will also be music, refreshments, drinks, and entertainment.

Hopefully, by causing a sort of ebb and flow of members and patrons between our two organizations we'll achieve a critical new level of synergy."

"And raise needed funds," added Drayton.

"Raise funds," echoed Timothy. "Absolutely." He slipped into his seat as Arthur Roumillat stood to address the group. Arthur gave a ten-minute overview of how the orchid show would be presented and how many Orchid Society members would be attending.

Overall, Theodosia thought the pairing of the two groups was a particularly brilliant maneuver on Timothy's part. It was a way to expose donors and patrons of the Orchid Society to the Heritage Society. And it gave long-time Heritage Society members a fun evening that included an outdoor show featuring one of nature's most coveted floral species. She also perceived both events as upscale entertainment that would bring out the cream of Charleston society.

"And the entire outdoor patio will be awash with orchids," finished Arthur Roumillat with an expansive gesture.

"Excuse me," said Drayton, putting a hand up. "But we need half of that patio for tables and chairs. We're already planning on glass-topped tables with festive centerpieces."

Arthur Roumillat frowned at Drayton. "First I've heard of that."

"Check your notes from last month's meeting," Drayton reminded him. He was a fourth-term board member as well as the Heritage Society's parliamentarian.

Timothy Neville suddenly looked unhappy. "Can you two work this out, please?" he asked. "Divvy up the territory so to speak."

"Certainly," said Drayton. "And I want to remind you

that Theodosia here has graciously volunteered to donate tea and desserts for Saturday night."

Warm smiles were suddenly focused on Theodosia. Celerie Stuart, one of the newest board members, said in a loud whisper, "You do so much, Theo."

Theodosia waved a hand as if to say, *It's nothing.*

Drayton continued.

"And Parker Scully, owner of Solstice Bistro and Wine Bar, will be donating and serving select alcoholic refreshments." Drayton peered over his half-glasses at Parker. "Do we know exactly what those libations will be yet?"

"White wine spritzers and a fancy cocktail as yet to be determined," replied Parker good-naturedly.

Drayton picked up his pen and scratched a note on his yellow legal pad. "Yet to be determined," he murmured.

Timothy Neville took that opportunity to grab the floor again. "And our newest board member, Celerie Stuart, has been working with numerous volunteers to coordinate our silent auction." Timothy turned his dark, piercing eyes on Celerie. "As I understand it, some rather exotic items have been donated. Celerie, would you care to enlighten us? Give us a little taste of what's to come?"

Celerie Stuart scratched the tip of her nose with her pencil eraser as she consulted her notes. Midforties, with a cap of reddish-blond curls, Celerie was a consummate volunteer and Junior Leaguer. "We've actually had an amazing amount of donations," she told the group. "Some of the items we've received include harbor cruises, a weekend at a Hilton Head resort, an exquisite collection of toy soldiers, oil paintings, a fishing charter, handcrafted silver jewelry, golf clubs, fifty pounds of raw oysters, and even a ride in a fighter jet."

There were excited murmurs all around the table.

"And we're still selling tickets?" asked Theodosia. "For admission this Saturday night?"

"Absolutely," said Timothy. "Thirty-five dollars if you phone in your reservation, forty dollars if you purchase your ticket at the door."

"And there's been fairly good publicity?" Theodosia asked.

Timothy nodded again. "We've already had a sidebar in the Arts section of the Charleston *Post and Courier*, plus listings on the community calendars of most major radio stations." He hesitated. "We've also received an invitation from Channel Eight to appear on their *Windows on Charleston* show this Saturday morning." He gazed around the table, casting an appraising eye at the group. "We still need a volunteer for that. Preferably someone who's media savvy."

Drayton immediately thrust an elbow into Theodosia's ribs. "You," he said in a loud stage whisper.

Sitting on Theodosia's other side, Parker immediately took up Drayton's cause. "Theodosia would be perfect," agreed Parker.

Timothy turned gleaming eyes on her. "Yes," he said, as if the idea had just that moment occurred to him. "You did work in marketing, didn't you? And you've appeared on television before."

Theodosia held up both hands in protest. She didn't feel she was the best spokesperson for this event. Didn't think she was all that convincing on camera. "I would think *you'd* be the logical candidate, Timothy." Her eyes sought out Arthur Roumillat. "Or Mr. Roumillat."

But Arthur Roumillat shook his head dismissively. "Can't," he said. "Way too much to do this Saturday. The

Orchid Society has never set up at this location before and it looks like we've got some serious logistical problems to work out. We've got plans for at least a dozen tables to showcase perhaps seventy-five individual entries, so I couldn't possibly take time out to do a media appearance."

Timothy placed both hands flat on the table and smiled at Theodosia. It was a wide, barracuda smile. A smile that meant he'd finagled his way. "The matter's settled then," said Timothy. "Theodosia will be our media spokesperson and do the on-air appearance with *Windows on Charleston.*"

"Good for you," said Parker, patting her on the back.

"I didn't exactly volunteer," muttered Theodosia.

"The television appearance was the last thing on the docket," said Timothy, gazing down the length of the table. "So we seem to have matters well under control."

"What about a photographer?" asked Celerie. "Were you able to line one up?"

Timothy grimaced. "I have one. Suffice it to say he was not my first choice. Nor even my second or third. Unfortunately, all the really good photographers seemed to be booked."

"Who did you get?" asked Drayton.

"Bill Glass," replied Timothy. "The fellow who publishes *Shooting Star.*"

"Oh no," groaned Drayton. "The man's an absolute pain." He turned to Theodosia. "You remember *him.*"

Theodosia nodded. She *did* know Bill Glass and she wasn't a bit thrilled with Timothy's choice, either. Bill Glass's weekly publication, *Shooting Star*, was a glossy, gossipy tabloid. People devoured it, but that didn't make it good.

"Mr. Glass may be slightly more *commercial* than the Heritage Society is used to," responded Timothy, staring at them with hooded eyes. "But he's given me assurances that *Shooting Star* will carry a front-page promo article for Orchid Lights. And his paper does come out Friday, the day preceding our event."

"It's a rag," snipped Drayton.

Timothy, who was old enough and rich enough to face anyone down, merely said, "It's free PR."

6

A *former cotton* warehouse, the century-old brick building that stood near the corner of President and Bee streets had been updated, rehabbed, and rewired. Now it was an elegant showpiece that housed the offices of Loveday and Luxor Commodity Brokers.

Theodosia crossed the gleaming wood floor of the reception area, glancing at colorful, geometric paintings that hung on the old yellow-brick walls. Under foot was a contemporary red-and-purple area rug. A receptionist was perched behind a sleek glass desk you probably wouldn't care to sit at if you were wearing a miniskirt.

The young woman looked up from her silver laptop as Theodosia approached. "May I help you?" she asked. Her long dark hair swished at her shoulders.

"I'm here to pick up a few things from Mark Congdon's office," explained Theodosia. "I'm Theodosia Browning. I spoke with Bobby Wayne, your senior partner, yesterday?"

"Of course," said the receptionist. Her hand moved toward the intercom system, flicked a flat button. "Mr. Loveday's in a meeting, but I'll buzz Fayne. She was Mr. Congdon's administrative assistant."

"Thank you," said Theodosia. She rocked back on her heels, taking in more of the decor. And wondered why it was that when interior designers got their hands on a graceful old building, many of them felt compelled to pack it full of contemporary art objects. Wondered why they felt driven to juxtapose old with new. Was it . . .

"Miss Browning?" came a timorous voice.

Theodosia interrupted her art critique to find a young woman gazing soulfully at her. "Yes," she answered. "That's me."

The young woman extended her hand in a cordial, businesslike manner. "I'm Fayne Hamilton, Mr. Congdon's assistant."

As Theodosia shook her hand, she studied the young woman. Fayne Hamilton was midtwenties, with long brown hair, a sprinkle of freckles across her nose, and serious brown eyes. But what struck Theodosia the most was Fayne Hamilton's manner. She seemed prim and proper almost to the point of being stiff. Of course, Theodosia reasoned, her boss had just died and Fayne was undoubtedly upset, was probably still in shock.

"Are you okay?" asked Theodosia. It was not the opening she'd planned for. Her sudden concern for this young woman just sort of popped out unexpectedly.

Fayne put a hand to her chest and blinked rapidly. "Mark . . . Mr. Congdon . . . his death caught us all completely off guard. One minute we were working together and then . . ."

"Unexpected tragedies such as this," said Theodosia, "are hard on everyone. Family, friends, and certainly coworkers."

"We all thought the absolute world of Mark," said Fayne as she led Theodosia down a long hallway. "When he joined Loveday and Luxor he was a breath of fresh air."

"Had you worked with Mark for long?" asked Theodosia.

Fayne stopped in front of a closed wooden door. A gleaming brass name plate off to one side read *Mark Congdon*.

"I was his assistant the whole time he was here," said Fayne. "Which was, what? Almost six months, I guess."

"He hadn't worked here all that long," mused Theodosia, as Fayne pushed open the door.

"No," said Fayne, stepping inside Mark's office. "But he was a terrific guy. And a really smart broker, too. All his clients loved him. And trusted him."

"I suppose we should start with . . ." began Theodosia as she followed Fayne into Mark's office. She paused midsentence and gazed, startled, around Mark's office. Empty bookshelves and a cleaned-out credenza met her eyes. Two brown cardboard boxes sat atop a bare expanse of wooden desk. "Everything's packed already," said Theodosia, sounding both surprised and a little flustered. This was not what she'd expected at all.

Fayne nodded sadly. "Surprised me, too. But I was told that Martha was asked to sort through everything last night. So Mark's personal things would be all ready to go."

"Really," said Theodosia. She'd been under the distinct impression that it would be her task to go through Mark's desk. To sift through his personal items. Theodosia put a hand on one of the cardboard boxes. "Not too much here."

"I suppose most of what was in here really belonged to the firm," said Fayne. "Client records, company documents, things like that. So Martha removed all that stuff and packed up Mark's personal items." She hesitated. "Which I thought was going to be *my* job."

"Who exactly is this Martha?" asked Theodosia.

"She's Leah Shalimar's private secretary," responded Fayne. "Ms. Shalimar is taking over all Mark's accounts. She's a senior vice president just like he was."

"I see," said Theodosia, realizing what Fayne said probably made sense. Except it all felt just a little bit rushed.

"Would you like to speak with Ms. Shalimar?" asked Fayne, sensing Theodosia's hesitation. "I know she's in."

"Sure," said Theodosia. "I'd like that very much."

Fayne escorted Theodosia farther down the corridor and rapped gently on a closed door. Then she pushed it open and led her into an expansive corner office with dark red walls and black Chinese-style furniture. Leah Shalimar was on the phone, but smiled brightly and waved them in. Then she held up an index finger to indicate she'd be with them in just one minute.

While Leah Shalimar purred to her client, or whoever it was she was talking to, Theodosia studied her. Leah Shalimar was superskinny in her plum-colored suit, with a sweep of dark hair, expressive eyebrows over darting eyes, and a hyperactive manner. Though she was on the phone, Leah Shalimar was in constant motion. She paced back and forth behind her desk, drummed her lacquered nails on her file cabinet, flipped through her Rolodex, all the while grabbing sips from an oversized coffee mug. Leah reminded Theodosia of a shark, the one ocean creature that must keep moving in order to stay alive.

Theodosia decided that Leah Shalimar had to ingest more than a few cups of espresso a day to generate that much activity. In fact, with the nervous energy she was putting off, South Carolina Electric & Gas could probably harness Leah and power half of Charleston.

"Hell-ooo," said Leah Shalimar once she was off the phone. She dashed around her desk, grasped both of Theodosia's hands, and flashed a dazzling smile. "So nice to finally meet you. Bobby Wayne has told me so much about your tea shop. And . . ." Now she favored Fayne with a quick smile, too. ". . . how supportive you've been to Mark's poor wife."

"Angie and I have been friends for a long time," murmured Theodosia.

Leah Shalimar took a step backward. "So, are the police any closer to discovering what really happened to Mark?"

"I'm not exactly privy to that sort of information," said Theodosia, wondering if Leah Shalimar actually knew something or if she was just fishing around.

"The police are *investigating*?" asked Fayne, looking worried. "I thought Mark died of a heart attack."

"Don't believe everything you hear," said Leah, her gaze drilling into Theodosia.

"You mean something *happened* to Mark?" asked Fayne. "Like foul play?" She seemed suddenly upset and on the verge of tears.

"That's for the authorities to determine," said Leah. She turned an unsympathetic eye on Fayne. "Why don't you run and tell Bobby Wayne that Miss Browning is here. I'm absolutely positive he'll want to pop in and say how-do."

Fayne hesitated a moment and cast a glance at Theodosia. "If you need any help going through those boxes . . ." she said.

"Thank you," said Theodosia, watching as Fayne turned reluctantly and left the office.

Leah, wasting no time, hunched her shoulders forward and gestured for Theodosia to take a chair. "Come. Sit down," Leah urged. She was obviously a high-energy woman used to having her way. Her stiletto heels sounded like rifle reports as she scooted back around her desk and plopped down in her chair, smiling at Theodosia across her ocean-sized desk.

"Lovely to finally meet you," said Leah. "I understand you were a good friend of Mark's. In fact, he mentioned your name to me several times."

"Mark was a terrific person," said Theodosia. "All of us at the Indigo Tea Shop will miss him very much."

Leah put a hand to her chest. "As will we. His passing is a terrible blow." She closed her eyes for a moment, as if the memory of Mark Congdon was almost too much to bear. Then her eyes popped open and she leaned forward across her desk. "You know," said Leah. "I've heard some amazing things about your little enterprise. It's reputed to be terribly cozy and charming. With marvelous food." Leah pronounced the word *mahvelous*, drawing out the "a" like an old silver screen actress might.

"We've gotten our fair share of good press," said Theodosia, wondering what the whole story was behind this slightly manic woman. "And we pride ourselves on having satisfied customers."

"Your stopping by has just sparked the most *brilliant* idea," announced Leah, dropping her voice in a conspiratorial manner. "I'm supposed to host a group of women for lunch tomorrow. Business women. Potential investors, actually. Wouldn't it be a kick if we came to your tea shop?"

"Tomorrow?" asked Theodosia. *Wow, this woman works fast. Maybe that's why she's a hotshot commodity broker.*

"Yes," said Leah, growing more and more enchanted with her idea. "I was going to take my group to Le Pouvre, but your place would be far more suitable. From what I hear it's extremely civilized." Leah grabbed her day-date book and scanned it eagerly. "Shall we say one o'clock?"

"Fine," said Theodosia, knowing she'd have to give a heads-up to Drayton and Haley. "We'd love to have you. How many guests?"

"Five in all," said Leah, holding up a hand and splaying out her fingers. "Oh, and make sure everything is *très* elegant, will you? We'll be expecting the unexpected."

"Will do," promised Theodosia, knowing in her heart that every single tea or luncheon that she, Drayton, and Haley catered and served was considered special. They wouldn't have it any other way.

"Knock knock," said a male voice.

"Bobby Wayne," exclaimed Leah. "Come in. Look who's here."

"Hello, Theodosia," said Bobby Wayne. He walked over to where Theodosia was sitting, bent down, and gave her a chaste peck on the cheek. "Good to see you."

"She dropped by to collect Mark's personal belongings," explained Leah. "To help expedite things I had Martha pack everything last night."

"Is that right?" said Bobby. He cast a warm and sympathetic smile toward Theodosia. "It's awfully nice of you to be so helpful to Angie. I spoke with her last night and she couldn't say enough good things about you and Drayton."

"And I understand you'll be giving the eulogy at Mark's funeral on Thursday," said Theodosia.

Bobby Wayne nodded sadly. "I didn't think it was my place, but Angie was so insistent I just couldn't say no."

"I'm sure you'll do a wonderful job," said Theodosia. A few months ago, Delaine had twisted Bobby Wayne's arm to serve as master of ceremonies for an Animal Rescue League fund-raiser and he'd done a wonderful job. So Theodosia expected Bobby Wayne would be able to find just the right words for Mark's funeral service. "And thank *you* for being there for Angie," added Theodosia.

"I told her anything I could do to help, she should just call. Day or night. After all," said Bobby Wayne, "Mark was family."

Leah's phone shrilled and she made a fast grab for it. "Hello? Leah here."

Bobby Wayne faced Theodosia again. "Can I give you a hand with those boxes you came to fetch?" he asked. "Apparently everything of Mark's has already been packed."

"So I've discovered," said Theodosia.

They waved good-bye to Leah, then trooped back down the hall to Mark Congdon's office. Bobby Wayne grabbed the two boxes off the now-empty desk and lugged them out to the parking lot.

"Thanks so much," said Theodosia as she popped open the back door of her Jeep.

"No problem," said Bobby Wayne, although his face was a little red and his breathing had become somewhat labored.

For some reason, Theodosia had forgotten all about the cardboard box containing the broken glass.

Good lord, she thought to herself as she gave that box a quick shove toward the front, then flipped a piece of tarp over it. But Bobby Wayne appeared not to notice as he struggled to load the boxes he'd just ferried down.

"Leah seems like a very capable executive," said Theodosia as she shut the back hatch. There was something about Leah Shalimar that didn't sit right with her and she wanted to find out more.

"Leah's not only smart, she's a hard worker, too," responded Bobby Wayne. He'd pulled out a white hanky and was mopping his brow. "She's especially stepped up to the plate now that she's going to be handling some of our very special accounts."

"I understand Leah is taking over for Mark?" said Theodosia, remembering what Fayne Hamilton had told her earlier.

"She is now," said Bobby Wayne.

"So in a way it's a kind of promotion for Leah?" prodded Theodosia.

Bobby Wayne cocked a sharp eye at Theodosia. "I never thought about it that way, but, yes, I suppose it is. To be honest, it was always a question of who would head the firm's FOREX Division, Mark or Leah. They were the two big stars of the firm." Bobby Wayne shook his head and sighed deeply. "Now, sadly, that question's been answered. Tragic circumstances spared us from making that difficult decision."

I wonder, thought Theodosia, *I wonder if that's completely true.*

7

❧

Hot crab casserole was one of Theodosia's favorite luncheon entrées. Loaded with good Carolina blue crab, the dish was creamy, cheesy, and sinfully rich. All the attributes Theodosia loved in food, but probably should be wary of. Plus, Haley was serving her crab casserole with traditional southern spoonbread. What a delightful combination!

"This looks fabulous, Haley," exclaimed Theodosia. She'd ducked in through the back door and dumped her handbag on top of a landslide of catalogs and correspondence that was mounded atop her perpetually messy desk. Now Theodosia slipped an apron over her head and threaded the strings around her waist as she admired Haley's cooking prowess.

"The crab casserole's a cinch," said Haley, pulling her first pan, all golden brown and bubbling, from the oven.

"And the spoonbread's just plain fun—there's no niftier way to combine butter, milk, cornmeal, and eggs. Anyway, I thought the combo would make for a nice luncheon duo today. Oh, and there's chilled crab salad, too. Just in case some folks prefer cold instead of hot."

"You hit the fish market this morning," observed Theodosia.

"Oh yeah," said Haley, who was a stickler for buying fresh food as well as making full use of local produce. On almost any given morning you could find Haley Parker, wicker basket in hand, stalking the open air farmer's markets. Prodding the red snapper, casting a watchful eye out for the best flounder, cobia, and bluefish. Haley picked up jars of local honey and jam, too. And knew a special few vendors who ventured out into the woods hunting for tasty yet short-seasoned morels. Of course, Haley's careful and discerning eye paid off big time. The customers who flocked to the Indigo Tea Shop were always delighted by Haley's traditional recipes as well as her imaginative nouvelle creations.

Theodosia glanced at her watch. It read eleven-thirty. "When will you be ready to serve?" she asked.

"Be about five minutes," replied Haley. "Drayton's already taken the orders, so maybe just go out and check that everyone's teacups are filled. Oh, and I made a pitcher of strawberry slush tea, too. It's chilling in the fridge."

"Haley, you're a wonder," said Theodosia as she slipped between the velvet drapes and out into the tea room.

"Well, hello there," said Drayton. He was behind the counter, ringing up a take-out order of tea and scones. "Everything go okay?" he asked once he'd packed the order in one of their signature indigo-blue bags and handed it over to the customer.

"Yes and no," said Theodosia.

Drayton raised an eyebrow. "Do tell," he said.

"Mark's things had already been packed by the time I got there," said Theodosia. "So the only real work was carting a couple boxes down to my Jeep, which Bobby Wayne kindly helped with."

"I don't see the problem," said Drayton as he ladled a scoop of rich black Darjeeling tea into a blue-and-white teapot. Wait a minute," he mumbled to himself. "Did table six want the Jungpana Estate or the Singel Estate?" He thought for a minute. "Jungpana." He glanced over at Theodosia. "Okay, now I'm listening."

"This was all done under the suggestion of Leah Shalimar, one of their VPs," said Theodosia.

"I think I remember Mark mentioning her once," said Drayton. "Said she was a firecracker. Or maybe it was a pistol."

"She's got firepower all right," said Theodosia. "In fact, now that poor Mark is out of the picture she's taken over all his accounts."

That got Drayton's attention. "Is that a fact?" he said. He stared at Theodosia, waiting for more. But she was silent. "There's something you're not telling me," said Drayton.

"I got a strange . . . what would you call it? A strange *vibe* from Leah Shalimar."

"Good vibe or bad vibe?" asked Drayton.

"Not one hundred percent good," admitted Theodosia. "Fact is, she didn't seem all that distressed by Mark's passing. And Bobby Wayne let slip that Leah and Mark had been up for the same job."

"Hmm," said Drayton. "Interesting. You don't suppose

this Leah Shalimar could have . . . um . . ." He stopped, unwilling to finish his sentence.

"I know exactly what you're thinking," said Theodosia. "And I have no earthly clue." She lifted the glass top off their pastry display, took out a peach scone, and placed it on a small Chinese-patterned blue-and-white plate. "But I'm sure as heck going to sniff around some more."

Just when things couldn't get any busier, Theodosia got a phone call. Haley called her name across the tea shop, trying to make herself heard above the chirp of tea kettles, the chatter of happy customers, and the gentle clink of teacups against saucers.

"Can you take a message?" Theodosia mouthed to Haley. She was pouring refills and balancing what she figured had to be their final tray of entrées to dispense.

Haley shook her head and her long blond hair swished about her shoulders. "It's important," she mouthed back.

Turns out, it was.

"Miz Browning?" came Sheriff Billing's booming voice once Theodosia had dashed into her office. "This is Sheriff Ernest T. Billings. We spoke yesterday?"

"Yes, of course," said Theodosia. When she'd called him late yesterday afternoon, Sheriff Billings had been somewhat skeptical about finding any kind of significant evidence on the broken painted glass.

"I've been noodling around what you said, so I made a phone call to the state crime lab? They think it might be helpful to analyze those broken pieces after all." He paused, mindful that he'd all but blown her off earlier. "Plus one of the docs at the hospital ran some new kind of test on Mr. Congdon's blood and tissue samples. Trying to narrow the diagnosis down a bit more." There was another pregnant pause. "So . . . do you still have those pieces?"

"I do," said Theodosia, her heart skipping a hopeful beat. The wheels of justice turned slowly, but at least they were turning. She could picture Sheriff Billings in her mind, looking slightly bulky in his khaki uniform, running a finger through thin, graying hair, his square jaw set firmly as he made this request and delivered his sort-of apology.

"Would you be willing to drop those pieces by my office?" asked Sheriff Billings.

Theodosia glanced around the tea shop. They were just finishing up lunch and had a tea-tasting group coming early afternoon. Plus she had to clue Drayton and Haley in about Leah Shalimar's special luncheon tomorrow.

"I'm awfully busy right now," she told Sheriff Billings. "But I could certainly drive out after work."

"That'd be just swell," said Sheriff Billings. "Just leave the whole shebang at my office, okay? You know where that is? Corner of Boone and Hopper? A couple of my boys will be there unless something else happens out this way. And I pray it does not."

"I'll deliver it," Theodosia assured him. "And you'll have the analysis done as soon as possible?"

"I'll send it to the state crime lab first thing tomorrow," promised Sheriff Billings.

Theodosia didn't get a chance to tell Drayton about Sheriff Billing's call until lunch and his tea tasting were over. But he was still wildly enthusiastic.

"That's wonderful news," said Drayton. "We should run right down and tell Angie."

"Are you sure we should both go?" asked Theodosia. She was torn between giving Angie her much-needed privacy and being a caring, supportive friend.

"Angie's already highly suspicious about the circumstances surrounding Mark's death," said Drayton. "It's just that she's still too stunned to do anything about it."

"So that's where we come in," said Theodosia.

"Exactly," said Drayton. "Besides, you wanted to give her Mark's address book . . ."

"Oh, man, I'll have to dig that out of my Jeep," said Theodosia, suddenly embarrassed that she'd forgotten all about the address book.

"And I need to fill Angie in on a few more details concerning Thursday's service," said Drayton.

"Okay," said Theodosia. "Then let's do it."

Teddy Vickers met them at the front door of the Featherbed House. He was carrying an armload of fresh towels and looked tired and grumpy. "Back again?" he asked.

"Is Angie around?" asked Drayton, ignoring Teddy's strangely brusque manner.

Teddy spun on his heels. "I'll get her."

Theodosia wondered why Teddy was so snarly. With no guests booked at the inn, he certainly couldn't be all that busy. After all, Drayton was pretty much handling all the details for the funeral service. Maybe, Theodosia decided, Teddy had been closer to Mark than she thought. And just displayed his grief in a different way.

"You're not going to believe this," said Angie, once the three of them were seated in the lobby again and she had Mark's address book clutched tightly in her hands. "Harlan Noble dropped by to see me not more than fifteen minutes ago."

Drayton frowned and adjusted his bow tie. "Are you serious? For what reason?"

Angie looked more than a little perturbed. "It seems Mr. Noble wants to purchase Mark's orchid collection."

"His orchids?" said Drayton, trying to digest what Angie had just told them. "You mean *all* of them?"

Angie nodded. "That's what he said. The entire collection, lock, stock, and barrel. But I got the feeling he was most interested in the monkey-face orchid."

"Good heavens," exclaimed Drayton. "Harlan is certainly a persistent fellow. What on earth did you tell him?"

"I thanked him for his offer and told him I'm not up to making any major decisions at this time," said Angie. "And I'm not." She followed her statement with a slightly worried frown. "And, frankly, I didn't much appreciate Mr. Noble's aggressiveness. Even though his offer was couched in a gesture of sympathy, I could tell what his true agenda was."

Theodosia shook her head. "Harlan Noble had no business coming over here and asking about Mark's orchids. He should be mindful of your privacy right now."

"I suppose he's dying to exhibit that monkey-face orchid in Saturday's big show," said Drayton. He gazed at Angie and shrugged, almost apologetically. "It *is* a lovely plant."

"It is," agreed Angie. She lifted her head and focused her gaze intently on Drayton. "Which is why I want *you* to exhibit it."

"What?" said a surprised Drayton, his voice suddenly rising a full octave. "Are you *serious*?"

"I couldn't be more serious," said Angie. "In fact, I want you to have the entire collection."

"Oh, no," stammered Drayton. "I'm truly touched, but I couldn't accept such a magnanimous gift."

"Of course, you could," said Angie. "You were Mark's friend and you have the skills necessary to keep the orchids going. If they stay here in our little greenhouse I'm sure I'll either under water or overfeed them, causing them to just wither away."

"It's too much," said Drayton, still protesting. He fingered his bow tie and gazed at Theodosia, hoping for moral support.

But she was firmly on Angie's side.

"You can do this, Drayton," urged Theodosia. "You've got the proverbial green thumb. Look how good your cultivation know-how is when it comes to Japanese bonsai. You're always winning awards at various exhibitions. Orchids might be a little trickier, I suppose, but I have complete faith that you can keep Mark's collection going. Besides, Drayton, your caring for Mark's orchids would be a kind of . . . well . . . a living tribute to him."

"A truly fitting memorial," agreed Angie.

"Goodness," said Drayton, still stunned. "I suppose when you put it that way . . ." He paused, wiped at the corner of one eye. "I'm just so very touched and honored. I mean, Mark's got a Fen orchid and a Southern Twayblade. Either one would be spectacular to own. But both of them. *All* of them!"

"Then it's settled," said Angie, looking slightly hopeful

for the first time in days. "Besides, passing the orchids on to you is the least I can do. You've given me so much help in planning Mark's service at the cathedral."

"Oh, I'm happy to," said Drayton. "Well, not exactly *happy*, but . . ." Drayton stopped abruptly, looking supremely flustered.

Angie patted his hand gently. "That's okay, Drayton, I know what you mean."

Once Theodosia and Drayton had said their good-byes and were standing on the front sidewalk, Drayton decided he wanted to pop into Mark's greenhouse. So they followed a stone footpath around the side of the large wooden inn to the secluded back garden.

Alternating squares of lush green lawn and redbrick patio were framed by well-tended flower beds. In the center a small pond teemed with goldfish. Wrought-iron tables and chairs and benches of woven river willow completed the relaxing scene.

The small greenhouse sat underneath the second-story walkway that connected the main house to the carriage house.

"This is amazing," exclaimed Theodosia as they pushed open the creaking door and stepped inside. Brilliant green foliage highlighted by bright blooms stood out like neon against the whitewashed windows. Gravel crunched underfoot.

Drayton nodded. "Like we've been instantly transported to a magical, tropical garden."

On either side of them large wooden tables were jam-packed with orchids, all in various stages of growth and bloom. Above their heads, flowering orchids were contained in wire baskets stuffed with sphagnum moss. Many of the longer roots dangled down, trailing in the air.

"Look at this white cattleya," said Drayton. "So simple, yet so magnificent. And over here, a Jewel orchid."

"What's this one?" asked Theodosia, indicating a small orchid with brilliant magenta spots spattered against yellow-green petals.

"Don't quote me," said Drayton, "because I'm still an amateur when it comes to orchid culture. But it's probably a Vandopsis."

Theodosia's eyes continued to take it all in hungrily. "And are these bromeliads?" she asked. Reaching out, she touched the tip of her finger to a stiff, spiny plant that boasted a brilliant purple-pink flower in the center.

"They are," said Drayton. "Sort of orchid second cousins."

"Everything looks so healthy," remarked Theodosia. "Mark must have been an amazingly gifted horticulturist."

"He was very particular about using only rainwater or distilled water," said Drayton.

"And the aroma in here is simply heavenly," sighed Theodosia. Inhaling the heady scents from the orchids reminded her of the poppy field scene in *The Wizard of Oz*. Dorothy, the Scarecrow, and the Cowardly Lion are all seduced by the heady scents from the flowers and decide to curl up and take naps. Almost forgetting about their visit to Emerald City.

"Just think," said Theodosia, gazing at the riot of blooming plants. "These all belong to you now."

Drayton shook his head, a perplexed frown suddenly descending. "Too much," he muttered. "It's simply too much."

* * *

When they finally got back to the tea shop, Theodosia coaxed Drayton into helping her unload the Jeep.

"Sure, sure," agreed Drayton. "No problem." He still seemed completely stunned by Angie's generous gift to him.

She led him around to the back alley where her Jeep was parked outside the back door, then popped open the back hatch.

"Just these two boxes?" asked Drayton, grappling for the two cardboard boxes that had come from Loveday and Luxor.

"Right," said Theodosia. "That smaller box is the one with the broken glass."

"Good lord," said Drayton as he struggled to pull out the boxes. "Just *having* those glass fragments around makes me nervous."

"After tonight you won't have to worry," she promised.

"Hey," said Haley as they tromped into Theodosia's office. "Good thing you guys came back. We just got a *mongo* delivery from FedEx! Five big boxes!"

"My new teas are here," exclaimed Drayton. "Outstanding!" He unceremoniously dumped Theodosia's boxes on top of her desk and dashed toward the front of the shop.

Theodosia, who'd been following in Drayton's footsteps, tried to stem the miniature landslide he'd set into motion on her desk. "I've just gotta clean this stuff up," she vowed to herself.

"You want a strawberry muffin?" Haley asked Theodosia. "There's still a few left and I just latched the front door, so they're yours if you want 'em." Haley paused. "And there's profiteroles, too. I could fill a couple with chocolate ice cream and top them with whipped cream."

"Just a muffin is great," said Theodosia as she slid her fingernails under the tape and pulled open the top of one of the cardboard boxes. "I'll be right out."

"Gotcha," said Haley, disappearing into her kitchen.

Theodosia dug into the box, wondering if there was anything else of Mark's that Angie might need right away. She sifted through a stack of business magazines and a week's worth of the *Financial Times*. "This can all be tossed," she muttered to herself, knowing it would be unproductive and wearing for Angie to sort through old publications.

Under a box of Cohiba cigars, Theodosia found an unused plane ticket, an invitation to an opening at the Cameo Gallery, and a brochure for the Plantation Ramble. She glanced at these three items idly as she carried them out into the tea shop, ready to sit down and enjoy her muffin and probably sample one of the new teas that had just arrived.

True to his nature, Drayton already had a teapot steeping as he hurriedly ransacked through the rest of his boxes.

"Here you go," said Haley as she hustled out and set a small plate that bore a single muffin in front of Theodosia. "Enjoy."

Theodosia took a nibble of strawberry muffin as she continued to glance at the three items she'd grabbed. The plane ticket was for a trip to Nassau in the Bahamas. She didn't know if it was related to business or pleasure, so she decided she'd better hand the ticket over to Angie. Let her decide. The invitation was for a fancy art opening last week, so that could just be tossed.

Theodosia studied the final item, the Plantation Ramble

brochure. It was a four-color foldout piece that was fairly well produced. Good paper stock, decent printing, lots of color photographs. She'd seen these same flyers all over town and out at Carthage Place Plantation, but had never really looked at one close up until now.

"Have some butter," said Haley, setting another small plate on the table. "It's unsalted."

"Thanks," said Theodosia. She picked up a tiny silver knife, carved out a small slice of butter, and spread it on her muffin. "Mmm . . . good," she remarked.

"What's in the two boxes?" asked Haley. "Junk from Mark's office?"

Theodosia nodded. "Stuff I was supposed to pack up, but got packed for me."

"You want me to carry 'em upstairs to your apartment?" asked Haley. "In case you haven't noticed, you don't have a lot of extra room in that office of yours." Haley was a neat-nik of the first magnitude and was always fighting to banish clutter.

"I think the boxes are pretty heavy," replied Theodosia. At least Drayton had made them seem so.

"I've been studying martial arts," bragged Haley. "Tae Kwon Do. So I'm a lot stronger than I look."

"Well, okay," said Theodosia. "Just be careful. Don't hurt your back or anything."

"Hey," said Haley, "you want me to get you another muffin? There's more left."

"No, thanks, I'm fine," said Theodosia as she perused the brochure with its impressive list of gardens at Carthage Place Plantation. Just as Delaine had mentioned, there was a rose garden, an English garden, a hedge maze, and a water bog. But there were more gardens listed here, too. A butterfly garden, an herb garden, and . . .

A small wrinkle insinuated itself between Theodosia's normally placid brows. Something had just struck her as odd. "Does anybody know about this nightshade garden?" she suddenly asked out loud.

"Hmm?" said a distracted Drayton. He was like a kid on Christmas morning, unpacking his new shipment of Darjeeling, Assam, and Nilgiri teas that had just arrived from India.

"The nightshade garden," repeated Theodosia. "At Carthage Place Plantation. Haley?"

"Don't know," murmured Haley as she moved off to clear the last of the tables.

"Drayton?" asked Theodosia.

"Not sure," he said, balancing a tin of Singbulli Estate Darjeeling in one hand and a tin of Doomni Assam in the other. "I'd imagine it's their contemplative garden. Probably very low-key and lovely, filled with lilies and evening primrose and such."

Nightshade, Theodosia thought to herself. *That doesn't sound all that contemplative. In fact, it sounds a little ominous.*

"I'd like to go out there and take a peek," Theodosia said to Drayton.

At hearing her words, Drayton spun around. She'd finally captured his attention. "Are you serious?" he asked. "Why?"

"Well, I have to deliver that broken glass . . ."

"And . . . ?" prodded Drayton.

"Chalk the rest up to curiosity," said Theodosia.

Drayton pulled a single furry eyebrow into a quivering,

disapproving arc. "If you recall," he told her in a somber voice, "curiosity killed the cat."

And maybe even Mark Congdon, Theodosia thought to herself.

8

Carthage Place Plantation at night seemed a totally alien environment. Sunday afternoon the grounds had been festive and fun, filled with tents, decorated booths, and strolling guests. Now it appeared as though a dark curtain had descended. The sprawling plantation house rose up like a solemn, stone sentinel, the gardens receded to dark tangles, the nearby woods seemed to encroach upon everything.

"You spoke with the owner?" asked Theodosia, as her Jeep crunched across gravel, then rolled to a stop.

"A Miss Maybelle Chase," replied Drayton as he unfastened his seat belt. "And I must say, she was most hospitable. Said to wander about the grounds to our heart's content, then ring the bell at the main house if there was anything we needed."

"Good grief, she lives out here all alone?" asked Theodosia as they climbed out of the Jeep. In the deep, inky darkness, the enormous live oak trees with their gnarled branches dripping long tendrils of Spanish moss seemed almost ominous. Fog stealing in from the Ashley River seemed to gather in ethereal puffs about their feet.

"I didn't ask," said Drayton, glancing about. "But I see what you're getting at. It's spooky out here."

"No kidding," said Theodosia as they set off across damp grass.

Fifteen‾ minutes earlier they had delivered the broken pitcher parts to Sheriff Billing's office. Now they were wandering about in darkness, trying to figure out exactly where the nightshade garden was located.

"If the hedge maze is over here," said Drayton, gesturing toward their old nemesis, "then maybe the nightshade garden is over this way."

"Okay," said Theodosia. "Sounds like a plan." She had no idea where the garden was located, but had a fairly healthy trust in Drayton's ideas and judgment calls.

Five minutes later she wasn't so sure.

"Drat," exclaimed a disgusted Drayton. "Stay where you are."

"What's wrong?" asked Theodosia, who was a few steps behind him.

Drayton lifted one foot up and Theodosia heard the telltale squish and suck of mud.

"I think I just discovered the water bog garden," Drayton told her in a disgusted tone of voice.

"Okay," said Theodosia. Feeling seeping moisture encroach on her loafers as well, she promptly wheeled to the left. "What say we try over this way." The clouds overhead had parted slightly and a small spill of moonlight had appeared.

"Give me a minute," said Drayton, more than a little cranky now. Pulling a hanky from his jacket, he backtracked, then balanced on one leg like a shaky whooping crane. Wiping a glop of mud from his shoe, he sighed dramatically. "Okay, lead on. Maybe you'll fare better than I did."

But this evening Theodosia's orienteering skills weren't exactly dead on, either. They wandered through bowers of trees, scrambled up a fairly steep slope, and tiptoed past the dark rose garden where tree frogs croaked out their evening medley.

"Didn't we just travel in a gigantic circle?" asked Drayton, peering through fog that continued to drift in and lend a fuzzy, soft-focus feel to the landscape. "Isn't that the main house?"

"Looks too small," said a slightly puzzled Theodosia. "And the wrong shape, too."

"You're right," said Drayton as they drew closer. "Oh, good heavens, you know what this is? We just stumbled upon what used to be an old rice mill."

"Now we know we're really off course," said Theodosia.

"I'll say," agreed Drayton.

"Look," said Theodosia as they approached the old building. "It's practically falling down. Pity." Silvered with age, the ancient rice mill was a small two-storied affair that leaned badly to one side.

"Just think, a hundred years ago these steam-powered threshing and pounding mills were commonplace," said Drayton. "You see over there, that's what's left of the chimney. That's where the firepower came from. An independent structure connected to the mill by an underground system."

"You really know this stuff," said Theodosia. Sometimes

she wondered if there was anything to do with South Carolina history, literature, or lore that Drayton *didn't* know.

"Not quite," responded Drayton. "I merely gave you a sort of Cliffs Notes version."

Curious now, Theodosia stepped up to the door and gave a tentative push. It swung inward with a loud creak, revealing cracked wooden floorboards. "I think somebody kept animals in here," sniffed Theodosia.

"Not all that recently," warned Drayton as a shaft of moonlight shone down through a large gap in the roof. He gazed in after her. "And be extremely careful, half the floorboards appear to be missing and the remaining wood is like tinder. If you lit a match in here, this whole thing would probably be gone in a heartbeat."

"Well," said Theodosia, taking two cautious steps in. "*Somebody* was here recently." She bent over and picked up a crumpled piece of blue paper.

"Someone likes to live dangerously," said Drayton.

"Let's just try to find that nightshade garden," said Theodosia as they exited the rice mill. Hunching her shoulders to the chill night air, she regretted that she hadn't dressed a little warmer or brought along a sweater.

"Maybe . . . over there?" proposed Drayton, pointing toward a wooden bridge that was barely noticeable in the darkness and increasing swirl of mist. "I tromped around here Sunday but never did explore the gardens across that footbridge." He paused. "If there even are any gardens."

"That's the only place we haven't looked," agreed Theodosia.

But crossing the bridge proved to be a rather strange experience. Suspended over a small burbling stream by a system of ropes that extended up into the trees, the narrow wooden bridge swayed dangerously and the planks echoed hollowly as Theodosia and Drayton marched across single file.

"This is like walking the plank," said Theodosia.

"Most unnerving," agreed Drayton, clutching the wooden railings as he shuffled along.

Once they'd crossed over the bridge they hesitated again. The forest was a lot darker over here, a lot more foreboding.

"This is certainly atmospheric," said Theodosia. "I sure wish we'd brought a flashlight."

"Agreed," said Drayton. "Where do you think *this* path leads?" He indicated a stone pathway that peeled off toward the right and disappeared into dense foliage.

"Let's find out," said Theodosia.

Gingerly, they followed the narrow pathway for about fifty paces, pushing aside branches and hanging vines.

"This isn't going anywhere," fretted Drayton. "Unless it leads to a caretaker's cottage or something."

"Hold on," said Theodosia. She was two steps ahead of him and had been watching the ground on either side of the pathway. "There's some sort of marker up ahead."

Drayton tiptoed forward and peered down. "Set way down there, who do you think it was designed for? Trolls?" He sounded snappy, almost cantankerous.

"This is it," breathed Theodosia. Carved into a small, knee-level wooden sign were the words *Nightshade Garden*.

"Strange little marker," muttered Drayton.

"Come on," said Theodosia as she turned off the stone path onto a narrow gravel path.

"I'm coming, I'm coming," Drayton said irritably as he followed behind. "But what I really want to know is . . ."

Drayton stopped dead in his tracks, mouth open. "Good heavens!"

Theodosia and Drayton both gazed in awe at a white marble statue that seemed to rise out of the forest floor. It was the figure of a giant angel, one knee bent as if in prayer, head down, wings fully extended.

"What's *that* doing way out here?" asked Drayton.

"I'd say she's guarding the garden," said Theodosia. In the dappled moonlight the angel appeared shimmery and ghostly.

"Is it a she?" asked Drayton. "Or a he?"

"Not sure," said Theodosia. "Although now that you mention it, all the important angels seem to be male. Michael, Gabriel, Raphael."

"Well, this certainly isn't much of a garden," sniffed Drayton, giving a perfunctory look at the mostly green plants that spread out in a dense circle around the statue. "I suppose I was expecting plants that flower at night. You know, like evening primrose, moonflower, or angel's trumpet."

Bending down, Theodosia studied a series of metal plaques. "These plants are a slightly different variety," said Theodosia, her voice suddenly tight. "Take a look. There's a reason this was dubbed the nightshade garden."

But Drayton was beginning to fidget. "Really, it's getting awfully late, Theodosia. Don't you think . . ."

"Belladonna." Theodosia's voice rang out as she read from the ornate metal plaque at the base of a leafy green plant. She moved a few steps forward, read off another name. "Banewort."

"What?" yelped Drayton. He spun around as if he'd suddenly been stung by something.

"Black nightshade, foxglove, poison rhubarb," continued Theodosia. She stared at him, her gaze level and serious. "That's what's growing in this garden," she told him.

"You've got to be kidding," said Drayton, backing up a couple of steps now. "Who on earth would want to grow that stuff?"

"Obviously Miss Maybelle Chase does," said Theodosia.

"How exceedingly strange," said Drayton.

"I agree," said Theodosia. "But the burning question in my mind is, could one of these plants be the nonspecific toxin that caused Mark Congdon's death?"

Drayton stared at her for a few long moments. "What a terrifying thought," he finally said.

They walked slowly back around the statue, letting the notion of a garden filled with deadly plants settle over them. Crickets and the occasional cicada chirped and clicked, from a distance came the low hoot of an owl. Dead-on sound effects for a very eerie setting.

"So why an angel out here?" Drayton finally asked as he stared at the marble statue with its cool, stoic face. "Surrounded by all these dangerous, awful plants. What on earth do you think it means?"

"Not sure," said Theodosia. "Maybe . . . an angel of death?"

Stepping into the big plantation house was like stepping back in time to the Victorian age. Tapestries hung on walls. Aubusson carpets covered gleaming wood floors. Lamps with fringed shades threw dim light on native cypress woodwork. Stuffed furniture was in shades of brown and apple green. Theodosia recognized a drawing by William Bartran, an early artist and naturalist who had sketched many of the South's indigenous plants and animals.

"This is a very impressive home," Drayton told Miss Maybelle once he and Theodosia had introduced themselves.

"Thank you kindly," said Miss Maybelle. She was a tiny woman, probably in her late seventies, with an aristocratic air about her. Her rich purple dress had a beautiful cameo brooch pinned to it.

"It was so generous of you to open your home to the Plantation Ramble this past weekend," said Theodosia. "And allow visitors access to your beautiful gardens."

"It's always a pleasure to work with the community and the different garden clubs," said Miss Maybelle. Her bright eyes peered sharply at the two of them. "You know, there just aren't that many authentic plantations left in South Carolina. It's important for folks to be able to come out and view a real slice of history. Of course, it gives the docents something to look forward to, as well."

"I take it you have docents that help with the gardens?" asked Drayton.

"You don't think I do it all myself, do you?" she asked with a mischievous grin on her lined face. "And, of course, the docents are tasked with taking visitors on guided tours, too. Usually on one designated weekend a month."

"Do you by any chance have a list of docents?" asked Theodosia.

"I suppose I do," said Miss Maybelle. She crooked a finger and they followed her into the library. She walked around a large rolltop desk and pulled open one of the narrow drawers. "This last Plantation Ramble was one of our most successful," Miss Maybelle told them as she continued to search through paperwork. "Raised a lot of money for charity. The only unfortunate incident was that poor fellow who suffered a heart attack!" Miss Maybelle looked up and clapped a small, gnarled hand over her own heart. "Wasn't that a shame?" She shuddered, as though the very thought of Mark's collapse still upset her terribly. "I certainly hope he's all right."

"Unfortunately, he did not survive," Theodosia told her.

Miss Maybelle's face crumpled. "Oh no. Isn't that *awful*. I had no idea."

Theodosia saw no point in telling Miss Maybelle how Mark Congdon had really died. Not yet anyway. Especially since no one was sure of the exact cause.

"Here's that list," said Miss Maybelle, handing a sheet of paper to Drayton.

"Thank you," said Theodosia.

"And were you able to find the nightshade garden?" asked Miss Maybelle, still peering up at Drayton. "That's what you called about earlier, wasn't it?"

"Indeed I did," responded Drayton. "And we most certainly did locate it."

"Miss Maybelle," began Theodosia. "I'm just curious. Why on earth would you want to grow plants such as those? I mean . . . they're all so . . ."

An unexpected smile flitted across Miss Maybelle's lined face. "Deadly?" she asked. "But, my dear, those plants have flourished on this plantation for a very long time. Psilocybin mushrooms, opium poppies, banewort, belladonna, black nightshade, foxglove, poison rhubarb, and three dozen other varieties of poisonous plants and herbs."

"Good heavens," exclaimed Drayton.

"Why, that nightshade garden and the statue of the angel was here when I moved in some thirty-seven years ago," continued Miss Maybelle. "After my uncle James died and bequeathed this place to me, God rest his dear, departed soul."

"Yes," said Theodosia, still trying to wrest an answer from Miss Maybelle. "But why grow them at all?"

Miss Maybelle turned wide eyes on Theodosia. "You see, Carthage Place Plantation has been granted special permission from the state of South Carolina to grow these plants. Many clinical chemists and researchers make use of them."

"Do you know the exact purpose?" asked a perplexed Drayton.

Now it was Miss Maybelle's turn to look slightly puzzled as she glanced from Drayton to Theodosia. "I'm afraid I really don't," she told them.

9

❧

Earl Grey's nose was out of joint. He'd lobbied hard to go along with Theodosia to Carthage Place Plantation tonight and she'd told him no. Then, when Haley came over to walk him, he'd gotten a four-block jog instead of his usual two-mile romp through White Point Gardens down along the Battery.

So Earl Grey, Theodosia's Dalbrador roommate and sometime service dog, was not a happy camper. Tonight he was a put-out pup.

"C'mon, Earl Grey," Theodosia coaxed. "Eat your dinner."

The dog sniffed his bowl of kibbles with its topping of steamed rice and looked away. When Earl Grey was upset he got finicky.

"Okay," said Theodosia, feeling guilty now for leaving him at home. "Then how about a turkey neck?" Turkey and chicken necks, because they contained gristle but no bones, were excellent for dogs. High in protein, with a serious chew factor to boot.

Opening the refrigerator door, Theodosia fished out a raw turkey neck, gingerly holding the slimy offering between her thumb and index finger.

Earl Grey's expressive brown eyes sparkled but still he feigned disinterest. He walked slowly over to Theodosia, sniffed at the proffered turkey neck, then hesitated. Finally he accepted it, giving Theodosia a look that clearly said, *I'm not happy about tonight, but a fellow's got to eat.*

As the dog started toward the living room with the turkey neck clamped securely in his mouth, Theodosia called out to him, "Whoa there, pal. Keep it in here on the tile floor."

Caught in the act, Earl Grey retreated to the kitchen.

While Earl Grey nibbled his turkey neck, Theodosia heated up a bowl of crab chowder, brewed a quick cup of chamomile tea, and grabbed an almond scone. Then she arranged everything on a wicker tray and carried it in to her dining-room table. True to her word, Haley had muscled both of Mark's boxes upstairs. So now they rested on the table, too.

Maybe I'll take a quick peek through them, Theodosia thought to herself. Although the big thing on her mind right now were the plants in the nightshade garden.

She wondered who would have known that such nasty plants were growing and actually thriving right there on the grounds of Carthage Place Plantation?

Drayton had procured the list of garden docents from Miss Maybelle Chase. So maybe, tomorrow morning, she'd take a look at that. But in the meantime . . .

Earl Grey, finished with his supper now, padded in and gave his mistress an inquisitive look.

"Okay, come on in," she told him. Earl Grey, used to having the full run of Theodosia's upstairs apartment, eased himself down on her green-and-cinnamon-colored Chinese rug and proceeded to groom his suede-like paws.

Theodosia stared at the two cardboard boxes. She was tired, the hour was late, and she was of a mind to forget the whole thing. On the other hand, some rather strange forces seemed to be at work. And some decidedly quirky people were beginning to look more and more like suspects. So maybe taking a quick look through Mark's stuff would shed some light on any number of things.

Shoving her dinner tray to one side, she flipped open the lid on the first cardboard box. Digging a hand in, she grabbed a stack of papers, notes, and miscellaneous items, then spread everything out on her dining-room table and stared at it.

No, she decided, *there's a better way to do this.*

She grabbed the box, tipped it upside down, and deposited the complete contents on her table.

Messy, she thought. *But now I won't miss anything.*

Slowly, Theodosia sorted through the contents spread out closest to her: a box of business cards, a Swiss Army knife, auto club membership decals, a desk calendar. She tossed those things back into the box, then swept another pile toward her. This time she found tickets for last year's Spoleto Festival, a few canceled checks, a small ceramic elephant, and an iPod.

Nothing very telling here, she decided as she stifled a yawn.

Theodosia was about to bag the entire search when her

eyes fell upon a square envelope. It was good quality linen paper and had but one word handwritten on it: *Mark*.

Should I? wondered Theodosia, worrying that she might be peeping where she shouldn't be.

She picked up the envelope, hesitated a moment, then opened it. Inside was a square note card, trimmed in gold with a tiny embossed bee at the top.

A short message was scrawled in looping handwriting:

Dear Mark,
Thank you for the lovely birthday lunch at Trocadero.
Maybe we can do it again sometime—my treat?
Holding my breath,
Fayne

Time stood still for a moment as Theodosia absorbed the contents and gist of this note. It was a note from an employee to her boss that seemed to cross the line of being merely friendly. The words seemed wistful, hopeful, and a little bit bold.

Theodosia scrunched around in her chair and stared at the oil painting that hung over her fireplace. It was a brooding seascape of a turn-of-the-century three-masted schooner caught in tempestuous waters far from the safe harbor of Charleston. With sails ripped and giant waves pounding onto its decks, there was no doubt the sailing ship would soon be lost. As she contemplated the painting she also contemplated the possibility that Fayne Hamilton had been in love with Mark Congdon. Or, if not in love with him, at least smitten.

Is that why Fayne seemed so discombobulated about Mark's personal belongings being packed up by someone else? Theodosia wondered. *Had Fayne realized the note she sent him might have been scooped up from his desk drawer and tossed into the mix? Maybe. Definitely maybe.*

Drumming her fingernails on the table, Theodosia decided there could be more notes of this nature contained within these boxes.

If so, what would that prove? she wondered. *That Fayne and Mark had enjoyed some sort of secret relationship? Or that Fayne had been rebuffed by Mark? And, as a result, been very, very upset.*

Upset. In a *Fatal Attraction* sort of way?

Theodosia stared at the old brass clock that ticked away on the top shelf of her mahogany secretary. It was ten-thirty now and it would probably take her at least another hour to sort through all this stuff.

She stared at Earl Grey, stretched out and snoozing comfortably. It was going to be a long night.

10

❧

"Are you serious?" squawked Haley as she stared at Theodosia with saucer eyes.

Theodosia nodded, then turned her gaze on Drayton. It was nine a.m. and she had just told both of them about the two notes she'd discovered among Mark's things last night.

"So the first note was a kind of simpering thank-you?" asked Haley.

"Pretty much," said Theodosia as she sipped a cup of Mango Verde, Drayton's house blend of an Assam green tea flavored with tiny bits of mango.

"And the second note?" asked Drayton, equally surprised by this revelation. "It was definitely more . . . uh . . . passionate?"

"I'd say so," replied Theodosia. She had both notes tucked in her pocket but didn't feel it would be proper to completely reveal their contents.

"Wow," said Haley. "Looks like Mark might have been having an affair with this Fayne what's-her-name!"

"Fayne Hamilton," murmured Theodosia.

"Of course he wasn't," snapped Drayton. He paused, then peered carefully at Theodosia. "At least I don't *think* he was."

"I seriously doubt if Mark was involved with her," said Theodosia. "Both of Fayne's notes seemed more sadly hopeful than anything."

"Then maybe Fayne Hamilton *murdered* Mark," proposed Haley. "Unrequited love is a very powerful emotion. Makes people do crazy things."

"It can," agreed Drayton. He picked up the floral teapot that sat in the middle of the table and poured himself another cup of Assam.

"When you talk to Fayne Hamilton in person," said Theodosia, trying to share her impression of the girl with Drayton and Haley, "she doesn't strike you as being capable of murder. She's a quiet girl, rather polite and unassuming."

There, thought Theodosia. *That's a pretty fair assessment.*

"But that's exactly what people said about that BTK guy," exclaimed Haley. "His neighbors claimed he was a nice guy, soft-spoken, helpful, always polite. And look what a monster he turned out to be!"

"Oh, Haley, please," said Drayton. "Now you've gone to the absolute *extreme.*"

"Listen," said Haley, still wound up, "if this Fayne person knew about the nightshade garden you guys found last night, maybe she snuck in, grabbed a handful of plants, and poisoned Mark's sweet tea. After all, you guys were sticking fresh sprigs of herbs and flowers in all the glasses. Who would notice? She could have slipped it right in!"

"Ah," said Drayton, looking supremely unhappy now.

"The nightshade garden. I have some information that could put a considerable wrinkle in your theory."

Haley eyed Drayton suspiciously. "What are you talking about?"

"Last night Miss Maybelle Chase shared with me her list of garden docents." Drayton paused. "I read through the names this morning and guess who cropped up?"

"Harlan Noble," guessed Haley.

"That's right," said Drayton.

"And Leah Shalimar," said Theodosia.

Drayton pointed a gnarled index finger at Theodosia. "Bingo. That lady also wins a prize."

"So both Leah and Harlan knew about the plants and had access to them," mused Theodosia. "That's fairly interesting."

"Some might say damning," said Drayton. "You're going to phone Sheriff Billings and see if he knows about the existence of the nightshade garden?"

Theodosia glanced at her watch. "That's definitely on my agenda. Soon as we get the tea shop prepped for the day."

"Are you going to mention Leah and Harlan's names to him, too?" asked Drayton.

Theodosia thought for a minute. "I almost have to. Especially Leah, since she was a docent at Carthage Place *and* she worked with Mark."

"It's certainly a major coincidence," said Drayton, narrowing his eyes. "I wonder if Ms. Shalimar will admit to being at the Plantation Ramble on Sunday."

"Was she there?" asked Haley.

"Don't know," said Theodosia. "But you can certainly ask her. She'll be here in a matter of hours."

"Oooh, that's right," said Haley.

"Uh, excuse me, but there's another big question on the table," said Drayton. "Do you plan to tell Angie about the notes Fayne Hamilton wrote to her husband?"

"I'm kind of agonizing over that one," admitted Theodosia.

"Well, I don't think you should tell her," said Drayton. "At least not right now. Angie's in a very fragile state. Seeing those notes might upset her even more."

"What do you think, Haley?" asked Theodosia.

Haley pushed her stick-straight hair behind her ears and exhaled slowly. Finally she said, "I think, as a friend, you owe it to Angie to be completely honest."

"I was afraid you were going to say that," said Drayton.

Theodosia slipped one hand into her pocket and fingered the two notes. "A dilemma," she murmured.

Midmorning, just as their customers had settled in, just as Drayton was pouring steaming cups of Irish Breakfast tea and Theodosia was distributing lemon–poppy seed scones, Delaine Dish came bustling in. She slalomed her way through the tea shop, delivering air kisses and emitting delighted squeals as she ran into friends on the way. Then she plunked herself down at the small table next to the stone fireplace.

"Angie Congdon tells me you're investigating Mark's death," Delaine said without preamble once Theodosia had drifted over with a small pot of Russian Caravan tea and a plate arranged with a trio of fresh-baked mini pecan muffins.

Theodosia gave a hesitant smile. She didn't feel it was appropriate to reveal everything to Delaine. "Somewhat," she hedged. "Angie kind of asked for my help with some things."

"Theodosia Browning," scolded Delaine. "Here you are snooping around over another mysterious death and you didn't tell *me*? Honestly, Theo, I thought we were friends. Dear friends at that." Delaine shrugged off her raspberry pink jacket revealing a matching raspberry pink sheath dress underneath.

"We are dear friends," said Theodosia, sliding into the chair across from her and noting that Delaine's lipstick matched her dress. Theodosia always found it a little bewildering that Delaine viewed her as a best friend. Delaine was often highly critical and short with her. Although Delaine was basically kindhearted where children and small animals were concerned.

"To tell you the truth, though," said Theodosia, "I'm thinking it's really best to let the authorities handle things." Theodosia hoped her statement might help stem the tide of questions Delaine probably wanted to ask. After all, Delaine always had a long list of questions.

"Definitely let the authorities take charge," concurred Delaine as she popped a bite of pecan muffin into her mouth. She chewed thoughtfully, then leaned forward in her chair, looking to all the world like she had a nice, juicy piece of gossip to deliver. "Especially since rumors about Mark's death are spreading like wildfire."

"Are they really?" asked Theodosia. Her front teeth worried her bottom lip.

Delaine gave a smug smile, then lifted her teacup and took a delicate sip. "*Nobody* is buying that heart attack story anymore," she finally said.

Theodosia tapped her fingertips against her silver tray and pondered Delaine's statement.

Delaine, supremely pleased by the response she'd elicited, arched her eyebrows and lifted her chin. "Maybe you should call your friend Detective Tidwell," she prompted. "He could help you sort this out."

"Tidwell's not her friend," said Drayton in a dry tone as he approached Delaine's table. "Not *exactly*, anyway."

"I'm afraid Dorchester County's not within Detective Tidwell's jurisdiction," replied Theodosia. Burt Tidwell was the rather brash and brilliant detective who headed the Robbery-Homicide Division of the Charleston Police Department. He would, of course, be the perfect investigator to ferret out and question certain prime suspects in this case. But Carthage Place Plantation was located at least thirty miles outside of Charleston proper. So definitely not Tidwell's jurisdiction.

"Just a thought," murmured Delaine. "I mention it only in passing. Oh, Drayton," she called as he started to move off. "So kind of you to help make arrangements for Mark's funeral tomorrow. Although I hear you tapped Floradora for flowers when Fig and Vine is really the hot new florist. In fact, they created the most *amazing* centerpiece for one of Marianne Petigru's recent dinner parties. Giant spider mums with Japanese irises and miniature callas."

"A funeral is a far cry from a dinner party," said Drayton in a slightly disapproving tone.

Delaine picked up a linen napkin and dabbed gently at her lips. "Perhaps," she said, shrugging her shoulders, "but they're still both important social events."

* * *

Ten minutes later, Theodosia found time to slip into her back office and call Sheriff Billings. When she told him about the nightshade garden at Carthage Place Plantation, he was completely blown away.

"I never even *heard* of such a thing," he said. " 'Course, me and Mrs. Billings aren't into gardening and plants and such. I'd rather watch NASCAR races and she's a die-hard quilter. No green thumbs in our household."

"Well, there's an absolute cornucopia of poison growing out there," said Theodosia, trying to keep a shrill note from her voice and barely succeeding.

"I'll for sure roust the crime scene guys and get them out to Carthage Place," Sheriff Billings assured her. "Take samples of all those plants." He hesitated for a moment. "Heck, maybe we'll even find a match to that nonspecific toxin the docs came up with."

"A match," repeated Theodosia. *Yes, that could happen.*

"And if we get real lucky," continued Sheriff Billings, we might even find a three-way match. Mr. Congdon's blood and tissue samples with one of those plants out there, and whatever residue that's found on that broken glass you brought in. Then we'd have it nailed."

"Not completely," said Theodosia. "You still have to figure out who the perpetrator is."

"Well . . . yeah," said Sheriff Billings, backing off somewhat. "There is that."

"There are . . . uh . . . a couple people you should maybe check out," said Theodosia. "What you might call persons of interest."

"And who might they be?" asked Sheriff Billings.

"A woman named Leah Shalimar. She's a vice president at Loveday and Luxor . . ."

"Same firm as Mark Congdon," grunted Sheriff Billings.

"She's also a garden docent at Carthage Place," said Theodosia.

"I already talked to this Miss Shalimar once already," said Sheriff Billings. "'Course, that was just a cursory meeting at Loveday and Luxor. It's routine to talk to people who worked with the deceased. Of course, if this lady really knew her way around those gardens . . . then she warrants checking out a second time. Who's the second one?"

"Harlan Noble," said Theodosia. "He's a docent, too. Plus he got into a sort of bidding war against Mark Congdon. Over an orchid."

"And I take it he lost?"

"That's right."

"Sore loser, huh? Yeah, we can run a check on him. Couldn't hurt."

"Thank you," said Theodosia. "And if you could get in touch with the various researchers who've been making use of those plants, maybe they can tell you something, too."

"Miz Browning . . ."

"Yes?" said Theodosia.

"Thank you. You've done some real smart police work on this."

"I appreciate that, Sheriff Billings. If you could sort of keep me in the loop, I'd be grateful."

"Count on it," said Sheriff Billings.

Well, thought Theodosia as she hung up the phone. *There's certainly a difference between Sheriff Billings and Burt Tidwell. One's polite, one isn't. One thanks me, the other tries to ignore me.*

"Uh . . . Miss Theodosia?" called an uncertain voice.

Theodosia looked up from her desk to find a young

woman staring at her. It took her a moment to figure out just who she was.

"Haley wanted me to come in and say hi," said the young woman, who was short, olive skinned, and had massive amounts of wavy, dark hair, almost as much hair as Theodosia had. "And I'm supposed to tell you that Haley wants everybody to get together for a quick meeting."

"You're our new intern," said Theodosia, suddenly springing up. "Welcome aboard." She closed the gap between them and stuck out her hand. "It's Charlotte Lynch, right?"

The young woman grasped her hand tentatively. "Yes, but call me Charlie, please. Everybody does."

"Charlie it is, then," said Theodosia. "Have you met Drayton yet? Did Haley introduce you?"

A panic-stricken look came across Charlie's face. "Yes," she said, her voice suddenly low and hoarse. "I sure have."

11

❧

"*I beefed up* our luncheon menu today," announced Haley, "since we've got special guests coming in."

"All our guests are special," snapped Drayton. He was leery of Leah Shalimar ever since he'd found out she was a garden docent. And was undoubtedly feeling jumpy about Charlie's presence, too.

Haley rolled her eyes. "You know what I mean." She'd called Theodosia and Drayton into the kitchen to go over the menu, even though Drayton remained, as Haley would say, "in a mood." Charlie was out front, prowling the tables with teapots in hand.

"What have you got?" asked Theodosia. Now that Leah Shalimar seemed to be on the docket as a potential suspect, she, too, wished the woman wasn't coming in today.

"We'll start with chilled strawberry soup," said Haley,

"accompanied by sliced pear and Stilton cheese tea sand-wiches. Then an entrée of pan-seared salmon with white asparagus and butter sauce."

"What about dessert?" demanded an impatient Drayton. Whenever they had a larger group coming in Drayton seemed to get more than a little unnerved.

"Dessert scones," said Haley. "Chocolate chip scones with Devonshire cream and black raspberry jam. Oh, and I'll probably do a batch of lemon jumble cookies, too."

"Lovely," said Theodosia. "I'm sure all our guests will be delighted."

"That's right," said Drayton. "The operative word here is *all*."

The bell over the front door tinkled and Drayton pulled back the green curtain to take a peek. He turned back to Theodosia and Haley. "Expensive cobalt-blue suit, model thin, lots of clanking gold jewelry?"

"That's her," said Theodosia, hurriedly brushing past him to go greet Leah Shalimar.

"Looks awfully high maintenance," murmured Drayton.

"But does she look dangerous?" whispered Haley.

"*Welcome to the* Indigo Tea Shop," said Theodosia, putting a friendly smile on her face.

"Hell-oooo," chirped Leah Shalimar. "I hope you don't mind that I'm a tiny bit early. But I wanted to write out place cards and, of course, I brought along hostess gifts. Darling little Rigaud candles. Don't you just adore them?"

Theodosia, who'd never purchased a seventy-dollar candle in her entire life, said, "I'm sure your guests will be thrilled."

"My, this *is* a sweet little place," said Leah, looking around as Theodosia led her to her table. "So cute and cozy." Then her eyes caught sight of the gleaming china and floral centerpiece. "And I *adore* this table setting. So very elegant."

"Due in no small part to the Valentina Chintz china by Royal Patrician and an ample bouquet of Anna roses and nerine lilies," said Drayton.

"Leah," said Theodosia, "this is Drayton Conneley, our master tea blender and catering manager."

"Hello," said Leah, extending a hand and suddenly turning all her intensity on him.

"Delighted to meet you," said Drayton. He grasped her hand in both of his and flashed a warm smile. "Besides setting a lovely table for you and your guests, we also have a superb menu planned."

"Oh, please don't tell me!" begged Leah. "Let it be a surprise. I simply *adore* surprises."

"As you wish," said Drayton. He pulled out a chair for Leah, waited for her to be seated, then sat down next to her. "Now . . . we have an ample repertoire of marvelous teas, but I've taken the liberty of selecting a few extra special ones for you today."

"I'm a complete neophyte when it comes to tea," admitted Leah. "So I'm going to have to leave the choices in your most capable hands."

"Then may I suggest we start with a Hyson tea," said Drayton, "a light, fragrant Chinese green tea."

Leah nodded enthusiastically. "That sounds wonderful."

"Moving on," said Drayton, "perhaps a Taiwanese Keemun, which is always lovely with a food course. And to compliment dessert, may I recommend our Orchid Lights house blend. It's a semi-fermented oolong with crushed orchid flowers. It's actually a sort of sneak peak at what we're serving this Saturday night at the Heritage Society."

"Good heavens," marveled Leah. "Three different teas?"

"For three different courses," responded Drayton. "Of course, if any of your guests prefer to stick with just one tea, that's certainly fine, too. Not too many rules when it comes to tea; one should always drink what one enjoys."

"I *love* it," declared Leah, seemingly entranced with Drayton. "You know," she said, studying him. "You'd be very good in sales. Have you ever done any work in financial sales?"

"Dear lady," said Drayton, giving her a baleful look, "I can barely manage a simple calculator."

"No, no." Leah laughed. "I already have a staff who do all the tedious number crunching. What's most critical in to-day's financial arena is building trust with potential clients." She peered at him speculatively. "You, Drayton, appear to possess that rather elusive quality."

"I really don't think so," said Drayton. He was clearly flummoxed by her words.

"Loveday and Luxor has recently stepped up our caliber of financial products," continued Leah. We are now branching out into foreign currency futures contracts. You've heard of FOREX?"

"Not really," said Drayton. "Sounds quite complicated."

"Not in the least," said Leah. "Foreign currency futures basically give clients a unique opportunity to speculate on the value of various world currencies."

"Mm-hm," said Drayton, his eyes beginning to drift away.

"And I was thinking," continued Leah, "that you'd be the perfect front man to manage cold calls and set up meetings."

That woke Drayton up. "But I work *here*."

"I haven't worked in this industry all that long, either," confessed Leah. "In fact, I used to be in high-end auto sales. Lexus, Mercedes, Porsche." Now she dropped her voice to a conspiratorial whisper. "But I can assure you, Drayton, that Loveday and Luxor's commission schedule is far more generous than anything you can earn serving tea." Leah smiled brightly at Drayton. Then, as if to signal that the matter was a fait accompli, she pulled out a large black Montblanc pen and began scribbling names on her place cards.

As the lunch hour wore on, Leah Shalimar's luncheon appeared to be a smashing success even though Drayton huffed and harrumphed in the background.

"She was rude to me," Drayton complained to Theodosia. "Telling me I'd make a good *front man* for her silly financial product and insinuating that I could make a lot more money working for her." Drayton snatched up a half dozen small glass plates of chocolate chip scones centered on white paper doilies, and dropped them onto his silver tray with a clatter. "Leah Shalimar assumes money is the most important thing in life."

"I hope this doesn't come as a shock to you," said Theodosia, as she garnished the chocolate chip scones with fresh mint leaves, "but an awful lot of people share that feeling." Some of her old coworkers had scoffed at her when she'd left her lucrative job in marketing to take a flier at running a tea shop. Of course, Theodosia's little flier had pretty much turned into a home run.

"Hey," said Haley, as she scooped dollops of Devonshire

cream into fancy cut-glass dishes, "money can be a good thing. There's a reason I'm studying business administration."

"But money's not the *only* thing," said Drayton as he lurched out of the kitchen. "It shouldn't rule your life."

Haley glanced quickly at Theodosia. "Drayton's really steamed."

"I don't blame him," said Theodosia, arranging a tray of truffles. "Leah Shalimar basically tried to devalue what he does. What's near and dear to Drayton's heart. And that's very disrespectful."

But Leah Shalimar proved to be a master of diplomacy as well as sales. She managed to broadly compliment all her guests, elicit delighted peals of laughter, keep the conversation lively, and pitch her new futures contracts. All at the same time.

Theodosia didn't catch all the details of Leah's pitch, but she heard enough as she moved about the tea shop. It appeared that foreign exchange currency futures were now the hot new investment in the global financial market. Leah cautioned that there was a limited time to buy in, with the initial investment being a minimum of fifty thousand dollars. But returns promised to be sky-high.

Theodosia shook her head. *Way too rich for my blood,* she decided, although the women sitting at Leah Shalimar's table looked quite moneyed. A couple were dressed in St. John knits, one in an Ungaro tweed suit, and the rest, including Leah, seemed equally well heeled. One woman, Theodosia was fairly positive, was the board chairman of the symphony orchestra.

I wonder if this is the new financial product Mark Congdon had been going to head up, Theodosia mused to herself. *Has to be. Although Leah looks like she's off to a successful and rousing start.*

Once the chocolate chip scones and lemon jumble cookies had been served and enjoyed by all, Leah's group proceeded to get up from their table and wander about the tea room to indulge in a little shopping. Theodosia had stocked her antique cupboards with teacups and saucers, pieces of old silver, antique teapots, glass slippers perfect for serving Devonshire cream, and sterling silver pendants of miniature teacups and teapots.

Of course, Theodosia's own creations were scattered about the Indigo Tea Shop as well. A large maple cabinet held stacks of silk-screened pastel T-shirts that Theodosia had designed herself. These were cotton shirts adorned with a whimsical drawing of a tea cup with a curlicue of steam rising above it and the words *Tea Shirt*. Some shirts featured a tea kettle and the words *Let off a little steam!*

Other shelves displayed Theodosia's proprietary T-Bath line. This included such delights as Green Tea Feet Treat, Lavender Luxury Lotion, and a tea-scented aromatherapy spray that, after much debate, they'd laughingly named Assam Enchanted Evening.

"Did you really design all this adorable packaging, too?" asked one of Leah's guests. She held up a package of T-Bath Green Tea Soak with its elegant celadon-green wrapper and typography done in a Japanese dry brush style. "It's so elegant and Zen-like," she exclaimed.

"I did," said Theodosia. "But I'm even more proud of the contents. All the tea-infused products are extremely gentle and soothing."

"Do you have a good facial moisturizer?"

"Right over here."

Just as merchandise was being heaped onto the counter and diaphanous sheets of indigo blue gift wrap were floating everywhere, an entire jitney packed full of tourists stopped in front of the shop and a dozen women came tumbling in for tea and treats.

"Good lord," cried Drayton, clutching a sweetgrass basket filled with T-Bath products, "we've hit the jackpot."

While the women oohed and aahed and shopped, Theodosia edged over toward Leah Shalimar.

"Looks like you had a successful luncheon," said Theodosia. Although she wasn't thrilled by the way Leah had initially "hustled" Drayton, the woman was still a guest in her tea shop.

Leah, who was picking out a half dozen teacups and saucers to take home as gifts, nodded in agreement. "We had a great time, thanks to you and your fine staff."

Theodosia took one of the cup-and-saucer sets from Leah and nestled it inside a small hexagon-shaped gift box. "We just did what we set out to do. Provide a quiet respite from the twenty-four-seven go-go world and serve a delicious luncheon with as much panache as we can muster." Theodosia favored Leah with a crooked grin. "Of course, some days we muster more panache than others."

"You are a dear." Leah laughed. "But, seriously, I think I may have learned a valuable lesson from all this."

"Which is . . . ?" asked Theodosia.

Leah cocked her head and gave Theodosia what appeared to be a rather heartfelt look. "I learned that slowing down isn't necessarily a bad thing. That I don't always have to operate in hyper mode. Which probably applies to my sales pitch, too."

"Does this mean you're switching from coffee to tea?" asked Theodosia. "And FYI, green teas and oolongs are far lower in caffeine. And herbal teas don't contain any caffeine at all."

"Which is probably why I feel so relaxed," admitted Leah. She paused, looked about again with a faint smile on her face. "But seriously, I meant what I said. Your little place is a sort of oasis of calm. A reminder that we shouldn't be afraid to take time for ourselves, to feed our bodies as well as our souls."

"That's a lovely thought," said Theodosia. "And very well put."

"Now I just have to live by those words," said Leah. "And pitch my little heart out on these futures contracts."

"Is that what Mark would have been selling, too?" asked Theodosia.

Leah nodded. With Theodosia's words, a look of sadness had fallen across her face. "Dear Mark," she murmured. "We surely miss him."

Here's my opening, Theodosia decided.

"Leah," said Theodosia. "Were you at Carthage Place Plantation this past Sunday?"

Now Leah looked sadder than ever. "Yes, I was. I stopped by with my dear friend Zoe Miller. But we were only there for maybe fifteen or twenty minutes at best. Then we drove on to visit the gardens at Magnolia Plantation."

"So you missed all the commotion," said Theodosia, realizing that calling it a *commotion* was probably a major understatement.

Leah nodded her head sadly. "I did. Although it would have been a horrendous shock to have witnessed Mark's collapse."

"That went well," said Haley, as the last of their luncheon crowd finally departed.

"It did, didn't it," said Drayton, a self-satisfied look on his lined face.

Standing behind the old brass cash register, Theodosia was busy tallying the receipts. "Do you know we sold an extra six hundred dollars just in house tea blends, antiques, sweetgrass baskets, and T-Bath products?" she asked them. "As well as every single truffle."

"Seriously?" asked Haley. "They even bought my truffles?"

"Every last one," said Theodosia. "Miss Dimple will be jumping for joy at our good fortune." Miss Dimple was their sharp-as-a-tack octogenarian bookkeeper who helped with monthly financial projections as well as occasionally serving lunches in the tea shop.

"So now what?" asked Drayton, glancing about at tables heaped with dirty dishes, low-burning candles, and empty shelves that called out for restocking. "KP duty I suppose." He spun on his heels and called out, "Oh, Charlie."

"Guys," said Theodosia. "Would either of you mind if I bugged out early?"

"Huh?" said Haley.

"I . . . uh . . . want to have a little chat with Angie Congdon," said Theodosia. "Remember?"

"Oh sure," said Haley. "Yeah, you better go do that. Charlie and I can take care of all this. And Drayton, too, if he can keep up with us."

"Haley Parker, don't you *dare* talk down to me," said Drayton. "I'll have you know I'm in the prime of my life. Middle-aged, in fact."

Haley winked at Drayton as she scooped up dishes and shoved them into a plastic bin. "Sure you are, Drayton. Just as long as you plan on living to be a hundred and thirty!"

12

Legs akimbo, toenails scratching against vinyl, Earl Grey
scrambled into the back of Theodosia's Jeep.

"Watch your tail," warned Theodosia as she slammed
the rear hatch. Then, noting that Earl Grey had ignored
the blanket she'd laid out for him in back and taken a flying leap into the front passenger seat, she sighed and
climbed in.

"Nice to see you're riding shotgun today," Theodosia
told him as she started the engine, then pulled into the alley. "But you'd better fasten your seat belt."

Earl Grey leaned over and touched his furry muzzle to
her ear, giving her a soft kiss.

"Flattery will get you everywhere," Theodosia told him.

Once she had her talk with Angie, Theodosia planned to
take Earl Grey for a good long walk. Let the old boy stretch

his legs, breath in the sea air, and sniff the Civil War cannons that lined up along the Battery.

But just as she turned down Murray Street with its showcase of elegant homes, Theodosia caught a quick glimpse of someone hurrying along. A young woman with long brown hair who looked very familiar.

"Wait a minute!" Theodosia cried out as she slammed on her brakes so hard Earl Grey had to scramble to brace himself. "I think that's Fayne Hamilton!" Earl Grey recovered, then gazed curiously at her as if to say *Who?* So Theodosia muttered, "Why would Fayne Hamilton be coming from the direction of the Featherbed House?"

Woof? responded Earl Grey.

"This is very strange," said Theodosia.

She accelerated, determined to make a right turn and race around the block to confirm her sighting. But just as Theodosia glanced left and caught the familiar profile of the Featherbed House, she was stunned to see flames shooting from its roof!

What? Oh, my lord! A fire?

Gunning her Jeep, Theodosia turned left instead, cutting directly in front of a blue van and sending Earl Grey sprawling again. Then it was only seconds before she pulled directly in front of the Featherbed House.

The fire was much worse than she'd initially thought. The entire second floor was engulfed in fire. Angry orange and yellow tongues licked and flicked at the roof line. A sudden loud explosion, almost like cannon fire, blew out a second-story window and shards of glass spattered the front walk like falling shrapnel.

Oh, my lord, what about Angie! Is she still inside?

Fear exploding within her, Theodosia threw her Jeep into park and jumped out. Closing the door firmly on Earl Grey, she sprinted for the front door, knowing she had to do something . . . anything!

Just as Theodosia hit the bottom step, the inn's double doors exploded outward and Angie came rushing out. Black soot covered her face like camouflage paint, her hair was wild and slightly singed, her eyes were filled with desperation.

At seeing Theodosia, Angie flung herself into her friend's arms. "We tried to put it out with fire extinguishers," she shrieked, "but it got away from us!"

Theodosia grappled for her cell phone to call 911, but someone had obviously beat her to it. Already she could hear the blare of sirens, the *whoop-whoop* of police cruisers as they sped toward the burning house.

Ten seconds later, Teddy Vickers came stumbling out onto the front veranda, clutching a fire extinguisher, his face blackened by smoke.

"What happened?" asked Theodosia, as three large fire trucks, lights flashing, sirens blaring, roared up and men in asbestos-and-rubber suits piled out. She clutched at Teddy's arm, trying to pull him away from the building.

Teddy coughed repeatedly, then shook his head. "No idea," he managed to choke out.

"What about guests?" cried Theodosia.

Teddy shook his head again. "None. They're all gone."

Now Theodosia, Angie, and Teddy clung together, a little island of people surrounded by giant fire trucks, a melee of firefighters, and the burning Featherbed House. They watched as ladders were swiftly unloaded, hoses unwound and coupled. Then great gluts of water were suddenly being sprayed out in giant arcs.

"You'll have to move back," one of the firefighters told them. He had a kind face and a name tag that read *Warren*. He led them back to one of the trucks, instructed them to stay put. Since they were now at a safe distance from the fire, Theodosia went to her Jeep and brought Earl Grey out on his leash.

But pandemonium was ratcheting up by leaps and bounds. Gawkers arrived and pushed forward, TV news vans and rescue vehicles clogged the streets. Inside, the Featherbed House was rocked by a series of small explosions.

Angie was beside herself. "I don't believe this!" she shrilled. "This can't be happening!" She dropped her head into her hands. "Mark and I sank all our hard-earned money into this place . . . all our dreams, too."

But it *was* happening. A deafening roar, like that from a blast furnace, filled the air as black smoke billowed from the top windows and hot flames danced atop the cupola. The updraft from the fire caused the little goose weathervane to spin madly, as if in utter panic.

Theodosia handed Earl Grey off to Teddy Vickers, then ventured twenty steps forward, edging toward the front lines, feeling intense heat prickle her face. "Can you save it?" Her fingers skittered off the rubber jacket of a firefighter who was muscling a giant hose, aiming his spurt of water directly through a blown-out window and into the interior of the building.

"Not sure, ma'am," he told her. "You gotta get back."

Returning to their little clutch, Theodosia found that Drayton had somehow made his way through the lines and was doing his best to console Angie and Teddy.

"How did you know?" Theodosia asked him. Earl Grey, excited by the goings-on, pressed up against her.

"Everybody knows," Drayton told her. "The news is all over the historic district. Timothy Neville phoned the tea shop, and so did Nell Chappel from the Chowder Hound. Look around, everybody's here!"

Peering over the tops of police cars, Theodosia saw a crowd that numbered in the hundreds. They'd come to gape at the fire, to stand transfixed by its power and devastating force.

Thirty minutes crawled by and finally the firefighters seemed to gain the upper hand. Three of them, suited up in asbestos gear, entered the house armed with axes.

"I can't stand this any longer," exclaimed Drayton. He slipped toward two firefighters who were conversing with their heads together. They turned when he approached and turned again when Drayton spoke to them and motioned toward Angie.

Theodosia watched Drayton's conversation closely, saw his look of concern change to dismay.

"It's a complete and utter disaster," said Drayton, when he returned to their little group. "The entire top floor has been gutted by flames. And of course there's major water damage on the first floor."

"What about the attached carriage house?" asked Theodosia. The second-story bridge connected the main building to the two-story carriage house where a restaurant and party room were housed. But Theodosia was unable to see that structure from where she stood.

"That at least was spared," said Drayton. "But the greenhouse . . ."

Angie put a trembling hand to her mouth. "Mark's orchids?"

Drayton looked distressed. "Pretty much devastated. If

they weren't fried by falling cinders they were pounded with water from the high-powered hoses."

"Theo! Drayton!" called a voice behind them.

Their heads turned in unison.

"Haley?" said a surprised Theodosia once she caught sight of Haley's young face. "What are *you* doing here?"

In response, Haley hoisted up a huge silver jug.

"Haley brought iced tea," Theodosia told the group. Tears welled up in her eyes. She felt overwhelmed by the fire, yet heartened by this single kind act.

"I'll run and help her," said Drayton.

Thanks in part to Drayton's persuasiveness and Haley's welcome offerings, the police allowed Haley to back her little blue hatchback up on the curb and set up a makeshift commissary. Within minutes, firefighters with soot-stained faces clustered around, gratefully accepting glasses of ice-cold sweet tea and helping themselves to scones and muffins. There was nothing more they could do now except hang tough and make sure there were no flare-ups from the red-hot cinders and ashes.

"Do you know how it started?" Theodosia asked one of the firefighters. He shook his head, unwilling to meet her gaze. A sick feeling was beginning to grow in the pit of her stomach. She searched the crowd, spotted a firefighter wearing a badge, figured he must be a captain or lieutenant or something like that.

Theodosia grabbed a tray of scones and edged her way toward him. He was on his cell phone, muttering excitedly. As she pressed forward, she distinctly heard the words *flash point* and *arson*.

Arson? she thought. *Meaning someone deliberately set this fire? Dear lord, no.*

As she stood watching him, the man with the badge punched a button on his phone and stared over at her. "Are you Angie Congdon?" he asked.

"She's over there," indicated Theodosia.

"Thanks." He moved off and Theodosia watched as he went over and introduced himself to Angie, put a hand gently on her shoulder, then lead her away to talk.

Theodosia passed out the rest of the scones, then headed back to Haley's car. Remarkably, Harlan Noble was standing there. But he looked grim.

"The orchids?" Harlan Noble asked. His dark eyes glowed while his face was as white as a sheet. "The orchids are ruined?"

"Everything's ruined," snapped Theodosia. She wondered how Harlan Noble could worry about orchids at a time like this, when Angie's only means of survival has just gone up in smoke!

"Give it a rest, will you, Harlan?" said Drayton, sounding more than a little cross. "And kindly move back."

Theodosia dropped the empty tray to her side and scanned the huge crowd that was still gathered. There were lots of familiar faces among the people who'd come to gaze in awe at the ruined Featherbed House. Neighbors, people who worked at the Heritage Society down the street, shopkeepers from around the historic district.

Why, there's Leah Shalimar, thought Theodosia, giving a little start as she spotted her in the crowd. *She must have still been in the neighborhood.*

And way over on the sidelines stood Fayne Hamilton. Theodosia gave a sharp intake of breath. She'd completely forgotten about Fayne.

Could she have had a hand in this? Theodosia suddenly

wondered as tendrils of suspicion crept into her mind. The love notes to Mark, the fact that Fayne had been in this exact vicinity when the fire started, and the mumblings about arson would seem to make Fayne a prime suspect.

Theodosia decided she'd better have a little chat with the fire captain once he was finished talking to Angie.

What was it fire investigators said about arsonists? Theodosia wondered to herself. *Oh yes . . . that arsonists often show up to view their own handiwork.*

13

❧

"Good heavens, Drayton," squawked Delaine, "those Eternal Peace bouquets belong over here!" Delaine Dish, looking both fashionable and sedate in a black knit suit and patent leather stilettos gestured toward two wicker plant stands and grimaced unhappily. "These dusty little tables are absolutely ghastly," she complained as she muscled them around and then repositioned them. "But I suppose there isn't time to make a change."

"Hardly," said Drayton. He was dressed in a severely tailored double-breasted charcoal-gray suit, white shirt, and black bow tie. His black shoes carried a high-gloss shine. Drayton could have gone anywhere in the world, Maxim's in Paris, the Metropolitan Opera in New York, the Breakers in Palm Beach, and looked smashing. But, today, his sad and tired eyes testified to the fact that he was helping prepare for a funeral.

Delaine frowned and fidgeted with two large bouquets. "Oh well, I suppose the spill of Rubrum lilies, roses, and gladiolas will hide the really nasty parts."

Theodosia stood in the nave of the Cathedral of St. John the Baptist and watched as Drayton and Delaine put finishing touches on everything. The imposing Gothic church with its vaulted ceiling and elegant columns looked magnificent as always. Candles flickered, light streamed in through stained-glass windows, saints peered down benevolently from their lofty windows in the clerestory.

There was a reason Charleston had been dubbed the "holy city." One hundred eighty-one church spires, steeples, crosses, and bell towers dominated its skyline. It was a fine procession of churches that represented a vast diversity of worshipers and served as a 300-year-old testament to the American ideals of religious freedom.

Theodosia squared her shoulders and stifled a yawn. She'd woken up early this morning. Around five o'clock, before the sun was even up. Unable to sleep any longer, she'd lain in bed fretting about her so-called investigation that seemed to be going nowhere. And dreading Mark's funeral, fearful that Angie Congdon had reached her limits as to the amount of tragedy one person could endure. From the fire yesterday that had reduced the Featherbed House to ruins, to her husband's funeral this morning—how much could she take?

But the human spirit is resilient, thought Theodosia. *And the Lord only doles out as much as we can handle, right?*

At the same time, Theodosia worried that there were now two separate investigations going on. Sheriff Billings's homicide investigation and the Charleston Fire Department's inquiry over yesterday's fire.

Theodosia was nervous that between the questioning, suppositions, clues, and paperwork, the two camps might get their lines crossed. Or, worse yet, not communicate at all.

So first thing this morning, Theodosia had taken it upon herself to telephone Sheriff Billings. He'd already heard from the fire department, so that had been a step in the right direction. Maybe, Theodosia decided, if Mark's death and yesterday's fire were somehow connected, someone would come up with a solid motive. Or at least a theory.

"What do you think, Theodosia?" called Delaine.

She'd moved the bouquets a fourth time, trying, Theodosia supposed, to achieve some sort of thematic design.

"Nice," called Theodosia. Her footsteps echoed in the great cathedral as she advanced down the aisle toward Delaine and Drayton. "Good." What could she say? There wasn't much of anything to say. It was a sad day and this was a funeral for Mark.

"I'm hoping Bobby Wayne arrives a little early," said Drayton. "Then we can do a microphone test instead of putting him up there to do his eulogy cold. There's nothing worse than being lulled by the music of Johann Sebastian Bach, then being jolted out of your pew by a buzz and an ugly hum from a bad PA system."

Delaine reached into her black silk clutch and pulled out a pair of black gloves. "Bobby Wayne will be coming with the Loveday and Luxor contingent. At least that's what he told me last night."

"You two were together last night?" asked Theodosia.

Delaine hunched her shoulders and gave a tiny giggle. It sounded incongruous in the solemnity of the church. "Date night," she whispered. "First we had dinner at Harbor Oaks over near the marina. Grilled grouper with huckleberry and orange chutney and the most glorious Pouilly-Fuissé. Then we sipped snifters of Armagnac brandy in their cigar room, after which we went on to the Gibbes Museum to hear a string quartet." She waved one hand and her gloves fluttered airily. "It was a small charity function. Very *chi-chi*. Oh," Delaine said, almost as an afterthought, "and when I got home I called Angie Congdon."

"Where's Angie staying?" asked Theodosia. When she, Drayton, and Haley finally left late yesterday, Angie hadn't figured out what her plans would be.

"She's holed up with her sister, Gwyn, down the street at the Bogard Inn," said Delaine. "I guess everyone down there really had to hustle. Most of the folks flying in from out of town for the funeral today had planned to stay at the Featherbed House."

"A dreadfully sad change of plans, eh?" said Drayton coming up behind them.

"Afraid so," said Delaine. She spun on her stilettos and surveyed the interior of the church. "But everything here looks wonderful. If we just move the Remembrance memorial wreath over to this side and, oh . . . I almost forgot about the Timeless Tribute casket spray. Don't you think we should . . ."

"Wait for the casket to arrive," said a somber Drayton.

As mourners filed in, filling the front pews and then spilling into the middle and back sections of the church, Theodosia and Drayton slipped into seats on the side aisle. Finally, a cousin of Angie Congdon, a tall man with a sad basset hound face, stepped up to the front of the church and gave a knowing nod to the organist. The opening tones of Mozart's

Requiem suddenly thundered in the vast recess of the church. Then, six pallbearers in dark suits wheeled the casket down the aisle. When they arrived at the front of the church, they seesawed it back and forth for a moment, then positioned it horizontally.

Twisting around in her seat, Theodosia studied the people who were already seated. Lots of people from the historic district had shown up, friends and neighbors who knew and cared for Angie and Mark. And there was Leah Shalimar, looking sedate in a navy suit, seated just behind Bobby Wayne. And way in the back of the church, Harlan Noble sat folded up like a praying mantis.

Then Angie walked in, looking small and tentative within her protective contingent of relatives. Once everyone had taken their seats, Delaine approached the large mahogany casket and placed a spray of long-tailed purple-pink Machu Picchu orchids on top. Then she took her seat with the rest of the mourners.

It was a traditional service, filled with fine words that should have brought great comfort and solace. But Theodosia found little consolation. Like most everyone close to her, she was convinced that Mark's death had been a wrongful death. And that justice was still waiting to be served. Swiveling in her seat once again, she surreptitiously scanned the crowd, wondering if anyone among them had come here today with a guilt-laden heart.

No, everyone looks very solemn and sad.

Drayton's shoulder gently touched hers. "Bobby Wayne," he said in a low murmur.

Slowly, as though moving with great effort, Bobby Wayne Loveday took his place at the podium. He had been

Mark's friend and employer. And lately, Angie's confidant and shoulder to cry on. It seemed fitting that Bobby Wayne deliver the final eulogy.

Bobby Wayne spoke eloquently, but with a warmth and down-home charm. He praised Mark, whom he called a dear and kind man, and wept openly when he spoke about Angie and Mark's marriage of twenty years. His words were heartfelt and touching.

Bobby Wayne finished up by reciting the poem "If Death Is Kind," by Sara Teasdale.

> *Perhaps if death is kind, and there can be returning,*
> *We will come back to earth some fragrant night,*
> *And take these lanes to find the sea, and bending*
> *Breathe the same honeysuckle, low and white.*
>
> *We will come down at night to these resounding beaches*
> *And the long gentle thunder of the sea,*
> *Here for a single hour in the wide starlight*
> *We shall be happy, for the dead are free.*

"Perfect," breathed Theodosia.

"Magnificent choice," whispered Drayton, pulling out a hanky to wipe his red-rimmed eyes.

The organ sounded a single note, then broke into the hymn "Abide with Me," as Bobby Wayne walked solemnly back to his seat. Theodosia's moist eyes followed him as he slid into a pew next to Delaine and fumbled for her hand.

Theodosia had been completely wowed by Bobby Wayne's choice of poems. The Teasdale poem was short, poignant, and contained some amazingly appropriate phrasing. References to honeysuckle, resounding beaches, and the gentle thunder of the sea seemed like tailor-made descriptors of Charleston!

As the final organ hymn concluded, a short blessing was bestowed on Mark Congdon's casket. Then Drayton rose from his seat and walked to the front of the cathedral.

"As you know," began Drayton, in an oratorical style that had been honed from dozens of lectures given at the Heritage Society, "we have invited all of you to place a flower on Mark's casket in tribute to his great passion for orchids and gardening. As the pallbearers wheel him out, please feel free to come to the center aisle and place your flower gently atop the casket. Then we shall all proceed to Magnolia Cemetery for brief prayers and the final interment."

Theodosia watched as Drayton placed a spray of fire orchids atop Mark's casket. There were at least two dozen flowers on the vine-like stem, yellow-orange blossoms dappled with bright orange spots.

Then the six pallbearers snapped to attention and took their place alongside Mark's casket. They wheeled it around, hesitated, then slowly made their way down the center aisle. A gentle rustle ran through the crowd and then arms were suddenly outstretched. Lilies, single roses, magnolias, stems of dogwood, and every kind of flower imaginable were placed on top of Mark's casket.

Theodosia smiled through a veil of tears. It was as though the heavens had opened and flowers were raining down.

She watched as the casket, now a veritable bower of flowers, slowly approached the doors at the back of the church. Then, a small figure rose unsteadily, hesitated, then placed a flower and ribbon-entwined wreath on Mark's coffin.

Fayne Hamilton! thought Theodosia. *And she looks extremely distraught.*

"Fayne," murmured Theodosia to Drayton.

He frowned, not understanding.

"Mark's secretary," she whispered. "The *notes*."

"Ohhh," murmured Drayton, finally understanding. The two of them stood, waiting until most of the mourners had retreated from the cathedral, then walked toward the altar to collect the flowers.

"She put a wreath on Mark's casket," said Theodosia. "And, I must say, she looked very upset."

"Who was upset?" asked Bobby Wayne, as he bent and, with a loud grunt, hefted one of the floral bouquets under Delaine's careful direction.

"Fayne Hamilton," said Theodosia.

Bobby Wayne peered at Theodosia through a jungle of orchids and vines. "You mean our Fayne? Mark's secretary?"

Theodosia nodded.

"Poor girl." Bobby Wayne sighed. "She's been awfully upset. Even called in sick yesterday."

A worried frown flickered across Theodosia's face. "Yes, poor girl," she murmured.

Theodosia caught up with Fayne Hamilton half a block from the cathedral. She waved at the girl, called her name, dodged through throngs of mourners who milled about on the wide sidewalk.

But when Fayne finally succumbed to Theodosia's entreaties, she seemed quite unwilling to talk. "Oh, hello," was all Fayne said.

Theodosia was not one to be put off or even mince words. "Fayne," Theodosia began, "I have to ask. Were you at the Featherbed House yesterday?"

Fayne shifted from one foot to the other, looking nervous. "No," she replied.

"Fayne," said Theodosia, shaking her head in consternation. "You strike me as a fairly straightforward person, an honest person. So this is not the time to twist words. Because I *saw* you. I saw you walking down Murray Street."

"Technically," said Fayne, "I wasn't really there. I was *going* to go there, but I changed my mind."

"Why were you going there?" asked Theodosia. Although she had a fairly good idea, she wanted to hear it from Fayne herself.

Fayne looked uneasy. "I wanted to talk to Mrs. Congdon."

"About . . . ?" prompted Theodosia.

"None of your business," snapped Fayne, suddenly mustering a modicum of anger and outrage. "I don't have to say a word to you."

"No, you don't," replied Theodosia. "But the fire marshal might be interested in asking you a number of questions. And I can pretty much guarantee he's not going to be nearly as polite as I am."

Fayne's gaze bordered on hostile now and her brown eyes fairly snapped with anger. "What are you talking about?"

"The fire," said Theodosia. She took a step closer to Fayne, daring her to answer. "Did you have anything to do with that fire?"

Fayne's anger seemed to suddenly crumble. Her eyes filled with tears, her chin quivered. "Of course not. How could you even *think* I had something to do with that?"

"You have no idea what happened?" pressed Theodosia.

"No," wailed Fayne.

Theodosia stared at Fayne, trying to detect any degree of deception in the girl's demeanor. But her emotions appeared genuine. Fayne just seemed unhappy. Supremely unhappy.

"The fire marshal still might want to talk to you as a witness," said Theodosia.

"But I didn't *see* anything," protested Fayne. "Really, I didn't. My being there was just a bad . . ." She struggled to find the right word. ". . . coincidence."

"Are you going back to work today?" Theodosia asked her.

Fayne bobbed her head and brushed at her eyes. "Yes. Probably."

"Okay," said Theodosia. She wasn't sure what to do now. Obviously the girl was upset, but Theodosia didn't think she was lying. Was pretty sure she wasn't. "I appreciate your talking to me," she added.

Fayne gave a tight nod.

Theodosia had turned and was heading back to St. John's when Fayne called after her, "Did she read the notes?"

"Pardon?" said Theodosia, stopping in her tracks. She was, perhaps, ten or twelve feet away from Fayne.

"Did Mrs. Congdon see the notes?"

Theodosia stared back at a somewhat confrontational Fayne Hamilton. "Not yet," she said.

"You have them, don't you?" said Fayne. "I know you do." Fayne gave an involuntary shudder, as though the day had suddenly turned cool. "Are you going to tell her?" Now there was a slight challenge in her eyes.

"I haven't made up my mind yet," said Theodosia.

* * *

The graveside service at Magnolia Cemetery was more of the same. Prayers, hymns, floral arrangements, final tributes. Finally, when that twenty-minute service concluded, Theodosia got in line at the tail end of the mourners who were filing past Angie, offering their last words of comfort. Teddy Vickers, looking serious in a dark suit, was right in front of Theodosia. Drayton, Delaine, and Bobby Wayne were directly behind her.

As the line gradually shuffled forward, Theodosia was struck by how monumentally beautiful Magnolia Cemetery was. It was an old cemetery that had borne the ages. Established in the 1850s, Magnolia Cemetery served as the final resting place for Civil War veterans, prominent southern politicians and planters, a few bootleggers, and ordinary folk, too. Crumbling brick tombs, wrought-iron crosses, and elaborate stone monuments were set against a dramatic backdrop of gnarled live oaks shrouded with moss.

So taken was Theodosia by an intriguing vista of marble obelisks and a hidden lagoon, that she barely paid any attention to the conversation going on between Teddy Vickers and Angie.

But Theodosia's ears perked up when she suddenly heard the words *reasonable offer.*

What? she wondered. *What's Teddy saying to Angie?* Theodosia took a step forward and tried not to appear as though she was eavesdropping. Even though she really was.

"Why do you keep pestering me about this, today of all days?" questioned Angie. Her voice was low and hoarse and she was visibly quivering, obviously deeply upset by Teddy's words.

"It's something I've been thinking about for a while," responded Teddy as he shifted about nervously.

Angie shook her head and swiped at her eyes with a linen hanky. "This is all too much," she murmured.

"My apologies," said Teddy, sounding downright unapologetic but still trying to keep the conversation between the two of them. "But I thought this might afford you some relief. Help you escape the pain of making so many difficult decisions."

"But this would be the toughest decision of them all," responded Angie. Her shoulders slumped, her voice dropped low and cracked.

"Fine," came Teddy Vickers's cool reply. "But please understand, my offer is good only for the next forty-eight hours. After that . . ." Teddy shook his head and stomped off.

"Angie," said Theodosia, stepping forward to put an arm around her friend. "Are you all right?" Actually, she thought Angie looked like she was on the point of collapse.

"I'm in shock," whispered Angie.

"Of course you are," said Drayton, coming forward to join them. "It's been an awfully trying day." He cleared his throat, trying to smile but managing only a nervous tick. "Really, a trying week."

"No," said Angie, shaking her head as if to clear away cobwebs. "This is something totally new. Something completely unexpected."

"Oh dear," murmured Drayton.

"What is it, honey?" asked Theodosia, as Delaine and Bobby Wayne, realizing something important was taking place, clustered about, too.

"On the way to the cemetery . . ." began Angie, her hands flailing helplessly.

"Yes?" said Bobby Wayne.

"In the limousine . . ." stammered Angie. "And then again just now . . ."

They all stared at her, waiting for her to finish.

"Teddy Vickers made an offer to buy the Featherbed House!"

14

❧

"Why is the Needwood out?" demanded Drayton. He and Theodosia had hurried back to the Indigo Tea Shop and now he was fretting over pots of tea that were steeping.

Charlie regarded him with a fearful look. "I was just . . ." she began.

"This is *hardly* our best Ceylon black tea." He snatched up the silver tin, hurriedly snapped the lid back on.

"But a customer requested it," said Charlie. "Asked for it specifically because it's organically grown."

"Well," said Drayton, tapping the lid with his fingertips, "that's entirely different now, isn't it? You should have *mentioned* that."

Charlie raised her eyebrows. "You really didn't give me time."

"Hey, tough guy," said Haley as she brought a glass pie keeper heaped with fresh-baked scones up to the counter.

"Ease up, will you?" She cast a sympathetic glance at Charlie. "He doesn't mean it, you know. Drayton's really a sweetie."

"Sure he is," muttered Charlie, as she fussed with the steeping teapots.

"You remember how to set up an individual tea tray?" asked Drayton, in a slightly kinder tone of voice. "Teapot, timer, cubes of raw sugar, sliced lemon, small spoon, linen napkin folded just so?"

"You showed me yesterday," said Charlie. "But if it'll make you feel any better, you can show me again."

"Maybe we *should* go over it one more time," said Drayton. "And did I mention we'll be doing a tea tasting this afternoon?"

"You sure did," said Charlie, obviously struggling to maintain a cool composure.

"What's your major again?" asked Drayton.

"Biology and chemistry," Charlie told him.

"Chemistry," sniffed Drayton. "What does chemistry have to do with working in a tea shop?"

"Everything," replied Charlie. "In fact, baking is really food chemistry."

Shaking her head, Haley wandered over to where Theodosia was clearing a table. Miss Dimple, their freelance bookkeeper and sometimes helper, was busy restocking display shelves nearby. With the luncheon rush almost over, the tea room was now only partially filled.

"How's it going over there?" asked Theodosia. She had picked up the drift of Drayton's paranoia.

"Drayton's not exactly exuding warm, fuzzy vibes," said Haley.

"We're talking cold prickly?"

Haley gave a rueful smile. "You might say that." She reached for a cup and saucer, pitching in to help Theodosia clear the table. "How was Mark's funeral?" she asked in a low voice.

"Strange," responded Theodosia. "Somewhere between the hymns and the final graveside benediction Teddy Vickers made a grudging offer to buy the Featherbed House."

Haley rocked back, stunned. "What? Are you serious? What was Angie's reaction?"

"Shock, disbelief, bewilderment," replied Theodosia. "I think the one-two punch of Mark's death and the terrible fire yesterday have hit her so hard she's still operating in trauma mode."

"Poor Angie," said Haley. "So the funeral was . . . pretty awful?"

"Aside from Teddy dropping his little bombshell, the funeral was actually quite lovely," said Theodosia. "Music, flowers, program . . . everything was planned and carried out perfectly. Right down to the smallest detail."

"Drayton always was a superb event planner," said Haley, carefully gathering up the lace placemats. "Must be that little touch of obsessive-compulsive disorder that spurs him to greatness."

Theodosia glanced across the tea room to where Drayton was still hovering and fidgeting. "Now if we could just get him to relax where Charlie is concerned."

* * *

"*Are you still* open?" called Delaine. "And do you have any food left?"

The little bell tinkled above them as Delaine Dish and Bobby Wayne Loveday stood in the doorway. While Delaine posed gracefully, looking all the world like an entitled duchess, Bobby Wayne was clearly unsure about entering an environment that was generally foreign to most men.

"Yes to both counts," Theodosia told them. "Haley made the most wonderful bacon and red pepper quiche for lunch. And I just this minute finished setting up a fresh table." She waved a hand and pulled out a chair at one of the tables for four. "Sit here. Give you plenty of room."

As Delaine and Bobby Wayne took their seats, Charlie was at Theodosia's side in a heartbeat. Looking like a real pro, she handed Delaine and Bobby Wayne the small luncheon menus that were laser printed daily, then set tall glasses of ice water in front of them.

Delaine regarded Charlie with open curiosity. "You're new here, aren't you, dear?"

"Yes, ma'am," responded Charlie.

"Charlie is Drayton's intern," explained Theodosia. "She's learning all about tea as well as the business of tea."

"There's that much to learn?" asked Delaine, wrinkling her nose.

"More than I ever thought," responded Charlie.

"So Drayton's actually a *good* teacher?" said Delaine, a little pussycat smile hovering about her lips.

Charlie didn't hesitate. "The best."

Theodosia had to check herself from doing a double take. Clearly, she decided, Charlie deserved an A in diplomacy.

*   *   *

"*And here I* was, worried about getting enough to eat," said Bobby Wayne, patting his somewhat ample stomach and leaning back in his chair. He had happily snarfed a cream scone, a bowl of oyster stew, and a wedge of bacon and red pepper quiche. Delaine, ever conscious of her size-eight figure, had eaten far more moderately, opting for a chicken walnut salad with lime vinaigrette.

Theodosia favored Bobby Wayne with a tolerant smile. His was a litany she heard frequently. In fact, women as well as men often expressed worry over the small tea shop portions. But once scones with Devonshire cream and jam were served, once a citrus salad or lovely cream soup had been offered as a starter, once the finger sandwiches, miniature quiches, tiny croissants stuffed with chicken salad, and endive stuffed with crab salad arrived at the table, it was no longer a question of *will there be enough to eat?* No, the problem quickly did an about-face and the subject instead was *how will I ever find room for dessert?*

And Haley had just delivered a plate of key lime dessert scones accompanied by peanut butter truffles to the table.

"Good heavens," groaned Bobby Wayne. "More food?" Still, his eyes roved hungrily over the golden-brown scones that had come steaming from the oven and the sinfully rich truffles covered in walnuts.

Theodosia had sat down with them and now Drayton sauntered over and joined them as well.

"These are some of Haley's finest," said Drayton, indicating the scones. "She always has the most amazing recipes up her tricky little sleeves. A highly inventive young lady, absolutely a whiz in the kitchen."

"Everything here is wonderful," Bobby Wayne rhapsodized. "The soup, the quiche, your desserts!"

Haley returned with a bowl overflowing with Devonshire cream and a tiny cut-glass bowl filled with lemon curd. "I'm probably going to be doing a recipe book," she told Bobby Wayne, after he'd lavished her with compliments.

Bobby Wayne stuck his spoon into the Devonshire cream and dropped another frothy spoonful onto his half-eaten scone. "When will that be?" he asked. He looked like he was ready to buy a copy today. Maybe even two copies.

"Not sure," said Haley. "I'm still . . . what would you call it? Dickering with publishers."

It wasn't long before talk turned to Angie Congdon and Teddy Vickers's strange offer.

"It just came sailing out of the blue," remarked Drayton. "Very bewildering. And highly inappropriate, too."

"Talk about a fire sale," remarked Delaine.

Drayton reared his head back. "Your choice of verbiage isn't particularly amusing, Delaine."

She waved a languid hand. "Oh, lighten up, Drayton. You know I positively absolutely adore Angie. I'm as shocked as anyone by Teddy Vickers's offer. But there's nothing I can *do* about it."

"Does Teddy even have the financial resources?" wondered Drayton. "I mean, he's awfully young. And he was just serving as her assistant."

"He can probably manage financing," mused Bobby Wayne. "Even though most of the Featherbed House is in ruins, it's still located on a prime piece of real estate."

"Maybe the Featherbed House could be rebuilt," offered Delaine. She glanced at Drayton, obviously trying to make amends for her flippant comment earlier.

"Smack-dab in the historic district and just a stone's

throw from the Battery," said Drayton. "I'll bet a lot of people would love to get their hands on that property."

Theodosia picked up a Brown Betty teapot and poured a stream of cinnamon spice tea into Delaine's and Bobby Wayne's teacups. "What bothers me is his timing. Why did Teddy Vickers suddenly wait until the day of Mark's funeral to spring this on Angie?"

"Don't know," shrugged Bobby Wayne, getting involved with his second scone.

"And what's with his forty-eight-hour deadline?" Theodosia asked.

"Maybe Teddy figured he was doing Angie a favor," said Delaine. "You know, taking the place off her hands."

"Sometimes," said Theodosia slowly, "actions that *appear* to be favors really benefit someone else."

"Theodosia?" said Charlie, suddenly appearing at their table. "You have a phone call. A Sheriff Billings?"

"Excuse me," said Theodosia, slipping quickly from her chair.

"*I thought I'd* get back to you on those plants," said Sheriff Billings, his voice booming loudly into Theodosia's ear.

"I appreciate it," she said.

"Apparently, the College of Pharmacy at the School of Medicine over in Columbia has been using those plants in an ongoing research study. They extract tannins, flavones, and alkaloids for use in antiviral research, if you know what that is."

"Sort of."

"Okay then. As far as the other stuff goes, we're still

waiting for lab results. You know, residue from the broken glass, tissue cultures from the victim."

Theodosia grimaced at the sheriff's rather clinical assessment.

"I assume you've been in touch with the fire marshal here in Charleston," she said.

"We've spoken a couple times," Sheriff Billings told her. "It does seem like a bit of a coincidence that Mrs. Congdon's husband was murdered and then her house or inn or whatever you'd call it suddenly burned down."

"You don't believe in coincidences?" asked Theodosia.

Sheriff Billings gave a rueful grunt. "No, ma'am, not that kind."

Good, thought Theodosia. *That means you're on top of things.*

But she found Sheriff Billings's next words rather disheartening.

"To tell you the truth, Miss Browning," he said slowly. "I'm a bit flummoxed by this case. In fact, I've been thinking about calling in SLED." The South Carolina Law Enforcement Division was a statewide agency that could be called in to assist with investigations.

"Really?" said Theodosia. She knew SLED was good, but she also knew that precious time would be lost if this happened. It would take days for Sheriff Billings and probably the fire marshal to get these new investigators up to speed. In the mean time, strange things seemed to be happening to Angie at warp speed.

Theodosia said her good-byes, then hung up the phone. She was still troubled by the fact that not much was happening. Where she'd once thought the wheels of justice were finally turning, now they seemed slightly derailed.

If only Burt Tidwell were investigating.

Burt Tidwell was the one detective, the only detective, that she truly trusted. He was tenacious, brilliant, and maddening. He'd helped her out before and had the keen ability to bull his way right into the heart of a thorny investigation. To make things happen. Fast.

Theodosia sat in her office chair and stared across at the montage of photos and memorabilia on her wall. An old photo of her and her dad on his sailboat. Framed exotic tea labels. An award she and Earl Grey had received for their work with Big Paws, the Charleston service dog organization. A framed copy of one of Haley's scone recipes that had appeared in the *Post and Courier*. More photos.

She thought about Angie and the terrible heartbreak her friend had experienced, was still going through. She thought about Mark, all excited about jumping back into the commodities game. Then his life coming to a screeching, gruesome halt as he lay convulsing in front of his wife and friends.

And the deep down, inner part of Theodosia, the part that despised bullies, rooted for underdogs, and believed that old-fashioned justice ought to prevail, quivered with outrage.

So Theodosia pulled herself together and did the most logical thing she could think of. She phoned Burt Tidwell at his office.

Unfortunately, the detective was not in residence.

"He's bone fishing down in Abaco," his assistant told her. "At Marvle Cay. Said he's not to be disturbed."

"Where's Abaco?" asked Theodosia.

"Bahamas."

"Do you know when he'll be back?"

"Lord willing," his assistant said, "he'll do us all a favor and stay out of the office for another week. Two would be even better."

"Okay," said Theodosia. "Thanks anyway." She dug into her red leather address book where she'd stuck Tidwell's business card. Scanning his card, she squinted at his cell phone number, hesitated for a few seconds, wondering if she could make a cell phone connection in the Bahamas. Then she punched in the number, deciding it was worth a shot.

Tidwell answered on the fourth ring. "Tidwell."

"Detective Tidwell, this is Theodosia. Sorry to disturb you but . . ."

"Theodosia who?" came Burt Tidwell's gruff reply.

"Theodosia Browning," she said. "You know, from the tea shop?"

"Who gave you this number?" he demanded.

Theodosia frowned. He was playing cat and mouse with her. One of his favorite games. "You did," she told him.

"Did you call my office first?" he asked.

"Yes, of course."

"And they told you I was in the Bahamas bone fishing?" he asked.

"Well . . . yes," replied Theodosia. "And I'm really sorry to disturb you, but . . ."

"Fish aren't biting worth a darn," complained Tidwell. "Stupid things are swimming all around me. I can see their *shadows* but they simply don't *respond*. That's the problem with fish. Dinosaur brains. Limited attention span."

"A lot of that going around," said Theodosia. She hesitated as she heard more loud splashing sounds, then a disgusted mutter. She conjured a mental image of Burt

Tidwell. Oversized, bobbling head, slightly protruding eyes. A big man, looking almost like a cross between a grizzly bear and a walrus. She wondered if Tidwell was suited up in rubber waders or just sloshing around in an old T-shirt and baggy Bermuda shorts. Either costume would be a strange sight to behold.

"So what did you want?" asked Tidwell. "Now that you've interrupted my vacation and completely obliterated my concentration."

"There's been a disturbing incident," Theodosia told him. "Mark Congdon, a friend of mine, collapsed and died last Sunday at Carthage Place Plantation. Initially the doctors thought he'd suffered a heart attack, now the medical report says he died from a nonspecific toxin."

"Not my jurisdiction," growled Tidwell. "I only handle homicides in Charleston proper."

"I realize that," said Theodosia. "It's just that I thought perhaps—"

Tidwell cut her off. "Who's heading the investigation?"

"Sheriff Ernest Billings."

Tidwell snorted. "I was part of a golf foursome with Billings once. Something called the Law Enforcement Officers Golf Scramble. Out at Shadowmoss. Man plays a terrible short game and cheats like a fiend."

Theodosia fervently wished they could get back on track. "I wouldn't know about that," she told him.

"Oh, mother of pearl!" Tidwell let out an excited whoop. "I actually snagged one of the buggers!" There were more excited mutterings, then a loud splash and a muffled burbling.

"Detective Tidwell?" Theodosia asked tentatively. She wondered if he'd been pulled underwater and was drowning.

Then there was more burbling and another Tidwell whoop. And then a faint *glub-glub-glub.*

Theodosia could almost picture Burt Tidwell reeling in his trophy-sized fish while his cell phone slipped through blue waters, finally settling on the sandy bottom of the Caribbean.

15

❦

Theodosia was pondering the whole dilemma. Thinking about how Angie Congdon had asked for her help. Feeling bad that she hadn't really been able to provide any. And was interrupted when Delaine and Bobby Wayne stuck their heads in her office to say good-bye.

"We're taking off now," said Delaine, giving a casual wave. "Oh, can we maybe slip out your back door? When we got here, Church Street was all parked up, so I had Bobby Wayne pull around back. I knew you had two reserved parking spots back there and figured you wouldn't mind.

"By all means go out this way," said Theodosia, starting for the back door. "But I'm going to have to move a couple things." She kicked at a carton of tea candles, then bent down and picked up a flat box. It was heaped with some of the spillover from her perpetually messy desk.

"Sorry," she told Delaine and Bobby Wayne as they edged past her. "I know I'm not the tidiest person . . ."

"You should see my office," said Bobby Wayne. "It's got . . ." He stopped abruptly, his eyes suddenly fixed on the box in Theodosia's hands.

"What?" she asked him.

Bobby Wayne looked puzzled. "That's some of the stuff that belonged to Mark?"

"Uh, yeah," said Theodosia, glancing down at it. "I guess it is. Some of it is." She almost forgot that she'd removed a few things from the two boxes before Haley carried them upstairs.

Bobby Wayne scratched at the back of his neck. "That little ceramic elephant . . . ?"

Theodosia stared at a shiny gray elephant with bright eyes and a curled trunk. It was a cute little collectible, the kind of thing you might put on a small shelf in your dining room along with other small knickknacks.

"I'd swear there's one just like it at our office," said Bobby Wayne. He frowned, his mind struggling to dredge up the exact visual. "Well, maybe not tucked in an office, per se, but sitting out on somebody's workstation."

Theodosia pounced on his words. "Whose workstation? Do you remember?"

Now Bobby Wayne looked nervous and a little unhappy. "I think it might be Fayne Hamilton's."

As if things weren't crazy enough, Drayton was running around like a chicken with its head cut off, trying to get organized for his afternoon tea tasting.

"Our customers will be here in less than ten minutes!" he

screeched, checking his watch for the umpteenth time. He was expecting a group of about a dozen women who had nicknamed themselves the Patriot's Point Tea Club and showed up at the Indigo Tea Shop three or four times a year. Obviously, Drayton wanted everything to be absolutely perfect for these repeat customers.

"Take it easy, Drayton," said Haley. "I've got everything lined up—scones, shrimp bisque, and cheese straws, plus cucumber–goat cheese sandwiches on herb bread. So the kitchen's good to go. And Miss Dimple has the two round tables all set up. She went with the French Garden china by Villeroy & Boch and the Ashmont pattern flatware."

"That's all fine and fancy," replied Drayton, "but I'm still playing catch-up and tinkering with tea selections." He rolled his eyes as if to punctuate his sentence.

Theodosia edged over to where Drayton was dithering amid the chirp and hiss of teapots. "What do you *think* might be on the menu?" she asked him. "Tea-wise, I mean."

"A Nilgiri for sure," said Drayton.

"Sounds like an excellent choice," said Theodosia. Nilgiris were fragrant black teas that imparted a slight "green" flavor. Almost vegetable-like.

"And a traditional black tea from the Ambootia Tea Estate in the district of Darjeeling," continued Drayton.

Theodosia nodded. As always, Drayton was spot-on with his tea selections. His vast experience as a master tea taster and blender always paid off big time. He had the know-how even if his confidence and patience occasionally faltered.

"And I'm thinking of tossing in a tea from the Gopaldhara Tea Estate," finished Drayton. He gave a slight shrug as if to indicate it *should* be okay.

"The Gopaldhara has a slight honey and sandalwood

essence," added Charlie. Despite Drayton's persnickety mood, she was hanging in there.

Theodosia gazed at the two of them as a smile played slowly at her mouth.

"What?" demanded Drayton. "You see a problem?"

"No," said Theodosia. "What I see are two people trying their darndest to put together a fantastic tea-tasting experience. All I can say is I'm delighted you're working together so well."

This last remark caught Drayton completely off guard. "We are?" he asked, fingering his bow tie and glancing nervously at Charlie. "Really?"

Just as Haley and Miss Dimple were delivering bowls of shrimp bisque to the Patriot's Point Tea Club ladies, just as Drayton and Charlie were pouring steaming pots of Darjeeling, Leah Shalimar strolled into the Indigo Tea Shop.

"I couldn't stay away!" she told a surprised Theodosia.

It was getting late and Theodosia hadn't really expected many more customers, but she gladly led Leah to a small table set for two.

"The idea of enjoying some of your wonderful tea and scones kept pulling at me," confessed Leah. "So I decided the best thing to do was drive over here." She peered up at Theodosia. "You're still serving, aren't you? I saw those other tables of . . ."

"We're delighted to have you," said Theodosia. "And Haley's been ferociously productive in the kitchen today, so depending on just how hungry you are you've got your choice of a full tea luncheon or an afternoon repast of tea and scones."

"What would the full tea luncheon be?" asked Leah. "I've been running errands ever since the funeral this morning and haven't had a bite to eat."

Theodosia thought for a moment. They still had quiche from lunch. And the sandwiches that Haley had made for the tea club. And then there was . . .

"Wait a minute," said Leah. "Why don't you just *surprise* me? You know I adore surprises." Her eyes wandered over to where Drayton was chatting with the tea club.

"All right," said Theodosia. "We'll fix a little tray for you." But at the same time she was wondering if Leah had really dropped in for tea or if she was scouting Drayton again. Or just . . . scouting?

Theodosia's questions were pretty much answered when, ten minutes later, Leah asked her to sit down at her table. And, out of the blue, began pitching her on investment products.

"A woman in your position really needs to employ a complete portfolio of financial products," said Leah, as she nibbled daintily at a cucumber-and-goat-cheese sandwich. In your younger years," said Leah, nodding sweetly at Theodosia, "it's important to *build* wealth. Of course, as you get older and your portfolio increases in value, your strategy should then shift to conserving wealth."

"This building wealth thing," said Theodosia. "What exactly are you recommending? Stocks? Mutual funds?"

Leah shook her head tolerantly, as though Theodosia had just given the wrong answer in a school spelling bee. "Way too conservative," she told her. "Even if you pick what you think might be a more volatile sector, like oil or telecommunications, you're not necessarily going to see guaranteed growth. Not in double digits anyway."

"I didn't think anything was guaranteed," said Theodosia. She knew a little bit about investing. Her father had been a lawyer, had left her a small portfolio when he died. And Theodosia knew that risk was always a factor in investing.

Leah reached for her teapot and refilled her teacup. "Let me tell you a little about FOREX," she began.

Uh-oh, thought Theodosia.

"FOREX basically means foreign exchange," said Leah. "You invest a certain amount of money to purchase a foreign currency futures contract."

"So it's speculating on the value of foreign currency," said Theodosia.

"I'm impressed," said Leah Shalimar, "that you grasped the basic concept so readily. Believe me, it took me a while to understand the nuances."

"Not having the best, uh, geopolitical understanding of the world's currency markets," said Theodosia, "I think I'd probably be pretty awful at this."

"Ah," said Leah, holding up a finger. "The beauty of our FOREX product is that you don't need to be particularly knowledgeable in this area. We work through a wonderful company called Sun Commonwealth Trust. They're the FCM, or futures commission merchant, who administers the plan."

"So Loveday and Luxor is basically brokering their product," said Theodosia.

Leah nodded. "In a way. And we feel extremely fortunate to be affiliated with Sun Commonwealth. As FCMs go they have a stellar reputation."

"Really," said Theodosia.

"They garnered a sidebar in *Futures* magazine not too long ago," Leah said knowingly.

"Ah," said Theodosia, who'd never read *Futures* magazine. It was as far from her daily realm as a gossip tabloid.

"So what I'm going to do," said Leah, reaching into her caramel-colored leather handbag, "is leave one of our brochures with you." She placed a small four-color brochure on the table and slid it toward Theodosia. On the cover was a montage photo of various foreign currency and gold coins. Leah's business card was stapled to the top of the brochure. "Read through it," urged Leah. "At your leisure, of course. Then we can get together and I'll answer any questions you might have." She favored Theodosia with a bright smile, a salesperson's smile.

"Great," said Theodosia, slipping the little brochure into her apron pocket and knowing this type of investment was way too rich for her blood. She gazed across the table at Leah, who was looking very pleased with her little pitch. "Can I ask you a question?" said Theodosia.

"Shoot," said Leah. She reached down, picked up her scone and took a dainty bite.

"Do you think Fayne Hamilton was in love with Mark Congdon?"

Leah stopped chewing and lifted her head to stare at Theodosia. "What a funny question," she said. "Impertinent, but a little juicy, too."

Theodosia sat there, letting Leah have her fun. Finally, the woman answered.

"It was probably just a silly little crush," said Leah. "After all, lots of secretaries fall in love with their bosses. Or coworkers." Leah shrugged. "Offices are kind of a breeding ground for that kind of familiarity. Everyone works close, you're together almost every day . . ."

"But do you think she was in *love* with him?" asked Theodosia, knowing that people caught in the throes of passion, or perceived passion, will sometimes go to extremes. Driven by sheer emotion, they often made unwise decisions.

"Was she in love," said Leah, drawing out the last word. "I don't know." She shrugged her thin shoulders. "Maybe. Probably."

Theodosia decided to finish out her day by going through some of the tea and tableware catalogs in her office. Dreaming over the new Wedgwood Bloomers plates that featured a giant, hand-painted rose, picking out a few tea novelty items. She was going to order some rock sugar as well as some green-tea anemones. The anemones were spring-picked tea leaves that had been bundled together, tied with string, and flattened into a rosette. They were basically display teas—you put an anemone in a glass teapot and watched it bloom. A couple of customers had requested anemones, so she was going to order a few. See if other people were charmed by them, too.

Then there was the silver samovar she had her eye on. An elegant, convenient way to heat water, brew tea, and then serve it as well. This one was an updated version of the classic Russian tea samovar and was in the four-hundred-dollar range. A little steep, but they could certainly use it when catering events.

Just as Theodosia jotted down the catalog number for the silver samovar, the phone rang. Knowing everyone was still busy pouring tea and serving the last course of fruit parfait, she picked up the phone herself.

The man on the line identified himself as John Darnell, the fire marshal for the Charleston Fire Department. Theodosia had known that sooner or later he'd get around to her, wanting to ask questions about what she'd seen or done the day of the Featherbed House fire.

Darnell wasted no time with his line of questioning.

"I understand you were one of the first people on the scene," he said, sounding conversational and rather low-key.

"That's right," replied Theodosia.

"Did you happen to see anyone on or near the property? Anyone who was lingering, or driving by, or maybe just seemed a little out of place?"

Theodosia hesitated. "Is this a criminal investigation?"

"This is an investigation," responded John Darnell. "*Did* you see someone, Miss Browning?" he prompted. His tone had suddenly turned a touch more official.

"There was one young woman," replied Theodosia. "I noticed her walking away from the Featherbed House just as I was driving toward it."

"You personally know this woman?" asked Darnell. "Or you can describe her?"

Theodosia took a deep breath, then plunged ahead. "Her name is Fayne Hamilton. And she actually works at the same company where Mark Congdon worked."

"Mark Congdon, the owner of the property," said the fire marshal. Now his voice was neutral, flat. But there was the sound of papers rustling in the background and Theodosia could tell Darnell was checking through reports as he chatted with her on the phone.

"Mark Congdon, the homicide victim," said John Darnell.

"That's right," said Theodosia. She felt bad about siccing the fire marshal on Fayne Hamilton. But what could she do? The girl *had* been seen in the vicinity. And Theodosia did have her own suspicions as well.

"Can you think of anyone else you might have seen that day?" asked Darnell.

Theodosia thought about Harlan Noble standing in the crowd, watching the fire with his dark, hooded eyes. He'd been coveting Mark's orchids earlier, had even tried to purchase them. Would Harlan destroy them if he couldn't get his hands on them? Theodosia thought about Leah Shalimar, too. Now heading up the division that Mark would have headed up. And she thought about Teddy Vickers, who was suddenly aspiring to be the new owner of the Featherbed House.

So many suspects, she thought to herself. *So many questions.*

But the fire marshal still had a few surprising questions of his own.

"Miss Browning, how long have you been personally acquainted with Angie Congdon?"

Theodosia thought for a second. "Maybe three, three and a half years."

"Do you know if there have been any recent problems at the Featherbed House?"

"Problems?" said Theodosia, wondering just where this line of questioning was headed. "I doubt they had any more problems than any other small business," she finally replied.

The fire marshal paused slightly, as if gathering his thoughts. "Do you know if there were any problems between Mrs. Congdon and her husband?"

Time stood still for Theodosia.

"You're asking about Angie?" said a stunned Theodosia.

"And your questions are leading to doubts about her character?"

John Darnell cleared his throat. "Look at it from our point of view, ma'am. In a complex situation such as this, we have to take a hard look at *everyone*."

It had been a long day and everyone was exhausted. Drayton and Charlie sat sprawled on chairs in the tea room. Miss Dimple was gamely clearing away dirty dishes. Haley rattled pots and pans in the kitchen. But it wasn't her usual "let's finish this up and get to night class" rattle. She seemed like she was done in, too.

"You look tired, Drayton," said Theodosia. "You, too, Charlie." Drayton was far from being a young man and Charlie wasn't yet used to flying around the tea shop all day, staying on her feet.

"I *am* tired," agreed Drayton. He glanced sideways at Charlie. "We both are."

Charlie nodded in agreement, seemingly too exhausted to utter a single word.

"Then you two scoot on home," said Theodosia. "I'll finish up here."

"Thanks," said Charlie. She pulled herself to her feet, undid her apron. "See you tomorrow."

"Bye." Drayton waved.

"Well, you've certainly mellowed," commented Theodosia.

"I'm like fine wine," said Drayton. "The older I get, the mellower my flavor."

"I'd say you were more like cheese," said Haley, ducking through the curtains with a tray of freshly washed cups and saucers. "The older you get, the sharper you get."

Drayton pursed his lips and arched a single eyebrow. "You see what I have to put up with?" he said to Theodosia.

Theodosia fixed him with a quirky grin. "Haley does have a point."

Drayton exhaled and shook his head, as if to clear it.

"What?" said Theodosia. "Surely you didn't take our little comments to heart?"

"No," said Drayton slowly. "It's just that I've been contemplating something all day long. Running it through my mind. And I don't know if it's a good idea or a very foolish one."

"Something to do with Mark's funeral?" asked Theodosia. She realized that Drayton had been jumpy ever since the service this morning.

"No," said Drayton. Then he stopped and thought for a moment. "Well, it's slightly related. What I've been noodling about in my head all afternoon is the notion of a quick collecting trip tomorrow morning."

"A collecting trip," repeated Theodosia. She wasn't quite sure where this was headed. Or exactly what Drayton intended to collect.

"You know," said Drayton. "Drive up to those swamps above Edgefield, see if I can find a monkey-face orchid to replace the one that was destroyed in the fire."

This grabbed Haley's attention. "What?" she squawked. "Are you *serious*?"

Drayton swiped at his cheek with the back of his hand. "I know it sounds slightly farfetched. But if I found a monkey-face orchid, I could enter it in the Orchid Lights show on Saturday." He dropped his voice. "In honor of Mark."

"I think that's a lovely idea," said Theodosia. It was just like Drayton to come up with that kind of thoughtful tribute.

"The thing of it is," said Drayton unhappily, "I'm going to need a canoe. Do you know anyone who has a canoe?"

"I can take care of that," said Theodosia, thinking of Parker Scully. He was an outdoor type of guy and she was almost positive he owned a canoe. Besides, Parker had invited her to drop by Solstice tonight, to taste test some new drinks with him. If she called him up now, he could probably have the canoe waiting for her.

But Haley was still incredulous. "Are you crazy?" she exclaimed. "You want to go paddling around in some snake-infested swamp looking for a rare flower? That's like searching for the proverbial needle in a haystack. Your chances are slim to none." She crossed her arms and shook her head. "No, Drayton, don't do it. It's way too crazy an idea."

"Maybe it's just wishful thinking on my part," said Drayton. "Still, I'm determined to give it a try."

"I'll go with you," offered Theodosia. "I think it's actually a fine idea."

"Wha . . ." began Haley.

Theodosia gazed at her earnestly. "It's Drayton's way of helping put things a little bit right."

"But who's going to mind the tea shop?" demanded Haley. "Friday's always our busiest day."

"Charlie will be here to help," replied Drayton.

"You mean you actually trust her?" asked Haley.

Drayton looked pained. "Well . . . yes. And of course we can always ask Miss Dimple."

"I suppose," said Haley.

"Ask Miss Dimple what?" said Miss Dimple as she emerged from the back, looking like a plump senior citizen elf.

"To help out again tomorrow," said Haley. She was still incredulous that Theodosia and Drayton were just going to take off in hope of finding a rare orchid. "Can you?"

Miss Dimple grinned from ear to ear. "Honey, I'd love to," she said. "You know this is like a second home to me."

"Then it's settled," said Theodosia. "Tomorrow we search the tropical wetlands of South Carolina for rare plants."

"Lots of luck," said Haley, shaking her head. "Because you're sure going to need it."

16

❦

"*Don't you ever* work?" Theodosia asked Parker Scully. They were sitting in the bar, a dark Mediterranean-themed room just off the main dining room of Solstice. She was comfortably perched on a black leather upholstered bar stool. Parker stood behind the bar, playing bartender. Thelonious Monk's "North of the Sunset," a cool, laid-back tune, purred over the sound system.

"Are you kidding?" said Parker. "I'm here all the time. I practically *sleep* here."

"But what do you actually *do*?" Theodosia asked, playfully.

"I run things, ma'am. Just like you do at your place."

"But I don't have a staff of thirty people like you do."

Parker's right hand toyed with a small glass bowl of mixed nuts that sat on the counter. "Yes, lucky me. I do have an executive chef, a manager, and a bartender to oversee the really tough things, don't I?"

"Exactly my point," said Theodosia. "So what do *you* handle?"

He leaned forward until he was just a few inches away from her. "I handle the customers."

Theodosia could feel energy coursing between them. It felt good, electric almost.

"Lately, however, I've been working on a very secret project," Parker told her, his blue eyes dancing with mirth.

"I'll bet," said Theodosia.

"No, it's true," said Parker. "I've been trying to develop a signature drink. You know how Pusser's Landing has the Painkiller and Andalucia has their sangria?"

"Yes . . ." said Theodosia slowly.

"Well, Solstice needs one, too."

"I suppose," she allowed.

"Hey," said Parker. "Even your tea shop has signature blends, right?"

Theodosia nodded. It was true. Customers were always asking for their Lemon Mint blend or their famous Lamplighter blend. And during the holidays their Berry Red blend pretty much flew off the shelves.

"So how are you coming with this signature drink?" Theodosia asked.

Parker gave a small shrug. "Please understand, there's a serious amount of specialized research and development involved. In fact, I expect there'll probably be at least six more months of grueling experimentation."

"Okay, smarty," said Theodosia, "then how are you coming with your drink ideas for Saturday night?" Parker Scully had offered to serve a special cocktail for Orchid Lights. He'd mentioned a few ideas to her, but nothing was carved in stone yet.

"Ah, that's where you come in," said Parker, reaching overhead for a pair of glasses. "I've actually got *three* drinks in mind, but I obviously need to winnow it down. Do a little focus-group testing." He grabbed a silver cocktail shaker, dipped it into a bin of crushed ice. Then he reached for a bottle of dark rum, grabbed two more bottles, and started pouring. He snapped the top on the shaker, gave everything a quick, efficient shake, then poured out his concoction into stemmed glasses.

"This is called a Black Orchid," he told Theodosia. "Curaçao, rum, and grenadine." He pushed a glass toward her. "Try it."

Theodosia took a sip. It was icy and tasty and just a little bit strong. "Nice," she told him. "I really like the sweet undertones."

Parker held up a hand. "We're not finished. You still have to see what's stashed behind door number two and door number three."

Theodosia sat there, amused, as Parker turned his back to her and fussed at the back bar. There was the pop of a champagne cork and then, seconds later, a lovely pink drink was set in front of her.

"I could get used to this," she told him.

Parker looked her straight in the eyes. "So could I."

Slightly flustered, Theodosia gazed down at her drink. "What do you call this one?"

"This, my dear, is a Strawberry Shangri-la. I know it sounds dreadfully exotic, but it's basically a scoop of strawberry sherbet with champagne poured over it."

Theodosia tried Parker's iced concoction. It was, of course, incredibly delicious.

"Careful," warned Parker, "don't sip too much at once. You'll get a brain freeze."

"You mean like a Mr. Misty headache?" said Theodosia, laughing. "Like I got as a kid when I slurped too much ice cream or shaved ice?"

"Yup," said Parker. "But you like the drink. Right?"

"It's fantastic. But I'm pretty sure Drayton is planning to serve something called an ice angel. Which is basically iced tea with gelato."

"Okay," said Parker. "So this might be a little too similar."

"Afraid so," said Theodosia. She took another sip. "Even though it's really quite wonderful."

"Okay," said Parker. "On this last one I'm pulling out all the stops." He busied himself, whipping up another drink. "This is my final offering, a Toasted Almond and Cream. Which is basically Kahlua, Irish Cream, Grand Marnier, and a splash of milk." He raised a single eyebrow as Theodosia lifted her glass to taste it.

"Excellent," she told him, "but your first one gets my vote."

"The Black Orchid," said Parker. "You're sure you're not just swayed by the name?"

Theodosia pushed back a mass of curly auburn hair and smiled at him. "No," she said, "it's not just the name."

Parker brought out a bottle of wine then, a Rancho Sisquoc Pinot Noir, and a plate of tapas from the kitchen. They sat together at the bar, shoulders touching, talking quietly, until Toby Crisp, Parker's executive chef, interrupted them.

"Going to take off now, boss," said Toby.

"And you want me to move my car," said Parker, easing off his bar stool.

"I better get going, too," Theodosia announced. She didn't really want to leave, but she'd promised Drayton they'd get an early start tomorrow. After all, they were planning to drive almost as far as the Sumter National Forest.

"We have to load that canoe," Parker reminded her.

"Thanks for zipping home to get it," Theodosia told Parker as she followed him out into the alley behind Solstice.

"No problem," he told her. "It's just been sitting in my garage gathering dust. Glad you want to toss it in the water. Although from what you tell me, it's sounds like you're just going to do some gentle paddling."

Parker reached up, unfastened a couple of lines on top of the canoe, then hefted the silver aluminum canoe onto his shoulders. Then, almost effortlessly, he flipped it onto the roof rack of Theodosia's Jeep. Together they stretched bungee cords around the canoe's thwarts then fastened them to the metal roof rack to hold everything in place.

"Be careful," Parker told her when they finished. "Don't take any chances tomorrow. From what I've heard, that's pretty wild territory you're venturing into."

Theodosia smiled up at him. "I'll be careful," she promised. "Just gentle paddling. Nothing tricky."

Parker stared at her, a crooked smile on his boyish face. "My dear Theodosia, you strike me as someone who's always smack-dab in the middle of the fray."

"Not always," said Theodosia. *Just lately*.

Parker put his arms around her and pulled her close. "Okay then, you're a magnet for trouble. Well, maybe not a magnet. Maybe trouble just kind of finds you. Like a heat-seeking missile."

Theodosia laughed. Parker wasn't all that far off. "How's the cat?" she asked him.

Parker gave a wry smile. "I visited Tiger Lily at the Riverbanks Zoo last week. She's almost eighty pounds now."

"Kind of big for a house cat," grinned Theodosia.

"Hey, you know me," said Parker. "Everything's gotta be larger than life."

Theodosia was still grinning when he leaned down and kissed her.

When she was just a couple of blocks from home, Theodosia suddenly remembered the little box of junk she'd stuck in the back of the Jeep. It was the stuff Bobby Wayne had remarked on earlier today. Stuff that included the little ceramic elephant. And the plane ticket, too.

Theodosia was especially curious about the fact that Mark or Fayne might have bought a pair of elephants. Had it been some silly little shared joke between them? Or had the little ceramic elephant been a gift from Angie? Just knowing that answer would go a long way in clearing up the mystery of whether Mark had been involved with Fayne Hamilton.

Pulling in front of the Bogard Inn, Theodosia sat in her Jeep and listened to the engine tick down. Should she go in? Should she bother Angie on what had to have been a thoroughly terrible day?

Theodosia gazed at the Bogard Inn, where lamps seemed to burn in every window and old-fashioned lanterns lit the way up the winding walk. The inn itself was built in the rococo revival style and featured four large pillars in front and a fanciful assortment of scroll, shell, and foliage motifs adorning the windows and roofline.

Yeah, I am going to go in.

Following the curving walk, stepping from one puddle of light to another, the question of the ceramic elephant burned in Theodosia's mind.

Okay, I'm just going to ask her outright. Hand her the junk, then ask about the elephant.

The young man standing behind the front desk greeted her with a smile. His horn-rimmed glasses and navy blazer gave him a slightly studious, schoolboy look. "Checking in?" he asked, eyeing the box in her arms.

Theodosia waved him off. "I came to see one of your guests," she told him. "Angie Congdon."

"Oh, sure," said the young man. "I'll ring her room." His fingers punched in numbers as he looked back over at her. "Who shall I say is here?"

"Tell her it's Theodosia."

The young man smiled at her and nodded. "Mrs. Congdon?" he said into the phone. "This is Jeremy from downstairs. There's a Miss Theodosia here to see you?" Jeremy listened for a few moments, then hung up. "Someone will be right down," he told her.

"Thank you, Jeremy."

"No problem." He stood behind the desk, looking at sixes and sevens. Then he finally said, "We've got a big party checking in tonight and I'm hoping they show up before I get off at twelve."

"Otherwise, what?" asked Theodosia.

"Wake up the owners?" said Jeremy. His smile morphed into a slightly frazzled look. "Except I'll probably end up staying. Be a nice guy about it." He glanced over at the stairway that curved down into the lobby. "Here comes your friend now, I think."

Theodosia's first impression was that the woman who

was descending the stairs looked like a slightly fuzzy Xerox copy of Angie Congdon. But as the woman crossed the lobby, her heels clacking loudly, Theodosia realized this was Angie's sister. A woman who was a couple of years older than Angie, had a few gray hairs, was perhaps a little bit thinner.

She was also angry. Extremely angry.

"What on earth do you want now?" asked the sister in a voice that grated like gravel. Her eyes blazed, her mouth was pulled back in a snarl.

"Excuse me," said Theodosia, confused. "You're Angie's sister, Gwen?"

"Gwyn," snapped the woman. "And you really don't have any business showing up here!"

Theodosia was racking her brain, trying to figure out why Angie's sister was so spitting mad at her. "Uh . . . perhaps you have me confused with someone else?" Theodosia ventured. *With Delaine? Did Delaine cause some sort of problem?*

"You're Theodosia, right?" spat out Gwyn. "Then you're the one who advised the fire marshal to investigate Angie!"

"I did no such thing," protested Theodosia. *Did I? No, of course not. I just answered a few of his questions. Truthfully at that.*

"As if my sister doesn't have enough problems, now she's under investigation for *insurance fraud*!" said Gwyn, her face contorting into a hard mask of anger. "And it looks like you're the one pointing the finger!"

17

It was still dark when Theodosia stopped in front of Drayton's home and tooted her horn. His small house, also located in Charleston's historic district, had been built and occupied by a prominent Civil War doctor. Today the tidy wooden structure remained weathered, old fashioned, and slightly elegant. Not unlike Drayton himself.

"You're wearing a jacket to go canoeing in a swamp?" Theodosia asked Drayton as he clambered into her Jeep. She chuckled to herself. "Seems a little dressy."

"This is a bush jacket," said Drayton, a trifle defensively. "One I ordered from L.L.Bean. Two-ply cotton duck with cargo pockets and a lined game pouch. Supposed to be water repellant, too."

"Well," said Theodosia, glancing at him again as she pulled away from the curb. "I'll have to admit it exudes a certain bwana-type charm."

"How did it go with Parker last night?" asked Drayton as they spun across the newly finished Cooper River Bridge.

"Hmm?" said Theodosia, her cheeks suddenly turning a bright shade of pink. "Oh, good. Fine."

"I didn't mean your *personal* relationship," said Drayton. "I was referring to the drink choices. For Saturday night's Orchid Lights. You *did* get around to selecting one, didn't you?"

"Oh, that," said Theodosia. She'd been replaying the tape of last evening's encounter with Angie's sister in her mind and had almost blanked out the part with Parker and his drink choices. "We settled on a yummy cocktail called a Black Orchid."

"Sounds apropos," said Drayton, stretching out his legs and leaning back. "Sophisticated name, probably very appealing to our patrons." He tried to stifle a yawn. "Goodness, it's early."

"Crank your seat back and take a nap," suggested Theodosia. "We've got a long drive ahead of us."

"You don't mind?" asked Drayton. He'd already slid his billed hat down over his eyes while one hand fiddled with the seat mechanism.

"Doesn't bother me at all," said Theodosia. "Gives me time to think."

Two and a half hours later, the thin layer of cloud cover had burned off and sunlight dappled the road ahead of them. An hour earlier they'd passed through Edgefield, a town known for its pottery and peach harvest. Now they were nearing the town of Carmel, just outside Hickory Knob State Park on the Georgia–South Carolina border. They'd just topped a ridge and were descending toward the Savannah River and the thousands of acres of dams, waterways, lakes, and swamps that seemed to string together and were often referred to as South Carolina's "freshwater coast."

As glorious as the scenery was, Theodosia found herself staring intently into her rearview mirror, snatching a glance whenever she could.

"What?" asked Drayton drowsily. He'd been awake for a few minutes and had just seen Theodosia glance into her rearview mirror for about the fifth time.

"There was a car back there that I thought was following us," she told him.

"Are you serious?" said Drayton. He squirmed about in his seat, anxious to check the road behind them. "What color?"

"Um . . . white. Cream."

"I don't see a thing."

"Neither do I anymore," said Theodosia. "I guess it must have turned off."

"You're just being paranoid," said Drayton. "In light of everything that's happened."

"I'll get over it," replied Theodosia, deciding that some time today she had to tell Drayton about the ceramic elephant, the fire marshal's probing questions, and the outrage expressed by Angie's sister, Gwyn. But not right now. Not when they were almost at their destination and about to embark on a swamp journey.

"You know where we're going?" asked Theodosia. "I mean precisely?"

"Of course I do," said Drayton. He had unfurled a little hand-drawn map and was studying it carefully. "Tommy

Draper, one of the Orchid Society members, gave me explicit directions. Said this was one of his premier collecting spots."

"And this is on private property?" asked Theodosia. "So it's perfectly legal?"

"Oh, absolutely," replied Drayton.

"I take it you just recently got the map from your friend?" asked Theodosia.

"Oh no," replied Drayton. "It's been maybe two . . . three years."

Theodosia's hands gripped the steering wheel a little tighter. "So it might not be such an all-fired hot spot anymore," she ventured. "Things could have changed depending on local conditions. Dry spells . . . or wet spells?"

"I suppose," said Drayton. "Still, this is supposed to be *the* best area."

"Where are we going?" asked Theodosia. "Give me a landmark."

"We should be passing Blazetree Corners."

"That was a half mile back."

"Okay," said Drayton. He studied his map again, glanced out the side window, looked suddenly startled. "Oh, goodness me, here's our turn! Hang a right! We're just coming up on County Road Ten."

Cranking the wheel hard, Theodosia made the turn, and took the Jeep down a jouncing, gravel road.

"Exciting," said Drayton, hanging on for dear life.

"Isn't it," said Theodosia, praying her shock absorbers would hold out.

* * *

Another twelve miles of rough road brought them to a small farm. According to Drayton's map, this was supposed to be their start point.

"Since this is private land," said Drayton, climbing out of the Jeep, "I have to go clear it with the owner. That was Tommy's advice anyway."

"Okay," said Theodosia. Squinting, she watched Drayton approach a small white clapboard house that was badly in need of paint. A barn stood behind it, but Theodosia could spot no animals nor see any planted fields. If this was some kind of farm, she had no clue what they actually raised.

The good news, however, was that there was a small, meandering stream some forty yards away from where she was parked. The land sloped gently down, with a minimum of underbrush, so she figured she could drive her Jeep right down. Then, all they had to do was slide the canoe off the roof and toss it in the water.

Drayton came hustling back, looking pleased with himself. "I paid the landowner twenty dollars to let us launch the canoe and another thirty for any plants we might collect."

"It sounds like a deal," said Theodosia.

"I thought so, too," said Drayton. "But the fellow, a Mr. Avery Walker, seemed to think we wouldn't find many plants. That he pretty much got the better of us."

"In that case," said Theodosia unfastening the bungee cords. "We'll just have to prove him wrong.

They leveraged the canoe off the Jeep and into the water. A skim of green parted as the canoe sluiced through. Dragonflies buzzed about pleasantly.

"You jump in first," Theodosia told Drayton. "You can be the bow man while I take the stern." She climbed onto the back end of the canoe, stabilizing the craft for Drayton. "Stay low."

"You realize I haven't been in a canoe since summer camp," said Drayton, as he clambered toward his end. "And I'm not about to tell you when *that* was." He eased himself down tentatively, then picked up a paddle and stared at it, as though trying to figure out which end to use.

"Paddling a canoe is a lot like riding a bike," Theodosia told Drayton as she tossed in his collecting baskets, then pushed off from the grassy bank. "You never forget the basics."

"But the consequences are significantly different," said Dayton. "If you fall off a bike you get a scraped knee or, at worst, a banged-up elbow. Fall out of a canoe and you drown."

"That's not going to happen," Theodosia assured him.

They paddled along, Drayton splashing away happily in the bow of the canoe.

"Feather the paddle," Theodosia advised him. "Like this." She held the flat blade of the paddle perpendicular to the water to make it more aerodynamic.

Drayton turned to watch her execute a few strokes, then caught on instantly. "Ah," he said. "I see. Less wind resistance."

As they continued to paddle along, the stream widened out considerably. Now it was more of a pond punctuated with stands of reeds. Carolina wrens flitted about, stands of tupelo and gum lined the banks. The occasional heron skimmed down to grab a shimmering little bream for lunch.

"What if we should run into an alligator?" asked Drayton.

"I think gator habitats are a lot farther south than this," mused Theodosia. "Down closer to Savannah where the water's considerably warmer."

"And snakes?" asked Drayton.

Theodosia stared straight ahead. "Let's not get into that."

"Oh, oh," said Drayton, as they rounded a bend and dozens of little inlets and tertiary streams came into view. "Now what?"

"This time I did bring a compass," said Theodosia. "Plus you've got your map."

"That was just to get us to the launch site," said Drayton.

"No X marks the spot for exotic orchids?"

"Sorry, no," said Drayton. They paddled some more. "So what do you think, just keep going straight?"

"For now," replied Theodosia. "Depending on what kind of plant life we encounter."

"Or don't," said Drayton.

But as the sun rose higher and stands of bog rose began to appear, luck was with them. And it wasn't long before Drayton's keen eyes spotted bright blooms through draperies of green vegetation.

"Can we edge in closer to the bank?" he asked. "I'm awfully sure that's a Showy Orchis."

Theodosia maneuvered the canoe in closer. The water had again narrowed to a stream with a fairly strong current. It made paddling easy, but pulling over a little trickier.

"Yes," came Drayton's excited voice. "It's definitely a Showy Orchis."

"That's good?" asked Theodosia as she drove the canoe into the muddy bank where the bow made a dull thud and then stuck fast.

"A fairly common variety," said Drayton. "But still a

beauty." He stepped carefully from the canoe, then leaned down and grasped the bow, pulling it up onto the bank a bit more so Theodosia could hop out without getting her feet wet.

"And you're going to collect it?" asked Theodosia. Drayton was tromping around, looking extremely pleased.

"Oh, absolutely. If only to display in the tea shop."

Theodosia's eyes searched the area for more orchids. It was damp and shady here, with stalks of puttyroot, too. Probably conducive, she decided, to native plant life. "Look at all this moss," she exclaimed. "Isn't it gorgeous?" At her feet were large lumps of bright green moss.

"Cushion moss," said Drayton. "Technically Leucobryum."

Loosening a clump with her hand, she scooped it up and hefted it gently. "It's like a big, fuzzy Christmas tree ornament."

"Very whimsical," agreed Drayton. "We should definitely collect some of the moss."

"Can't you just see these moss goobers as centerpieces at the tea shop?" asked Theodosia, still charmed by the balls of moss. "Four or five in a wicker basket, maybe surrounding a small bouquet of violets?"

"Or tucked into pots with some of my Japanese bonsai," said Drayton. "To lend the feeling of a Zen garden."

"What a great place," declared Theodosia. "Your friend with the map was right on. Hey, can I use one of your collecting baskets?" Theodosia had already grabbed one and had it half filled with moss.

"Feel free," said Drayton, plunging his trowel into the soil for about the fourth time. "While I try to disengage this rather large root ball from the soil."

Straining, Drayton bent into his task again. "Tough," he said.

"Want me to help?"

Drayton wiped at his face. "Maybe grab that other trowel and give me a hand."

"Sure," said Theodosia. "No problem."

But as they both bent forward, a loud pop split the air.

Drayton's head popped up like a startled gopher. "Huh? What?"

"Get down!" hissed Theodosia, clawing frantically at his sleeve. She knew there was only one thing in the whole world that made a loud, instantly identifiable report like that.

"What's wrong?" asked Drayton, still trying to straighten up for a look around.

"Get down, get down!" hissed Theodosia. "I think someone just took a shot at us!"

"They took a . . . what?" exclaimed Drayton. "Good heavens, is it hunting season?"

"C'mon," urged Theodosia, grabbing wildly for collecting baskets and equipment. "Back into the canoe!"

The canoe lurched wildly from side to side as Theodosia scrambled in first, hurling her daypack and baskets into the center. Drayton got his feet soaked as he pushed off fast then hefted himself in, shoving his paddle into the sandy bottom of the stream.

Settled onto her seat, trying to stay low, Theodosia struggled to swing the canoe around. She knew if she could get them out of the area, maybe slip down one of the smaller tributary streams, that would afford them some cover.

"What now?" asked Drayton, fear evident in his voice.

"Paddle!" came Theodosia's terse instruction as she

headed them away from the bank. "Paddle now and paddle hard!"

Another shot zinged over their heads as the two of them dug in, paddling like crazy, trying to put some distance between themselves and the gunman.

"Holy smokes!" gasped Drayton. He was leaning low, his strokes coming frantically. And already breathing hard.

Theodosia dug deeper, worried at Drayton's ability to maintain this frantic pace. Drayton wasn't a young man and Theodosia had no idea how heart-healthy he was.

As they splashed frantically downstream, Theodosia caught sight of a faster-moving, burbling stream that split off to the left. They could veer off into that channel, she decided, or take their chances and keep heading down the main stream.

"Which way?" screamed Drayton.

Theodosia snuck a quick glance over her shoulder. The right river bank was flatter and a lot more open, certainly more conducive for a gunman to run alongside and track them. But if they took the left stream, they'd be plunged into dense undergrowth which would, hopefully, slow their pursuer and afford them some cover.

"Head for that left fork," Theodosia shouted at Drayton. "Switch your paddle over to the right side and dig in like crazy." She drove her own paddle deep into the current, using it as a rudder to execute a sharp turn.

Then they were moving along, caught up in the current, hopefully being carried away from the gunman.

Drayton ventured a quick look back at Theodosia. His face was drawn and tense, filled with bewilderment. "Was someone shooting at *us*?" he gasped.

18

❧

Theodosia shook her head to indicate she had no idea what was going on. Things had gone from benign to bedlam in a matter of seconds. They'd been digging up an orchid, taking care with the root ball, congratulating themselves on their good fortune. And suddenly they were under siege. The entire scenario was utterly bizarre.

"Keep paddling," Theodosia encouraged Drayton. But she could see from the set of his shoulders that he was flagging now, and she knew it was up to her to keep them moving forward.

For several minutes Theodosia was only aware of her own ragged breathing and the burning sensation between her shoulder blades as she dug her paddle, feathered it, dug and feathered again, then switched sides and repeated her motions.

Drayton was leaning forward now, breathing heavily, his paddle resting across the gunnels of the canoe. He lifted his head slowly, seemed to spot something up ahead, then called out to her, "There appear to be some rapids ahead!"

"Good," Theodosia muttered as they tucked right into the current and their speed increased dramatically. She knew hitting a little white water was definitely a lucky break. The fast-moving stream would carry them along swiftly. So they'd hopefully be out of range of whoever had been shooting at them.

Clunk!

The right side of the canoe slammed into a rock. Wobbling slightly, they caromed away and promptly slammed into an even larger rock on the opposite side.

Using her paddle as rudder, Theodosia bent hard into the task, trying to steer them around rocks and boulders as the riverbank flashed by. The little stream that had started out as their savior was rapidly turning into a swiftly moving river that carried them helplessly along.

If only I could maneuver us toward the bank, she thought. *We've made enough distance that we should be safe now.*

But no matter what technique she tried, Theodosia wasn't able to head them over to the bank. They were caught in the middle and moving too swiftly.

"What are we going to do now?" cried Drayton. He'd picked up his paddle again and was dipping it helplessly. "Will we be stopping soon?"

"Just hang on," said Theodosia gamely. She knew Drayton was terrified, could read it on his face and see it in the way he'd stiffened his shoulders. "We'll be okay," she yelled at him.

She in no way reassured him.

"This feels like a scene out of *Deliverance*!" Drayton cried, twisting in his seat to glance back at her again.

"I hope not," prayed Theodosia. Sweat streamed into her eyes and she took a quick moment to wipe it away. When she again glanced at the river ahead, Theodosia couldn't believe what she was seeing.

Just a thin, blue line.

Swirling rapids around them, a thin, blue line ahead, and then . . . nothing!

"Waterfall!" came Drayton's sudden, terrified cry. But it was far too late to do anything about it. Too late to fight harder for shelter on the rocky banks. The canoe was held fast by the current and heading directly toward that fast-approaching, terrifying edge. An edge that appeared to have nothing beyond it!

"Hang on!" screamed Theodosia as they slipped closer to the top of the waterfall. "Brace yourself with your legs!"

The canoe seemed to hesitate for a moment on the edge of what appeared to be a twenty foot vertical shoot. Then slowly, inexorably, the bow of the canoe tilted out over the falls, and they pitched forward with a jolt. There was a loud whooshing sound and then they were caught up in the mad rush of their downward plunge.

"Hang on!" Theodosia screamed again as they plummeted headlong down a steep curtain of water, gaining momentum as they dropped. Water drummed on her head and poured down the back of her camp shirt. A loud roar filled her ears. Once, Theodosia had gone on the White Water Falls ride at Carowinds park over near Rock Hill. This plunge almost replicated that terrifying experience, except there was no underwater track to keep them headed straight, no friendly employee to offer a helping hand at the end of the ride. This was a horrible, excruciating freefall into a swirling cauldron of water below.

As the bow of the canoe sliced into the whirlpool's roiling spume, the canoe began to spin. Theodosia could see Drayton clutching the gunnels, his knuckles white with fear. Then slowly, inexorably, Drayton pitched overboard and disappeared into a terrible swirl of white foam.

"Oh no," moaned Theodosia. Knowing Drayton could barely swim a stroke, she drew a deep breath and, without hesitation, dove in after him.

It was like being inside a washing machine. Currents and eddies pulled at her from every direction. Spun her around, tumbled and tugged her, and slammed her hard against underwater rocks and boulders.

Theodosia floundered gracelessly in the pool, grabbing, kicking, coming up for a quick gasp of air, then diving down repeatedly.

Where was Drayton?

Heartsick, Theodosia searched underwater for him, fighting the current, fearing the worst. She was almost ready to give up when one flailing hand suddenly brushed against fabric.

Drayton?

She pinched hard, pretty sure she'd grabbed on to his jacket, then extended her other arm out and found more fabric. Pulling Drayton toward her, she wrapped both arms about him and began to kick. Kicked desperately until her legs began to feel like jelly. And just when she was about to despair, just when she didn't have another molecule of air left inside her lungs, their heads popped above water.

Theodosia gasped for a breath of air, then yelled, "Kick!"

Now they were both kicking like mad and, amazingly, moving away from the pocket of foam and swirling water into slightly more calm waters. Theodosia wrapped her left arm around Drayton's shoulders and paddled frantically with her right arm. At the same time she managed a tired but fairly decent scissors kick with her legs.

Finally, tiredly, painfully, they pulled themselves out of the river and up onto a series of flat, dry rocks.

"You okay?" Theodosia gasped. The back of Dayton's jacket was still twisted in her hands. She had to force herself to release him.

Drayton nodded his head even as he tried to scuttle farther up onto the flat rocks. His breathing was shallow and he seemed dangerously close to hyperventilating. "I . . . thought . . ." One hand pawed at the air as he struggled to catch his breath. ". . . I thought I was a goner."

Theodosia flopped over onto her back, stared up at sunlight and green foliage so bright it almost made her nauseous. "I thought we were both goners," she finally managed.

"Someone was shooting at us?" he said. "Why?"

"Don't know," said Theodosia.

"It felt like that last shot parted my hair," said Drayton. He coughed, patted himself nervously as if to make sure he was still in one piece.

Theodosia sat up and untucked her sodden blouse, then tied it loosely at her waist. "I think someone did follow us," she told him. "And that those shots were fired as a threat."

"What kind of threat?" asked Drayton as he pulled off a shoe, dumped out a stream of water.

"Warning us not to snoop. To mind our own business."

"You mean because of our investigation into the Mark Congdon thing," said Drayton.

"Gotta be," said Theodosia. "And because we've been skeptical about the fire, too."

"But we're not even *close*," wailed Drayton. "Sure, we've got suppositions and suspects, but nothing concrete."

"I'm guessing," said Theodosia, "that we've got more pieces than we think we do." She quickly told Drayton about the fire marshal's direct line of questioning and how Angie's sister had come after her last night like a rabid dog. Had left her standing in the lobby of the Bogard Inn feeling stupid and guilty and still clutching Mark's box of junk.

"The fact remains," said Drayton, after he'd listened to all Theodosia had said, "we didn't *cause* any of those events to happen. We're only peripherally involved. Bystanders, really."

"Somehow we've touched on something, an important clue," said Theodosia. "We just haven't been able to put two and two together." She shook her head, frustrated, still shaken from their escape and headlong plunge, feeling more than a little angry. "I don't know . . ."

They sat for a few minutes, pondering their harrowing escape from the river, wringing out clothes, examining their various bumps and bruises. Then Drayton pulled himself into a seated position. "Where's the canoe?" he asked in a funny, high-pitched voice.

Theodosia waved an arm. "Gone. Probably still shooting down the river like a runaway bobsled." The image of Parker's silver canoe sluicing through the rapids all by itself, the notion that they were finally safe after being shot at, then plunging down a twenty-foot waterfall, caused her to choke out a strangled laugh.

Drayton wobbled his head toward her. "You can't seriously see humor in any of this, can you?"

Theodosia lifted her shoulders and rotated them, trying to loosen the knot of tension in the back of her neck. "Look at it this way," she said. "You've been hankering for a little break."

"A break in my *routine*," Drayton shot back somewhat crossly. "Not my neck." He stood up, dripping water. "You know what?" he said.

"What?"

"This jacket is definitely not waterproof."

Amazingly enough, they located the canoe some fifty yards down stream. It had hung up on a fallen tree and remained securely wedged there.

"We're in luck," announced Theodosia. "We've also got paddles, baskets, your hat, and a plastic thermos of tea. Everything's a little bedraggled but still functional, I guess."

"But how on earth are we going to get out of here?" asked Drayton. He gazed upstream at the pounding waterfall. It looked majestic, but lethal. "We certainly can't go back the same way we came."

Theodosia's brain was finally beginning to fire again on all eight cylinders. "First we'll wade in and get the canoe and stuff," she suggested. "We're already wet so what's another dunking? We can probably just kind of walk it across the river to this bank. See . . . the stream isn't that deep here and the current slows way down."

"Then what?" said Drayton. "I hope you don't expect us to carry the canoe out of here. Or make a portage, as they say in voyageur-speak. It could be miles back to where we started."

Clambering up the rocks and onto solid ground, Theodosia pushed through clumps of horse nettle and ventured a few yards into the woods.

"Whoa," said Drayton, scrambling after her. "Kindly wait for me."

He found her, hands on hips, studying the ground.

"We're in luck," she told him.

Drayton cocked an eyebrow. "We could use some."

"There was a road here at one time. See?" Theodosia pointed at two muddy ruts that were still faintly visible through the high grass. "All we have to do is follow this trail out, find the Jeep, then drive back here and pick up the canoe."

"Oh, that's all, is it?" said Drayton. "You make it sound like a wonderful romp in the park. Pardon me while I fetch my umbrella and picnic hamper."

Theodosia turned toward Drayton with sympathetic eyes. "Tell you what, why don't you hold down the fort right here. I'll jog back and try to locate the Jeep. Then I'll drive back here and pick up you and the canoe."

"Not on your life," said Drayton, squaring his shoulders. "After all we've been through today, we're sticking together!"

After the dousing they'd experienced, it felt almost pleasant to wander along the old trail with the sun shining down on their backs. Birds twittered in the trees, the scenery was nothing if not spectacular, and their clothes and lightweight baskets dried out with every step they took.

"Nobody would believe what we've just been through," said Drayton. "A veritable comedy of errors." He thought for a moment. "Or maybe a tragedy of errors, if there is such a thing."

"Whatever you choose to call it," said Theodosia. "None of this was any fault of our own." Then she reconsidered her words. "*Almost* any fault," she added.

"Yipes!" exclaimed Drayton, suddenly jumping back and grabbing her arm in a viselike grip.

"What?"

"Snake," he said in a low voice.

Theodosia stood stock-still for a few seconds, then finally worked up the courage to peer down at the ground. "Uh . . . where?"

No quick motions for Drayton; he kept his arms clamped tight against his body. "Right where that tall grass is parting slightly," he told her in hushed tones.

"Did you see any markings?" Theodosia asked nervously. She hadn't seen the creature, but that didn't mean the snake wasn't nearby, ready to pounce or coil or whatever it was snakes got in their head to do.

"There were brownish bands. Yes, I'm quite sure they were a chestnut-olive shade," said Drayton. "Or maybe dun-colored. Or umber."

"Easy, Drayton," said Theodosia in a low voice. "We're trying to identify a snake, not pick a paint sample."

Drayton nodded tightly. "Right. Of course." He was obviously nervous and his teeth were just this side of chattering.

"What about the nose?" asked Theodosia. "Pointy or blunt-nosed?"

"What's the difference again?"

"Pointy is nonvenomous and . . ."

"Blunt-nosed is the bad guy," finished Drayton.

"Yeah, that's it."

Drayton turned slightly to face her. "While we've been standing here like frightened ninnies, pondering its coloration and physiognomy, Mr. Snake has slithered off on his merry way. Leaving us to wonder just what his intentions might have been."

"Whew," said Theodosia. She made a broad gesture of wiping her brow, like a cartoon character would. "Freaky."

"Terrifying," agreed Drayton.

They continued their trudge down the trail. What had been woods and a little bit of meadowland had now turned more forested and swampy.

"Getting boggy," said Theodosia as her shoes squished unpleasantly in the mud.

"I hope we don't lose this trail," worried Drayton.

"As long as we keep the sun at our back we should be okay," replied Theodosia as frogs and katydids chirped at them, unseen.

"Do you have your trusty compass?"

"Uh . . . no," responded Theodosia. "I think it flew out of my shirt pocket when we went through that final spin cycle." She knew she was lucky to have the clothes on her back. And luckier still that she'd left her car keys behind, tucked under the floor mat of her Jeep.

"Good heavens," exclaimed Drayton. He stopped, took a hesitant step, frowned, then halted again.

Nervous about the possibility of another snake sighting, Theodosia glanced about, wondering what had suddenly caught Drayton's eye.

"Do you see what I see?" asked Drayton.

Theodosia let down her guard a bit as she continued to

glance about tiredly. "No snakes in sight," she told him. "But I do see mud, tupelo trees, slimy water, more slimy water, and, if I'm not mistaken, maybe a modicum of quicksand to top things off and make us really feel welcome."

"No," said Drayton, his voice suddenly trembling with excitement. "Over there. Look!"

Theodosia's eyes followed Drayton's finger as he pointed toward a stand of straggly willow saplings. And there, growing out of a little copse of green was a pure-white flower.

"Is that what I think it is?" she asked.

Drayton nodded tightly. The rare *Platanthera integrilabia*. The monkey-face orchid."

"Well, I'll be," said Theodosia.

"Pass me the collecting basket, quick," said Drayton. "I've got to hurry," he mumbled as he stumbled rapidly toward it.

"It's not going to walk away," laughed Theodosia.

"It better not, after all we've been through," said Drayton. "Do we still have a few balls of that moss to help hold the moisture in?"

"Talk about a lucky save," said Theodosia. She watched as Drayton gently freed the little orchid, then placed it in a basket and packed moss around it.

Fifteen minutes later the sketchy trail they'd been following turned into a bona fide path.

"Look," exclaimed Drayton, putting a hand up to his brow, "if my old eyes don't deceive me, that's the farmyard we started from."

"And there's my Jeep," said Theodosia, spotting her little red vehicle hunkered down next to the stream where she'd left it. She was glad to see nothing had happened to it.

"And there's Mr. Avery Walker," added Drayton. "Think we should mention something to him about the gunshots? Or stop and make a report to the police or sheriff?"

"I'm not sure exactly what we'd report," said Theodosia. "We never actually *saw* anyone, so it would be tough to give any sort of meaningful description."

They walked up to Mr. Walker, who peered at them curiously from under a battered straw hat.

"We have returned," Drayton announced tiredly but cheerily. "And with a rather fine orchid at that."

Avery Walker slid his straw hat off his head and gaped at them with pale blue eyes that conveyed shocked surprise. "My lordy," he said. "You poor folks look like you've been lost in these woods for a week!"

19

❦

"*Must have been* a fun outing," said Haley when Theodosia walked in the back door of the Indigo Tea Shop mid-afternoon. "Because you look really good."

"I do?" said a surprised Theodosia. After she dropped Drayton at his home, she'd hustled herself upstairs, jumped in the shower, washed her hair, changed clothes, and tried her best to undo some of the damage that had been done earlier. It hadn't been easy.

"Your complexion is glowing and you kind of look like you came from a spa," said Haley.

"A whirlpool treatment maybe?" asked Theodosia, a little smile playing about her mouth. "And a mud scrub?"

"Yeah," said Haley, still studying her. "Something like that. Anyway, it looks like spending time outdoors agrees with you. Maybe you and Drayton should go orchid collecting more often."

"Maybe so," said Theodosia, knowing she probably wouldn't be venturing into *that* part of South Carolina again. At least not without a band of Eagle Scouts and an armed guard at her side.

"So where is Drayton?" asked Haley. "You did bring him back, didn't you?"

"He'll be along shortly," said Theodosia, grabbing for an apron. "He's taking care of the plants he collected."

Haley's eyebrows shot up. "Did he find *the* one? The mysterious elusive orchid?"

Theodosia nodded. "Amazingly, yes. And a really lovely specimen at that. But tell me, how did things go here? How *are* things going?"

"Oof," said Haley, scrunching up her face. "Lunch was a real crush. Practically standing room only. Thank goodness Charlie and Miss Dimple were here to help out. Charlie handled the tea brewing like an old pro and we had Miss Dimple scurrying around like crazy. Now things have finally settled down to a dull roar with the usual gang of Friday afternoon tourists out front. Most of them have been tromping around the historic district since early morning, doing the sightseeing thing, so they're ready for a little tea shop pick-me-up."

"Do we have enough food left?" asked Theodosia.

"Barely," said Haley. "Which is why I have batches of blueberry scones and banana-walnut muffins in the oven now."

"I'll dash out front and see what I can do to help," said Theodosia, glancing in the small mirror by the door, thinking to herself that she *did* look rather fresh and alive. It was amazing what a twenty-foot drop and a soak in the river could do for one's complexion.

"Oh, and Delaine and Bobby Wayne are out there, too," added Haley as she darted back into her kitchen.

"I'll go say hi," said Theodosia, pushing her way through the green velvet curtain.

But with every table filled to capacity, Theodosia had to plunge right into the fray. She delivered refills of Assam and Nilgiri tea, as well as the last of the cream scones and cran-apple muffins. And she placated waiting customers with news that more fresh-baked goodies were on the way.

When the rest of Haley's baked goods finally came out of the oven, when everything seemed under control, when every customer was sipping tea, Theodosia made it over to the table where Delaine and Bobby Wayne were seated.

"Where have you been?" was the first question that popped out of Delaine's mouth. "You're usually not such an absentee owner. Especially on Friday."

Theodosia brushed off her friend's question. "Drayton and I had some business to attend to."

"Bobby Wayne and I have been frantically busy ourselves," said Delaine. She reached down and picked up a shiny black tote bag. "See this? We've been running around, collecting last minute donations for tomorrow night's silent auction." She set the bag back down, sighed mightily. "Celerie Stuart was *supposed* to take care of all this, but she ran into trouble with the decorations, so she begged me to finish up." Delaine smiled sweetly at Bobby Wayne, who was busy buttering a scone. "I tried to handle everything myself, but I was going absolutely bonkers, so I finally picked up the phone and asked Bobby Wayne here to lend a hand. Which he did, dear gentleman that he is."

"No problem, my sweet," Bobby Wayne told her, even though his mouth was full.

Haley came scurrying over with a plate of banana-walnut

muffins. "Here are those muffins you asked for, Bobby Wayne."

"Thanks, honey," he said.

Haley lingered at their table. "Did you guys collect a lot of good stuff for the silent auction?"

That was all the prompting Delaine needed. She reached into one of her tote bags and hauled out what she deemed the "special" pieces. Which, in Delaine-speak, meant jewelry.

"Brooke over at Heart's Desire donated one of her hand-tooled silver bracelets. See?" Delaine dangled a shiny charm bracelet from her fingers. "Strung with her Charleston charms—tiny trolley, palmetto leaf, an oyster shell. And see, she added some new ones. A little wrought-iron gate and a magnolia."

"I just adore her charm bracelets," said Haley.

"And Van Stern Jewelry donated this necklace." Delaine pulled out a chunky gold chain with a bright green stone dangling from it."

"What's the stone?" asked Bobby Wayne, squinting at it. "A peridot?"

"Lemon citrine," Delaine told him.

"So what else?" asked Haley. "What about the businesses around here?"

"The Chowder Hound donated a hundred-dollar gift certificate," Delaine told her. "And Hattie Boatwright at Floradora is donating a Think Pink bouquet of gerbera daisies and Anna roses. See, here's a photograph of it. Nice, no?"

"Nice, yes," said Theodosia. "But I thought you preferred Fig and Vine."

Delaine gave a careless shrug. "We *always* welcome donations," she said. "No matter where they come from."

"You've done a lot of work on this," said Theodosia. Delaine could be a pain sometimes, but she was a hardworking volunteer.

Delaine rolled her eyes in a gesture of supreme exasperation. "I was hoping some of the Orchid Society people would pitch in and garner donations, too. After all, they're *supposed* to be an equal partner in Orchid Lights. But so far not one of them has lifted their little pinky. The only thing they're focused on is the orchid show itself."

"I suppose they're not accustomed to staging fund-raisers," said Theodosia. "After all, they're more of a social club, while the Heritage Society is a nonprofit organization, used to hitting people up for contributions."

"Still," said Delaine, "the orchid people could be a lot more cooperative." She took a delicate sip of tea, looked around, suddenly threw up one hand and waved wildly at Drayton. "Drayton!" she gushed. "There you are!"

Drayton came scurrying over to their table, looking none the worse for wear. "Nice to see you," he told Delaine. Then directed a solemn nod toward Bobby Wayne. "You, too, Bobby Wayne."

Bobby Wayne nodded pleasantly as his silver knife cut into another of Haley's muffins.

"I'm doing the final round of collecting for the silent auction," Delaine told Drayton.

"I trust our fine neighbors up and down Church Street have been more than generous," he replied.

"Some have, some haven't," Delaine said cryptically. "Your friend Harlan Noble was grudging at best."

"I wouldn't go so far as to characterize Harlan as my friend," said Drayton.

Theodosia's ears perked up. "You asked Harlan Noble for a donation?"

"Yes," said Delaine, rolling her eyes. "But all he gave us was an old dog-eared copy of some book on Civil War history. Not terribly appealing. Certainly not to me, anyway. I'm not even sure we should include his meager contribution in tomorrow's silent auction."

"You stopped by Harlan's shop this morning?" asked Theodosia. She wondered if Harlan Noble had somehow found time to drive north, take a potshot at them, then whip back to Charleston. He seemed like a mild-mannered fellow, but you never really knew about people.

"No, we just saw Mr. Noble maybe . . ." Delaine narrowed her eyes, thinking. ". . . something like forty minutes ago. That was the first place we hit together, right, Bobby Wayne?"

Bobby Wayne nodded as he chewed.

Delaine leaned forward in her chair, a conspiratorial look suddenly spreading across her heart-shaped face. "But even if Harlan Noble isn't the most generous donor, we *did* pick up some rather juicy gossip." Now Delaine's eyes positively gleamed.

Theodosia and Drayton stared at Delaine, well aware she was bursting to share her news with them. They didn't have to wait long.

"It's about Angie," said Delaine, flashing a cat-that-ate-the-canary smile.

"Angie Congdon?" said Theodosia. Now what was going on?

"It seems that Angie is under investigation for insurance fraud!" Delaine delivered this shocker of a line with wide-eyed wonderment.

"That can't be so," piped up Drayton, even though Theodosia had mentioned to him earlier today that the fire marshal had asked pointed questions concerning Angie.

"Are you serious?" blurted out Theodosia. *So she really is being investigated? No wonder Gwyn was so upset last night.*

"Doesn't that just take the cake!" crowed Delaine.

"This is all a mistake," said Theodosia. She didn't for one minute believe Angie was guilty of anything.

"I don't think so," said Delaine, reveling in her bearer-of-bad-news status. "Tell them, Bobby Wayne." She sat back in her chair with a satisfied look on her face, happy to pass the gossip baton to Bobby Wayne.

Bobby Wayne blotted his lips with a napkin and turned serious eyes on Theodosia, Drayton, and Haley. "Apparently it *is* true."

"Explain, please," said Drayton, motioning with his fingers.

Now Bobby Wayne looked thoughtful. Regretful, almost. "Well, there was a one-point-five-million-dollar life insurance policy on Mark."

"Really?" said Drayton, doing a slight double take. "That much?"

"Sure," said Bobby Wayne. "And the Featherbed House was worth far more than that," he continued. "Even though it did sustain fire damage, a prime property located near the Battery is still worth several million dollars in today's real estate market." Bobby Wayne put both hands flat on the table, looking grim now. "So you add together life insurance as well as property, content, and business insurance and you probably end up with a sizeable pile of money."

"How sizeable?" asked Drayton.

Bobby Wayne thought for a moment. "Maybe six, seven million dollars that Angie will come into."

"*That* much?" exclaimed Delaine. Now she sounded almost envious.

"Oh, easy," said Bobby Wayne. "Maybe more."

"The thing of it is," said Delaine, lowering her voice to a stage whisper, "now the authorities are looking hard at Angie for Mark's death!"

"That is so wrong!" exclaimed Theodosia.

"I won't even consider the fact that Angie Congdon might have murdered her own husband then torched the Featherbed House," said Drayton. "That scenario makes no sense whatsoever."

"I completely agree with you," said Theodosia. "Angie would be systematically destroying everything that was important to her. The husband she loved and everything she worked so hard to create."

"Still," said Delaine, happy to interject a sour note. "People have been known to do exactly that."

Now Bobby Wayne looked unhappy. "They have, indeed," he said.

"And you heard all this from Harlan Noble?" asked Theodosia. Perhaps he was just full of sour grapes.

"And other people, too," confirmed Delaine. "People all over the historic district are whispering."

"Poor Angie," said Drayton. "Her reputation will be in shreds."

"To say nothing of her life," murmured Theodosia.

A few minutes later, when Bobby Wayne took off, Delaine's tote bags clutched in both hands, Theodosia accompanied him to the door.

"Have you talked to Angie today?" she asked him.

"No, but I'm planning to go see her," said Bobby Wayne.

"Mark was like family to me and I can't stand to see Angie bear the brunt of this preposterous investigation." Bobby Wayne stared earnestly at Theodosia. "You know she's completely innocent and so do I."

"Agreed," said Theodosia.

"So we have to help her get through this," said Bobby Wayne.

"If she'll let us," said Theodosia, thinking back to last night and the wrath of Angie's sister, Gwyn.

"I'll talk to Angie," said Bobby Wayne. "Get her the best lawyer I can find. Really straighten things out."

"Bobby Wayne," said Theodosia, as he pushed open the door, "a couple days ago, you said there'd been a sort of competition between Mark and Leah to head your FOREX division. Tell me, if Mark hadn't been killed, would Leah have been your first choice?"

Bobby Wayne chewed at his lip thoughtfully. He knew darn well what Theodosia was asking. "No, probably not," he finally responded.

Delaine was waving at Theodosia to come join her again. So Theodosia grabbed a fresh pot of tea and headed back to Delaine's table.

"Drayton was just telling me about your new summer tea blend," she said. That was the thing about Delaine. She had the ability to jump from nasty gossip to tea shop news in a split second.

"You're privy to one of his big secrets then," said Theodosia. "Because Dayton hasn't even told me about it yet."

Drayton focused a solemn gaze on Theodosia. "It's a

rather novel house blend I want to call Starry Night. I'm blending a mixture of Chinese and Indian black tea and flavoring it with star anise and wild cherry bark."

"To die for," said Delaine.

"Good heavens, let's hope not," replied Drayton as he slid his chair back, jumped up, and headed for the counter.

Delaine watched Theodosia refill her teacup, then turned a coy smile on her. "I have something for you," she said.

"If it's another tidbit of gossip, I don't think I want to hear it," said Theodosia. She was still disturbed that Delaine seemed to derive subtle pleasure from talking about Angie Congdon's misfortune.

"No, silly," said Delaine. "It's the perfect dress for you. For tomorrow night."

"I have a dress," said Theodosia. She was planning to wear a simple cream-colored sheath and maybe add a wrap if the evening turned chilly.

"This is better," Delaine said knowingly. "Fine Chinese silk dyed to a wonderful shade of apple green. Enormously complimentary, of course, to your auburn hair. And the dress itself is very romantic and ruffled." Delaine took a sip of tea and pursed her lips. "Somewhere between Laura Ashley and Monique Lhuillier."

"I'm not sure I'm the romantic, ruffled type," commented Theodosia. In fact, her own personal style seemed to have evolved into simplicity and comfort. Colorful, slinky silk T-shirts, tailored capri slacks, lower-heeled shoes that let her fly about the tea room relatively unencumbered. Kind of a modern-day Audrey Hepburn. With the addition of exceptional amounts of auburn hair, of course.

"The romantic look was *made* for you," pressed Delaine.

"Case in point, you own an adorable little tea shop that people flock to. And you're a southern hostess with a warm, caring sensibility. Ergo, this dress will be perfect!"

Theodosia still wasn't convinced. "Ruffles," she said. "I'm just not feeling the ruffle thing."

"Nonsense," said Delaine. "The dress is utterly *divine*."

"You promise I won't look like something out of *What Ever Happened to Baby Jane?*"

Delaine's brows knit together as she peered at Theodosia. "We're talking romantic, Theo, not spooky Southern Gothic." She drummed her perfectly manicured fingertips on the tabletop. "Tell you what, why don't you come over this afternoon and try it on. I've got my assistant, Janine, holding it for you in the back room."

"No way can I make it today," Theodosia told her. *In fact, I'd rather not come at all.*

"Tomorrow then," said Delaine. "Come tomorrow morning."

"I promised Timothy I'd do that on-air segment at Channel Eight," said Theodosia. "Kind of a final push for Orchid Lights."

"Then drop by *afterward*," insisted Delaine. "Of course," she said, leaning sideways and casting a critical eye toward Theodosia's khaki slacks and comfortable loafers as though they were fashion roadkill, "we'll have to find you some decent shoes as well. I'm thinking perhaps a pair of four-inch stilettos that show a little toe cleavage."

"How about a comfortable pair of two-inch mules?" asked Theodosia. "And forget trying to make my toes look sexy. I'll probably be on my feet all evening. Helping Drayton set up, then serving tea at the event . . ."

"You're no fun at all," complained Delaine. "You never want to go all-out glitz or glam. If I had to depend on you for a customer, Cotton Duck would be plum out of business!"

"I'll be there." Theodosia sighed. "Tomorrow."

"Try to get there by eleven, dear, will you?" said Delaine with a self-satisfied smile. "I've got that marvelous woman, Leah Shalimar, coming in to talk about investing."

20

❧

"*What did you do* to it?" asked Parker Scully as he ran a hand over the giant dents in the hull of his canoe. "Beat it with a baseball bat? Take it over a fifty-foot waterfall?"

"No, no, nothing *that* disastrous," Theodosia assured him even as she felt a tiny twinge of guilt bubble up inside her.

"Well, it's pretty banged up."

"I know," said Theodosia. "And I feel just *awful* about all the wear and tear. Drayton and I hit a few patches of white-water and, of course, there were rocks, too. I guess my navigating skills weren't as sharp as I thought they were. So, again, I apologize. I'll be happy to replace the canoe or pay to have the dents pounded out. Whatever you'd prefer."

"No no," said Parker, still looking supremely puzzled. "I'm not upset about the canoe. Heck, I haven't used the darn thing in years. I'm just kind of stunned that one little woman and a somewhat older gentleman could put it through such a tough workout."

"Have you ever canoed the rivers up near Hickory Knob?" asked Theodosia.

Parker Scully shook his head. "No," he said, almost cautiously.

"They're tricky. One could almost say treacherous."

"Uh-huh," said Parker. He wanted to believe her, but wasn't quite buying it.

"I understand kayakers train there," said Theodosia. "For serious competitions."

"Serious competitions," repeated Parker. His eyes narrowed as he studied her carefully. "What is it you're not telling me?"

"Nothing," said Theodosia, hoping she looked a lot more innocent than she felt.

"Something happened," said Parker Scully. "Something you don't want me to know about."

Theodosia flapped a hand helplessly. They were standing in Parker Scully's back alley, just outside his garage. She was anxious to help unload his canoe and be on her way. If Parker kept up this line of questioning, she'd for sure break down and tell him exactly what happened. That someone had taken a shot at her and Drayton. That they'd headed down the wrong fork and gone headlong over a waterfall. Then Parker would want to call in the police about the shooter and her own investigation might be . . . well, not ruined, but possibly derailed. Just when everything was at its most twisted and tangled, and she was struggling to unravel it.

Besides, Theodosia decided, if Parker knew she was hip deep in this murder and arson investigation, he might worry about her safety and ask her to quietly extricate herself. And that was the last thing Theodosia wanted to do right now.

Pop. Theodosia loosened a bungee cord and let it snap against the back window of her Jeep.

"Careful," said Parker. "Those things ricochet like crazy." He moved in to help. "Here, let me . . . I'll lift it down."

Theodosia retreated to a safe distance, watching him unload the canoe, hoping he was distracted enough to drop his line of questioning.

She followed Parker into his garage as he carried the canoe, stooping to go through the doorway. "Watch out!" she told him as he hefted it up onto two metal struts that stuck out from the wall. "Be careful of your fishing stuff."

Parker slid the canoe onto the rack and peered at Theodosia in the dim light of the garage. "You want to come in? I have to be at Solstice in an hour or so, but there's time for a quick drink."

Of course Theodosia wanted to join him. But she also didn't want Parker to start asking his probing questions again. Better wait, she decided. There were a few things she had to check out first. Then there'd be time, plenty of time, for the two of them.

The next order of business was Earl Grey. Theodosia had contemplated taking the old boy along this morning. Now she was thankful she'd left him at home. It would have been tricky enough to have a squirming, curious dog in the canoe, and a terrible disaster if he'd been swept over the falls with them. Unthinkable, really.

Once Theodosia got home, she changed into a T-shirt,

leggings, and running shoes. Then she snapped a lead onto Earl Grey's collar and the two of them took off. Loping gently down Church Street, cutting over at Tradd, then hitting Meeting Street.

At this time of night Charleston's historic district was a sight to behold. Enormous three- and four-story mansions were bathed pink and purple from the sun's final rays. Lights twinkled from tall windows, wide verandas beckoned. One could imagine baked oysters and soft-shelled crab being served on gleaming silver trays, sparking crystal, and the gentle pop of wine corks.

When they hit the broad vista of White Point Gardens, Theodosia and Earl Grey pounded past the lineup of antique Civil War cannons. Hugging the shoreline, they reveled in the salty air that rode the insistent Atlantic breeze. Underfoot, bits of flotsam mingled with rough sand and broken shells.

They passed the Bogard Inn where Angie and her relatives were holed up. Then slowed their pace as they came upon the burned-out hull of the Featherbed House. Poking jaggedly into the night sky, the remnants of the old B and B looked eerie. Spooky almost.

As Theodosia reached front and center of the Featherbed House, she came to a stop. Stared up at it, wondered if it would ever be brought back to its former grandeur. Her thoughts were interrupted by . . .

Swish, swish.

Theodosia stared at her dog as he stared back at her.

What's that weird sound? she wondered.

Tiptoeing up the front sidewalk, Earl Grey at her side, Theodosia peered toward the Featherbed House. Large pieces of plywood were nailed where doors and windows had once been. So there was no way anyone could be inside.

Theodosia and Earl Grey ducked under a tangled flutter of black-and-yellow police tape, then stepped gingerly around the side of the Featherbed House, staying on the sidewalk as best they could, but mindful of the charred timbers and debris that were scattered about. Theodosia supposed it wouldn't be long before workers in huge dump trucks showed up to cart everything away. Then Angie would be faced with a really tough decision—rebuild or tear the whole thing down.

Swish, swish.

That sound. There it was again. Theodosia and Earl Grey rounded the house, heading toward the backyard. Finally as they drew closer, Theodosia could make out a single figure laboring away in the dim light.

Teddy Vickers was using a kitchen broom to clear away debris from the back patio.

Theodosia's first inclination was to laugh. Teddy looked so strange and the scene was so incongruous. Trying to clean up a major disaster using just a simple broom!

Once she got over her initial surprise, Theodosia began to wonder exactly what Teddy was doing here. Sure, Teddy had been an assistant manager. But that was over now, wasn't it?

"Teddy," Theodosia called out. Her voice sounded hollow and low, dampened by the fog that was starting to roll in.

Teddy jumped as though someone had touched him with an electric wire. He straightened up spasmodically, his head jerking left, then right, until he finally spotted Theodosia standing in the shadows, Earl Grey at her side.

"What are you doing here?" Teddy called out, sounding a trifle unnerved.

"A better question might be, what are *you* doing here?" replied Theodosia.

"I work here," answered Teddy as he continued sweeping.

"Are you planning to open for business in the near future?" Theodosia asked him. "Because things do seem a trifle iffy right now." She stepped closer and gazed around. The patio that had once been so gorgeous, had served as a model "Charleston garden," lay in utter ruin. Flowers and shrubbery were a sodden mess. Part of the roof had collapsed on top of the gazebo. A sooty scum of ashes floated atop the small fish pond. Theodosia wondered briefly if the charming little goldfish that had darted about so joyfully in the pond had perished. Decided they probably had. The thought of those tiny lives lost saddened her heart.

Teddy pointedly ignored Theodosia's words.

"Does Angie know you're here?" asked Theodosia. She glanced toward the carriage house, where lights shone from inside. "Are you living here?" she asked.

Teddy stopped sweeping and leaned on his broom, staring at her now. "Somebody has to keep watch," he said in a flat tone. "You never know what could happen. Anyone could just walk in."

But Theodosia wasn't particularly impressed by Teddy's sudden show of loyalty. "Why," she asked him, "did you make Angie an offer to buy this place?"

Teddy continued to stare at her. "Because I love the Featherbed House. Because I don't for one minute believe it's finished."

"You think it can be rebuilt," said Theodosia.

"Read your history," snapped Teddy. "Anything can be rebuilt. Look at London after World War II. Or Dresden."

"Your history lesson notwithstanding," said Theodosia, knowing a flimsy smoke screen when she saw one, "please tell me why *you* want to take this on?"

Teddy stood there for a while, contemplating his answer. Finally, he spoke slowly. "I know some investors," Teddy told her. "Real estate people who'd put up money to rebuild this place."

Sparks ignited inside Theodosia's brain. Finally, *finally* they were getting to the heart of the matter. "Rebuild this place as the Featherbed House?" she asked him. "Or something else?"

Now Teddy looked more than a little uncomfortable.

"Some real estate people approached you, didn't they?" said Theodosia, filling in the blanks herself. "Probably condo or hotel people. And asked you to be their go-between."

"What if they did?" said Teddy. "There's no law against it."

"What about Angie?" asked Theodosia, trying to appeal to his better side. "Think of her. She's upset over Mark's death and shell-shocked from this fire. That puts her in an extremely vulnerable position."

Earl Grey strained forward on his leash, muzzle tipped up, and Teddy retreated a step.

"I didn't mean any harm," he told Theodosia. "They said they'd pay me a commission."

"And the forty-eight-hour deadline?" asked Theodosia. "What's that all about?"

Teddy Vickers shrugged, looking sheepish now. "I only said it to add impetus to the offer. To hopefully move Angie along in her thought process."

Theodosia couldn't believe what she was hearing. "Teddy!" she admonished. "Angie has no thought process right now. She's completely shut down emotionally and intellectually. This has all been way too much for her."

"I suppose," he said grudgingly.

"You were her assistant," sputtered Theodosia. "She *trusted* you."

Teddy shifted sullenly from one foot to the other. "I didn't do anything wrong."

"You didn't do much right, either," said Theodosia. She shot him a thunderous look. "Teddy Vickers, swear to me you had nothing to do with this fire!"

Her words served to shake him up. "I swear," Teddy muttered. "I'd never pull anything like that. Arson's a serious crime."

"It certainly is," said Theodosia, as anger suddenly flooded her. She'd tried to remain calm, but now her emotions were taking over. "Do you know that the fire marshal has been questioning Angie? That there's a serious criminal investigation going on?"

"What?" squawked Teddy. "I thought the fire started because of faulty wiring."

"Somehow I doubt that," said Theodosia. "And rest assured that the fire department will dig deep and look at all the angles. I also imagine that sooner or later—probably sooner—they'll get around to questioning you."

"I already talked to them," Teddy told her. "Right after the fire."

"I'm quite positive they'll be talking with you again," said Theodosia.

"Because you'll make sure of it, won't you?" said Teddy. He sounded bitter, defeated.

Theodosia tugged on Earl Grey's leash and the dog turned toward her, eager to get moving again. "Count on it," she told Teddy.

Theodosia was still furious with Teddy Vickers when she arrived home. She decided that he'd basically betrayed Angie. Not by doing anything illegal, but because he'd betrayed her trust. Angie had hired Teddy and given him a lot of responsibility. Now Teddy was repaying her by attempting to profit on her terrible misfortune.

Feeling unsettled by her conversation with Teddy and apprehensive about appearing on television tomorrow, Theodosia stomped into her kitchen and put her tea kettle on. She'd brew a cup of jasmine tea. That sweet, flavorful elixir always served to soothe her nerves.

Carrying her tea into the bedroom, Theodosia hoped that somewhere in her overstuffed walk-in closet she'd discover the perfect outfit to wear for tomorrow's TV appearance.

She also prayed she could dash in to Channel 8, do a fast forty-five-second pitch on Orchid Lights, and remind viewers that tickets were still available. Then she'd get the heck out of there with a minimum of fanfare. Head off to Delaine's.

Delaine's. Thud.

Somehow, the notion of trying on a romantic, flouncy dress did little to cheer her. It was the idea of ruffles, she decided. Ruffles were great on christening gowns, prom dresses, and some wedding gowns. And relatively cute when tastefully adorning silk blouses or a full skirt you might wear to a garden party.

Ruffles were definitely not good on men's tuxedo shirts,

dog and cat collars, and, probably . . . that dress. The mysterious dress that awaited her at Cotton Duck.

Plopping down on her bed, Theodosia tilted her head left, then right, detecting a few sore spots on her back. She'd definitely banged a shoulder in her headlong plunge this morning. And put a strain on her lower back with all the frantic swimming and diving. She wondered how Drayton was faring this evening. Decided he'd probably retired early with a steaming cup of rosehip tea, his calming tonic of choice.

Theodosia clasped her fingers together at the base of her neck, massaging with her thumbs. She tried to hit the pressure points that might relieve those nagging aches. Sliding her hands upward, she massaged the back of her head with her fingertips and instantly felt better. She closed her eyes, working her fingers up over her occipital ridge to the top of her skull.

Better now. Much better with the old magic fingers massage.

As feelings of relaxation seeped through her, Theodosia's eyes gradually fluttered open and she found herself gazing at the top of her dresser. It was a little messy, just like the top of her desk, with its collection of perfume bottles, a Baccarat crystal Labrador, and a little ceramic Buddha that had multiple strands of colored beads wound around it.

Then Theodosia's eyes landed on the box she'd brought back from the Bogard Inn last night. The box she'd been going to deliver to Angie.

Little ceramic elephant, iPod, and that ticket.

As she eased herself down onto her bed, she thought to herself, *Ticket. I've just got to ask someone about that ticket.*

21

❧

Constance Brucato, the producer for *Windows on Charleston*, was waiting impatiently for Theodosia when she arrived in the Channel 8 lobby.

Dark haired, broad shouldered, always slightly out of breath, Constance's only greeting was "Hurry up!" as she motioned impatiently for Theodosia to follow her. When Theodosia complied, Constance turned and hurried down a long white corridor hung with trendy pieces of art. Stopping at a door marked Edit Room, Constance knocked softly, then pushed her way into a dimly lit control room.

"What, no hair and makeup?" quipped Theodosia. "No green room?"

But Constance was in no mood for humor today. "I don't know if you've had a chance to watch *Windows on Charleston* lately," she said as she paused near a console where a dozen monitors flickered and two men slouched over a huge panel of buttons. "But we've got a brand-new show host."

Theodosia, who was usually at the Indigo Tea Shop by eight-thirty, rarely had time to catch *Windows on Charleston*, which aired at ten. She shook her head, offered a rueful smile. "Sorry," she told Constance. "Haven't seen it lately."

"Well, our new host, hostess really, is a *wonderful* woman," trilled Constance. "*Tons* of personality. Hand-picked by our general manger."

Theodosia peered at Constance. She'd spent time in marketing, she knew a sell job when she heard one.

"Here's the other thing," began Constance. "We had to change the format a touch." She tapped her pen nervously against her clipboard. "We have another guest that's going to appear *with* you."

"Really," said Theodosia. "Because I was under the impression I'd be going on alone. Just to give a quick reminder about tonight's Orchid Lights."

"That may have been the case a few days ago," said Constance. "But we've reshuffled things." She shrugged. "That's the nature of television. Always in flux."

"So who . . . ?" began Theodosia.

But Constance was on the move again. "This way," she said sharply, pushing her way through another set of double doors and leading Theodosia directly into a dimly lit studio.

"Excellent," muttered Constance. "He's setting up now."

Theodosia peered across the studio, but cameras and set components blocked her view. "Who is?" she asked, picking her way carefully through thick black cables that snaked underfoot. She could see a small table packed with orchids, lit overhead by a row of extremely bright lights. Curious now, Theodosia moved a few steps forward, easing herself around a large TV monitor. Then her tentative smile turned to sudden dismay as she recognized the second guest.

"Harlan Noble?" Theodosia reached a hand out and squeezed Constance's plump arm. "I'm appearing with Harlan Noble?"

"Yes," said Constance, shaking herself free of Theodosia. "He very graciously agreed to bring in some of his most prized orchids."

"And you want us to go on . . . together?" Theodosia's normally well-modulated voice had turned into a protesting squawk.

"My executive producer had strong feelings about this," said Constance. "*Showing* actual orchids versus just talking about them in the abstract."

"I can understand that," said Theodosia. "And I think putting Harlan Noble's orchids on camera is a wonderful idea. So why not let Mr. Noble go on alone and present his collection?"

"No, no, no," protested Constance Brucato. "That's not the way we visualized the segment." She held up a fistful of six-by-eight-inch cards and riffled them in Theodosia's face. "I've already written out cards for Abby Davis, the host of *Windows on Charleston*. Abby's very meticulous about preproduction, so I'm not about to burden her with any deviation in the plan. Besides, if I changed anything now, she'd *kill* me!"

Apprehension building, Theodosia waited off camera while Harlan Noble fussed with his orchids. He looked just as hostile as he always looked. And Theodosia couldn't seem to shake the image of Harlan Noble, standing in a crowd of gawkers, watching the Featherbed House burn. Especially since it had come on the heels of Harlan trying to purchase Mark's collection and being turned down by Angie.

This is silly, Theodosia told herself. *I'm acting like a frightened school kid. When what I really should do is go talk to him.*

Theodosia edged closer to the table. "Your orchids look lovely," she told Harlan.

He looked up at her as though he had no earthly idea Theodosia had been standing there. "You think so?" he asked. "I'm dreadfully nervous about these hot lights." He glanced upward. "But the producer promised they'd only be on for ten minutes at most."

"Orchids don't like heat?" asked Theodosia. "I always thought they were hothouse plants."

Harlan Noble gave a quick frown. "That's what everyone thinks. But these are mostly *native* varieties. Used to a little more shade and a subtropical climate versus tropical."

"So most of these were collected locally?" asked Theodosia.

"All of them," replied Harlan. He moved a Spider orchid, replaced it with a Northern Green orchid.

"Interesting," said Theodosia. "I take it you have a few favorite haunts where you go to collect?"

Harlan Noble straightened up, then seemed to really look at Theodosia for the first time. "I'm originally from a little town called Plum Branch," he told her, his dark eyes boring into her. "Best collecting in the state."

"Aha," said Theodosia, the hair on the back of her neck suddenly standing on end. "Up near Sumter National Forest." She wasn't about to tell Harlan she'd passed that way yesterday. Then again, he might already know that.

"So you really know that area," said Theodosia.

"I know it *very* well," responded Harlan Noble. "Very well, indeed."

Luckily, they didn't have to wait much longer. Abby Davis, the show's new host, strode across the studio. Attired in a slim-fitting pink suit, Abby had a cap of dark spiky hair and a no-nonsense look about her. Oohing and aahing over Harlan's orchids, she greeted him first. Then she approached Theodosia, cards in hand. "You're Theodosia," she said. "I'm Abby Davis. Host of the show."

Theodosia smiled warmly at Abby. There was something familiar about this woman. Or maybe it was her name. Had she heard it before? Before today? "Your name sounds awfully familiar," said Theodosia. "Perhaps we've met before?"

Abby's brown eyes carried a hint of merriment mingled with challenge. "You think so?"

"Pardon me?" said Theodosia, slightly puzzled. *Why,* she wondered, *is this woman coming on so strangely?* She thought for a moment. *Unless she's . . . oh no, she can't be. Please don't let her be . . .*

"You're . . ." began Theodosia.

Abby Davis leaned forward, dark eyes glittering, her face pulled into a hard smile. "I'm Jory Davis's cousin. And, yes, we *have* met before."

"Nice to see you again," said Theodosia. Her response sounded lame, but she wasn't exactly sure what she should say to the cousin of her ex-boyfriend. She filled in the conversation gap by adding, "I understand you've recently joined the station. Congratulations."

"Yes," said Abby. "I just moved back from Tampa."

"Where you were also an on-air personality?" asked Theodosia, trying her best to keep the momentum going.

"At the top-rated station," purred Abby. "And you, I'm sure, are still doing your little tea shop thing."

"Not so little," said Theodosia. No way was she going to stand there and let Abby pick at her. "The Indigo Tea Shop is thriving, the catering business is developing nicely, and I created a line of T-Bath products." *There,* she thought, *I may not be the CEO of a Fortune 500 company, but I am an entrepreneur who's growing and nurturing a small business.*

"Good for you," said Abby in a bored tone. She spun on her heels, gesturing for Constance to join them. "Let's lay this down," said Abby. "I don't have all day."

Then they were all crowded around a small table overflowing with pots of orchids. Abby stood in the middle with Theodosia on one side, Harlan on the other. The lights burned bright and hot as Abby chatted breezily, dimpled prettily for the camera, and asked the exact right questions so Harlan could talk about the enticing orchids on display at tonight's Orchid Lights show and Theodosia could make her pitch that tickets were still available.

The cameras moved in close to pan the orchids several times, and then it was over. The klieg lights dimmed, the cameras with their giant eyes rolled back on soundless, rubber wheels, and a production assistant rushed in to unclip Theodosia's microphone.

Abby stood a few steps away, reviewing her cards for the next segment as a woman from the makeup department twirled a fat brush in a compact and dabbed powder across Abby's cheeks. All the while Abby completely ignored everything that was going on around her. The makeup lady. Harlan packing up his orchids. And Theodosia.

"Miss Davis," Theodosia said, mustering a strong, no-nonsense tone. It was the same tone she'd used years ago when she'd had to rein in impossibly pushy clients.

Abby Davis looked up. Surprise widened her eyes.

"If this segment hadn't been a promotional pitch for the Heritage Society," said Theodosia, "I want you to know I would have walked out. You've been nothing but rude to me."

"You broke Jory's heart," spat out Abby.

"Jory moved to New York!" said Theodosia, surprised by the emotion that resonated in her own voice.

"He asked you to go along," said Abby.

"And leave everything behind, yes," replied Theodosia. "Family, friends, and my business. It was a hard decision to make and sometimes I still wonder if it was the right one." And with that, Theodosia turned and walked off the set.

22

❧

"*Theodosia!*" *Delaine's shrill* voice greeted her. "I see you *finally* showed up."

Theodosia stared across racks of gossamer silk tops, cropped pants, cotton sweaters, and long skirts. "I told you I had to do an appearance at Channel Eight this morning."

"And how did it go?" asked Delaine, hastening toward her on four-inch stilettos, a saffron scarf trailing behind her.

"Fine," said Theodosia. "Great." *Well, not great. Pretty darn terrible if you want to know the truth. But you probably don't.*

"Wonderful!" exclaimed Delaine, giving Theodosia a succession of air kisses and enveloping her in a soft cloud of lilac perfume. "Things have been absolutely *frantic* here. In the last couple days we've literally blown through our entire inventory of embroidered T-shirts and our Sea Island cotton sweaters are simply flying off the shelves."

"So business is good," said Theodosia. "You should be delirious." She picked up a silver sandal from a display. It was feather light with a wedge heel of smooth cork.

"All I am is exhausted," said Delaine, clasping a hand to her chest. "Between ordering inventory, handling sales, and making plans for a buying trip, I just can't seem to keep up."

"What's the problem?" asked Theodosia. Usually Delaine thrived on chaos.

Janine, Delaine's longtime assistant suddenly appeared. "She was out with Bobby Wayne again last night, that's the problem." Janine's face, perpetually red from juggling a gazillion things while trailing around after Delaine, carried a knowing look.

"You were?" Theodosia said with a surprised look on her face. "Another date?" It would appear the two of them were getting very close indeed.

"Just one of our romantic little dinners," confided Delaine. "We drove over to Summerville. There's a lovely little bistro there called the Bluebird Grill, located just on the edge of Old Town. The herb-crusted sea scallops are to die for."

"That's your second date this week," remarked Theodosia.

"Third," corrected Delaine. She whirled about, suddenly shouted, "Janine," at the top of her lungs.

Janine popped her head up from behind a display of long evening gowns.

"The dress," Delaine hissed. "Bring out Theodosia's dress."

"It's not my dress yet," said Theodosia. She browsed through a rack of silk tops, found two or three that were really adorable.

"Ta-da!" said Delaine, as a green froth of ruffles and frills suddenly materialized.

For some reason, the dress reminded Theodosia of the wall of green in her old nemesis, the hedge maze. "Good heavens," she exclaimed. "That really is apple green."

"Like it?" asked Delaine. Her head nodded in the affirmative, willing Theodosia to say yes.

"And it certainly is . . . ruffled," said Theodosia, neatly dodging the question.

"Ruffles connote romance," said Delaine, holding the dress up against Theodosia. "And, lord knows, you could certainly use a little romance in your life."

"Does she like it?" Janine called from the back counter.

"She adores it!" yelled back Delaine.

"Actually," said Theodosia, turning to finger one of the fluttery silk tops that had caught her eye. "Something like this would probably be more practical."

Delaine's nostrils flared. "Might be apropos for a garden party," she sniffed. "But it certainly won't make a strong statement like this dress."

"No, it won't," admitted Theodosia. "But to tell you the truth, with all I have to do tonight, pouring tea, handing out tea sandwiches, helping Drayton serve his ice angels, this dress might not really get showcased properly."

Delaine paused, trying to mentally assess just how serious Theodosia was.

"This dress is beautiful," continued Theodosia, "but I worry about the ruffles on the sleeves. I'd hate to drag them through the lobster salad and lemon gelato.

"That would be a disaster," allowed Delaine.

"I'd be heartsick if it was ruined with just one wearing," said Theodosia.

Reluctantly, Delaine pulled the dress back toward her.

"You make a good point," she said slowly. "Hmm. The fluttery tops, huh? You think one of those would work?"

"I think so," said Theodosia. "And you do have some really cute ones." She sorted through the rack. "In your expert opinion which one do you think might work best? Colorwise, I mean."

Delaine debated for a couple seconds, then reached forward and snatched up two of the tops. "I like the copper-colored one and the sea-green one. But I'd wear *oodles* of turquoise beads with the copper, and gold jewelry with the green. Good statement gold."

"Not silver?" asked Theodosia.

"No," said Delaine. "Gold is dressier and will give it more of an edge."

"So let's try them on," said Theodosia.

"Okaaay," said Delaine, still finding it difficult to give up on the green dress. "I suppose."

"Oh, now that's awfully cute," said Janine when Theodosia emerged from the fitting room a few minutes later.

"Not bad," said Delaine. "I *do* like that copper color against her hair."

"I love it," said Theodosia, posing in front of the three-way mirror. "Do you think I should try the green top, too?"

Delaine studied her carefully, then shook her head. "No, that top's really perfect. Do you have a stash of turquoise beads to put with it?"

"Maybe one strand."

"Janine!" screamed Delaine at full volume. "Turquoise beads!"

Janine came panting up, carrying multiple strands of turquoise beads.

Delaine stepped back while Janine proceeded to decorate Theodosia like a Christmas tree.

"Enough?" asked Janine.

"One more strand," declared Delaine. "Now take a look, Theo. Tell me what you think."

Theodosia turned back toward the mirror to study her image and decided she was delighted with the look Delaine had grudgingly helped orchestrate. The silk top and beads managed to convey dressy, comfortable, and bohemian chic all at the same time.

But Delaine wasn't quite finished. "Earrings," she declared. "Those coin-shaped pearl earrings we got in last week."

The pearl earrings were the finishing touch. Just a final dash of shimmer to polish the look.

"And you're to wear this with flowing cream slacks," admonished Delaine. "And cream or bronze sandals. Remember, the higher the heel the better. Let's get you up there with the really tall girls."

"Will do," promised Theodosia, delighted to have escaped the snares of the frilly green dress.

"Look who's here!" called out an exuberant voice. "Two of my favorite female entrepreneurs!"

Both Theodosia and Delaine turned toward the front of the shop where Leah Shalimar was speeding toward them. Wearing one of her trademark elegant suits, she clutched a large, leather portfolio. A giant grin animated Leah's face.

"Leah!" shrilled Delaine. "Lovely to see you!" She scampered to meet her and they exchanged air kisses, missing each other by a mile.

"Hi, Leah," called Theodosia, still posing in front of the three-way mirror.

"Aren't you the adorable one," said Leah, favoring Theodosia with a wide smile. "New outfit? Must mean you have a hot date."

"No, no," Delaine explained hastily. "That's her *working* outfit. Theo's serving tea and sandwiches at Orchid Lights tonight. Which I hope you've made plans to attend."

"Haven't even thought about it," said Leah. "I've been busy, busy, busy, and never quite got around to buying a ticket."

"There are still tickets left," said Theodosia. "If you're interested."

"It's a benefit for the Heritage Society?" Leah asked politely. "What's the program exactly?"

"An orchid show, refreshments on the patio, and a silent auction," piped up Delaine. "With most of the proceeds benefiting the Heritage Society."

"That's right," said Leah. "Drayton did mention he was planning to exhibit some orchids. He's still doing that?"

"As far as I know," said Theodosia.

"Maybe I'll show up after all," said Leah. She glanced pointedly at Delaine. "Is now good for you? There's a small amount of paperwork you need to fill out, so maybe we should go in your office. It's probably the easiest."

"Good idea," said Delaine. Her head spun around. "Janine? Can you finish up here with Theodosia?"

"Of course," said Janine, who always seemed to be juggling six things at once.

"I take it you're going to be doing some investing," Theodosia said to Delaine.

"Thanks to Leah's good advice," said Delaine. She giggled. "And a few choice words from Bobby Wayne."

"He's a charmer," said Leah. "And so darned smart."

"This is the FOREX product you mentioned to me?" Theodosia asked as Leah unzipped her portfolio and leafed through a sheaf of papers.

Leah nodded happily. "The one administered by Sun Commonwealth Trust," she said.

"And they're located where again?" asked Theodosia.

"The Bahamas," said Leah.

"Anything else you need, Theo, Janine will help you," called Delaine as she and Leah disappeared into her office and shut the door behind them.

Theodosia sat in her Jeep outside Cotton Duck, thinking about Leah Shalimar. All things considered, she had actually grown to like Leah, she really had. Leah seemed smart and convivial and fairly sharp. And she'd worked hard to make it in a sector that was traditionally dominated by men.

Still . . . Mark Congdon's death had allowed Leah to leapfrog to the top of the heap. Had put Leah square in charge of Loveday and Luxor's new FOREX division.

So the question remained . . . had Leah somehow engineered this move? Theodosia let that question wash over her once again.

Could Leah have been supremely jealous of Mark Congdon? Could Leah have caused his death?

If she had, who would know? Or even suspect? Bobby Wayne didn't seem to have any suspicions. He was caring and solicitous toward Angie and still seemed to be a booster for Leah. Certainly trusted her to head his department, even if she hadn't been his first choice.

So that doesn't go anywhere, thought Theodosia.

Okay, then what does?

Theodosia reached down, stuck her key in the ignition.

What about someone at that company in the Bahamas? Would they know anything? Would they have had dealings with Mark Congdon?

She figured they had to. After all, she'd found a ticket to Nassau stuck among Mark's things.

Would they know anything? Anything at all? Did they even know that Mark was dead?

Theodosia slowly removed the key from the ignition.

She had no idea if she could call outside the continental U.S. using her cell phone, had never attempted to do so before. But you never really knew about something until you gave it the old one-two. After slight deliberation, Theodosia pulled her cell phone from her handbag and leafed through her phone directory. Did she still have Tidwell's cell phone number? Yes, there it was, penciled in under the Ts.

Theodosia's index finger tapped the top of her phone for a moment. Then, she finally made up her mind and punched in the digits.

Tidwell's cell phone rang eight times before a prerecorded, tinny-sounding Tidwell voice erupted in her ear.

As you can no doubt ascertain, I'm currently unavailable to respond to your call. Since this probably won't stop you from bothering me, kindly leave your message when you hear the mechanical beep.

It was, Theodosia thought, a decidedly odd and Tidwell-esque message. But she plunged ahead and left her own message anyway.

"Detective Tidwell? It's Theodosia again. Browning. Sorry to bother you, but if you have any time at all, could you possibly check on a company by the name of Sun Commonwealth Trust? It's a FOREX company headquartered in the Bahamas. Oh, uh, FOREX means foreign exchange currency, in case you didn't know. Anyway, Mark Congdon had a ticket to the Bahamas, to Nassau. So could you possibly find out if he had a meeting scheduled? You could, uh, tell them you're investigating his death or something. So, uh, okay. Thanks so much. Bye."

23

❧

"*I really like* the moss you guys brought back from your collecting trip," said Haley. "It's so cute and cuddly-looking." She was sitting at one of the tables in the Indigo Tea Shop, wearing plastic food-service gloves and arranging her homemade truffles on several three-tiered serving trays.

"You better bag those trays in plastic when you're finished," Drayton advised her. "You don't want your chocolates to get all dried out and crumbly." He was standing at the table next to her, studying his newly potted orchid. He'd arranged the monkey-face orchid in an oxblood-red Chinese pot and snugged a small piece of moss next to it.

"Don't worry," Haley told him. "They'll be bagged and tagged and ready to go." She straightened up, studied his orchid. "When do you have to get your orchid over to the Heritage Society?"

"Everything's going over together," Drayton told her. "Food, tea, truffles, and my orchid. We'll load it all into Theo's Jeep."

"Think it'll all fit?" asked Haley.

"It has to," said Drayton. "We've got so much to do, there really isn't time to make two trips."

Haley nodded her head toward the front counter, where Theodosia and Charlie were packing up an order of scones and tea to go. "Is Charlie coming along?"

"Not tonight," said Drayton. "I told her we didn't need her."

"Did she want to come along and help?" asked Haley.

"Don't know," said Drayton. "I never asked."

"Drayton," said Haley in a scolding tone. "What's with you, anyway?"

"What?" asked Drayton, still focused on his orchid.

"Be nice," said Haley.

"I'm always a gentleman," Drayton assured her.

"Yeah, right," said Haley. She looked over toward Theodosia, made a motion for her to please come over.

Theodosia, who was juggling orders and trying to answer all the various and sundry business questions that Charlie kept firing at her, nodded toward Haley, even managed a few steps in her direction. But when the telephone on the front counter shrilled, Theodosia reversed course and grabbed for it.

"Indigo Tea Shop," said Theodosia. She tried to sound cordial, keep the tension out of her voice. They didn't have a lot of customers to take care of this afternoon, but for some reason phone orders kept pouring in left and right.

"Miss Browning?" came a man's voice.

"Yes?" said Theodosia, thinking he sounded familiar. Someone from the neighborhood?

"This is John Darnell, the fire marshal . . ."

"Oh yes," chimed in Theodosia, suddenly on full alert.

"Sheriff Billings asked me to call you. I'm not usually in the habit of doing this, especially in the middle of an investigation, but it seems we have some exceptionally good news."

"Okay . . ." said Theodosia.

"You are, of course, acquainted with one of the prime suspects, a Miss Fayne Hamilton?"

"Yes," said Theodosia.

"After obtaining a search warrant, investigators discovered a significant amount of dimethyl ketone, 2-propanone in Miss Hamilton's garage. In layman's terms, acetone. Definitely a fire accelerant."

"Dear lord," breathed Theodosia. She turned her back to Charlie, lowered her voice. "Do you think it might have been used to start the fire at the Featherbed House?"

"Again, our investigation is still in the preliminary stages," said Darnell. "We need to do gas chromatographic testing, but it would appear to be the same type of liquid ketone detected at the scene."

Theodosia put a hand to her chest, stunned. All she could think was, *Poor Fayne. Poor misguided girl. This one stupid, impulsive act has probably changed the course of her life forever.*

Theodosia cleared her throat. "Is she in custody?"

"She is."

Theodosia's voice still cracked as she asked her next question. "Will Sheriff Billings be questioning Fayne in the death of Mark Congdon?"

There were a few moments of silence at the other end of the line and then John Darnell said, "My understanding is he will be speaking to her at length about that particular homicide."

Theodosia let out a long sigh. So there it was. The conclusion to what had been a terrible, tragic week. "Have you spoken with Angie Congdon yet?" Theodosia asked as an afterthought.

"I'll be doing that in person very shortly," said Darnell.

Theodosia thanked the fire marshal, then hung up the phone and gazed around the tea shop. Tea kettles were blowing insistent little puffs of steam into the air, teapots released perfumed scents of oolong and chamomile, golden sunlight filtered through the leaded windows. It looked like any other day at the Indigo Tea Shop, but it suddenly felt like a heavy burden had been lifted from Theodosia's shoulders. The madness, the investigation, the pointing of fingers and nasty suspicions were finally, mercifully over. Now they could all get on with the business of coming to grips with what happened and work through the healing process. Tomorrow, Theodosia decided, she'd go talk to Angie Congdon. Sit with her. Offer more condolences. And, perhaps even more important, offer her friendship and help in whatever way possible.

Hurrying over to where Drayton and Haley were confabbing, Theodosia immediately broke the news to them.

"Wow!" exclaimed Haley. "That's great."

"Great?" scoffed Drayton. "Are you serious?"

"I mean it's great to finally *know*," amended Haley. "Before, we were all so tense and suspicious. Especially when it came to Leah Shalimar and Harlan Noble."

"And don't forget Teddy Vickers," added Theodosia.

"We didn't exactly have charitable thoughts concerning him, either."

Haley shrugged. "Teddy is an opportunist, as you pointed out."

Drayton was slowly coming around to Haley's way of thinking. "I suppose you're right. This is for the best. Now we know that all our previous suspects are in the clear."

"And we can focus on tonight," said Haley. "On Orchid Lights." She suddenly looked a little discombobulated. "I've got tons to do in the kitchen yet."

Theodosia readily agreed. "There is a lot to do."

"Too much," said Drayton. His eyes slowly traveled back to his monkey-face orchid on the table.

Theodosia picked up on Drayton's unease. "You're fretting about something else," she said. "What is it?"

He pointed to the monkey-face orchid in the Chinese pot. "What do you think?" he asked.

"I told him it looks real nice," piped up Haley.

"See?" said Drayton, throwing up his hands. "She thinks it looks *nice*."

"And it's rare," said Haley. "It's got that going for it."

Theodosia tilted her head sideways and raised her brows. She didn't quite see what was causing Drayton so much distress.

Drayton plunged ahead, hoping to enlighten her. "I was hoping for spectacular," he said, his words coming out overly loud and a bit theatrical. "So what do you think? Have I hopefully veered toward spectacular? With the orchid itself. And my arrangement?"

Theodosia studied Drayton's arrangement. The little orchid looked very lovely in its new pot. But was it a total showstopper? That was the big question, wasn't it?

"It's exotic-looking," admitted Theodosia. "And very beautiful."

Drayton was beyond nervous now. "All orchids are exotic and beautiful. But do you think *this* one is good enough to take home a blue ribbon?"

"After what we went through," said Theodosia, "I certainly think you deserve one. But . . ."

"But what?" prompted Drayton.

"I'm no judge of orchids," said Theodosia. "I barely know a Phalaenopsis from a bog rose. All I know is what you've taught me. And it's been, what one might call, a crash course. But tonight you're going to be judged by experienced orchid experts. It's going to be their call as to which one is a prizewinner or not."

"Oh dear," murmured Drayton, turning his full attention to the monkey-face orchid again. "And I so wanted to win a ribbon for Mark."

"You're doing this in his memory," Theodosia reminded him. "That's a win-win situation right there."

Charlie had suddenly joined them. "Drayton?" she said. "You have a phone call. A Mr. Timothy Neville?"

Drayton snatched up his orchid. "Now I suppose there's an *event* crisis, too," he said.

"Why don't you take the call in my office?" suggested Theodosia.

"Thank you, I will," said Drayton as he threaded his way across the floor of the tea room.

"What's the deal with Drayton?" asked Charlie. She seemed calm, unmoved by his hysteria.

"He's just being Drayton," laughed Haley.

"He's worried about his orchid," Theodosia told Charlie. "Thinks the display isn't showy enough."

"Really," said Charlie, studying Drayton's arrangement. "Not showy enough, huh?"

"Charlie," said Theodosia. "Could you do me a really big favor?"

"Sure thing," said Charlie.

"Could you put together a tea basket for tonight's silent auction?"

"You haven't done that yet?" asked Haley.

Theodosia shook her head. "Not yet."

"No problem," said Charlie. "So you want me to just arrange a few things in a basket? Like tins of tea, a jar of jam, cup and saucer, things like that?"

"Perfect," said Theodosia. "You're a very quick study."

"Not perfect," said Haley. "We're clean out of baskets."

"What about those woven grapevine baskets that have been sitting in my back office for months?" asked Theodosia.

"Gone," said Haley. "Dusted off and sold this past week when the contingent from Goose Creek stopped by."

"Really?" said Theodosia. "Okay then, maybe . . ."

"Why don't I just run out and get a basket," volunteered Charlie. "It's no big deal."

"Can you really?" asked Theodosia. "Gee, that'd be great."

Charlie was already slipping her apron over her head. "Be back in ten minutes," she promised.

Theodosia and Haley turned their attention to Haley's truffle trays.

"At any rate, these are all done," declared Haley.

"They're gorgeous," said Theodosia. Indeed, Haley had whipped up coconut-ginger truffles as well as raspberry-chocolate truffles and white chocolate–almond truffles.

"Once we get our tables all set up at the Heritage Society

tonight, I'm going to sprinkle edible flowers among the chocolates," said Haley.

"Edible orchids?" asked Theodosia.

"Not quite," said Haley, slipping plastic bags over her three-tiered trays and using a twist tie to fasten them securely at the bottom. "I'm going to put these in the back of your Jeep, okay?"

"No problem, doors are unlocked."

"When I come back I'm going to tackle the tea sandwiches," said Haley.

"I'll help," said Theodosia. "How many different kinds are you planning to do?"

"Probably three," answered Haley.

"Okay. We'll let Drayton tend to the few remaining customers."

"I heard that," said Drayton, coming back into the tea room.

"Everything okay with Timothy?" asked Theodosia.

Drayton rolled his eyes. "Arthur Roumillat and his Orchid Society members want to wait until the very last minute to set up."

"I suppose they're worried about their plants," said Theodosia.

"I can just see them circling the block," complained Drayton. "Waiting for the last possible moment to come swooping in."

Theodosia was starting to get a little worried herself. The patio at the Heritage Society wasn't all that spacious. And they had to set up their tea table, which she still wasn't certain was going to be one table or two tables put together. And Parker Scully had to set up his table for the Black Orchid cocktails nearby. And, of course, there were Drayton's ice angels to contend with. Plus there were circular glass tables for guests to sit at. "It's going to be chaos," ventured Theodosia.

"What isn't chaos these days." Drayton sighed.

When the front door flew open ten minutes later, Theodosia knew things were not only going to be difficult, they were probably going to get contentious, too.

"What are you doing here?" an unhappy Drayton asked their new arrival.

Bill Glass ran a hand over his dark, slicked-back hair and glanced around the tea shop. "Jeez," were his first words. "This place looks like a hurricane just hit."

"We're dreadfully busy," snapped Drayton. "Now what is it you require?"

Glass aimed one of his Nikons at the table where tea sandwiches were being stacked and packed. "Just a few quick photos. You know, document the whole event."

"I was under the impression you were retained to photograph the actual orchid show," said Theodosia. "The events at the Heritage Society."

"Nothing like getting a few candid shots," said Glass as he slid over toward the table where cellophane-wrapped sandwiches were being packed in wicker baskets.

"Stop right there," ordered Drayton. "Do not help yourself to one morsel of food. That's an order."

"C'mon," wheedled Glass. "You've got enough food here to feed an army."

Theodosia hustled over to Bill Glass. "You can help yourself to tea and sandwiches *tonight*," she told him. "With the rest of the guests."

Glass raised his camera and clicked off a quick sequence of shots in her face, causing Theodosia to blink.

"You're no fun, tea lady," he told her. "Why such a party pooper?"

"Is that who I think it is?" called Haley's strident voice. She came barreling out from behind the velvet curtains and rushed right up to Bill Glass. "Stop it," she told him, smacking his outstretched hand like she was reprimanding a willful schoolchild.

"Yow!" yelped Glass, pulling back his hand and laughing at the same time. "Aren't you a little spitfire."

Hands on hips now, Haley peered at Bill Glass. "Get lost, Glass," she told him. "It's bad enough you were hired to photograph Orchid Lights. We don't need you poking around here, too."

"Behind-the-scene shots," he told her, though his explanation sounded lame.

"Go bug somebody else," Haley told him. "Go annoy the Orchid Society. Or the staff at the Heritage Society." She fluttered her fingers, then turned her back on him to indicate the issue was closed.

It hadn't been that long ago that Bill Glass had tried to entice Haley with big plans to publish her recipes. But the publishing contract he'd delivered to her had been hopelessly in his favor and Theodosia's admonition to revise it had apparently fallen on deaf ears. So at the moment, Bill Glass was persona non gratis with Haley.

Charlie suddenly appeared in the doorway. "Drayton," she said. "Can you step outside with me for a minute?"

"Who's that?" asked Glass, raising his camera.

"Leave her alone," said Theodosia, shooing him away like he was an annoying, persistent hornet.

"What?" Drayton asked Charlie. "You mean in back?"

Between Charlie's beckoning to him and Bill Glass stalking the tea room, Drayton seemed like he was caught off balance.

"Outside," repeated Charlie. "Just for a minute."

"Whatever for?" asked Drayton.

Charlie's shoulders sagged. "Drayton." She sighed. "Indulge me, will you?"

Bill Glass turned toward Theodosia as Drayton left the room. "You people are just as crazy as ever," he chided.

"Thanks. Thanks a lot," she told him.

Bill Glass followed her over to the counter. "I'm really just killing time until the event starts," he told her.

"No kidding," said Theodosia, busying herself. She knew she'd need sugar bowls, silver tongs, stir sticks, and a couple of tea strainers for tonight. And what else? There had to be a million other things.

"I'm not a bad guy," Glass told her.

"That remains to be seen." Theodosia leaned down, grabbed a six-pack of votive light candles. She figured they'd look perfect flickering on the tables once it got dark. Or should she bring the candelabra? Yes, that was even better.

"What do you hear about the fire at the Featherbed House?" Glass asked her.

Theodosia straightened up and stared at Glass. "Just that it's a tragedy for Angie as well as the historic district." She gazed at him suspiciously. "Why? You fishing around for a front-page story for next week's *Shooting Star*?"

Glass shrugged. "Maybe. I already ran a short piece on the fire yesterday. But if you've got any new insight I'm all ears."

"Nothing besides the fact that poor Angie lost her husband and her livelihood." No way was she going to tell Bill

Glass about Fayne Hamilton. He could read about that in tomorrow's *Post and Courier* with the rest of Charleston.

"Yeah," said Glass, fiddling with his camera. "Too bad about all that."

Theodosia grabbed a blue-and-white teapot and poured out a cup of black tea heavily scented with jasmine. She shoved it across the counter toward Glass, hoping a few sips might settle him down. "Compliments of the house," she told him.

Bill Glass eyed the tea suspiciously, then picked up the cup and took a judicious sip. Surprisingly, it seemed to meet with his approval. "Good," he told her. "Tasty."

"I thought you might like it."

Glass leaned forward, getting ready to fix Theodosia with one of his trademark aw-shucks smiles, when his head suddenly swiveled right and he looked past her.

"What the . . . ?" said Glass, fumbling for his camera.

Curious, Theodosia also followed his gaze. And saw a grinning Charlie standing alongside a beaming Drayton. A beaming Dayton who was balancing a gigantic bell jar in his arms.

Then Theodosia realized what had taken place.

Drayton and Charlie had repotted the monkey-face orchid. The tall stalk with the white helmet-shaped flowers suddenly looked very dramatic and spooky in its new environment. Nestled at the base of the orchid were giant balls of moss that lent an overall effect of an orchid still growing in a natural, pristine forest.

Theodosia chuckled as Bill Glass clicked away. She figured Glass might just have found his dramatic cover shot for the next issue of *Shooting Star*.

24

❦

"*This is a* disaster," muttered Haley as she elbowed her way through the crowd, trying to keep her truffle trays level.

Theodosia, who'd already staked out their meager position on the Heritage Society's patio, had to agree. "Just ferry everything to the table first," she advised. "Then we'll figure out the logistics of setting up."

"The table?" asked Drayton, in a thunderous tone. "We're talking singular?"

"Afraid so," said Theodosia, pushing a puff of auburn hair back over her shoulder. Her hair looked lovely, her makeup was soft and glowing, her outfit was very boho chic. But the evening was starting off on a precarious note. "The Orchid Society set up four more tables than planned," she told Drayton, "so we've all got to do a little scrunching."

"Typical," said Drayton with a sniff.

"So where's Parker going to have his drink table?" asked Haley.

"Right over there," said Theodosia, indicating an empty table. "Just down from us."

"Where does that leave me with my ice angels ?" asked Drayton.

"Right here," said Theodosia.

"No way can we arrange everything on one table," fretted Drayton. "Tea, tea sandwiches, truffles, and my ice angels. What silly idiot gave our other table away, anyhow?"

"Yoo-hoo, Drayton, Theodosia!" called Delaine Dish as she scuttled across the patio, looking fetching in a diaphanous pink cocktail dress. "Can you people slide your table down just a smidge? I told Mr. Roumillat that his orchid people could have a tad more room."

"Three guesses who gave our other table away," muttered Haley. "And the first two don't count."

Drayton spun on his heels to face Delaine, launching into a rebuttal speech as if it were a college debate. "My dear Miss Dish, we're not about to slide this table one single millimeter in longitude or latitude. In fact we shall not be deterred in any way from serving an array of splendid, first-class refreshments.

Drayton's words slowed Delaine down for a few scant seconds. Then she leaned in close and fixed everyone with a peculiar bright-eyed gaze. "Did you hear about Fayne Hamilton?" she asked. "She's been *arrested*." Taking a deep breath she went on. "Arrested! Can you believe it?" Delaine looked almost delirious at the news. "It goes to show you just never know what lurks in people's hearts and minds."

"You never do," agreed Theodosia, hoping the news of Fayne's arrest wouldn't dominate the event tonight. "And I believe the correct terminology is *taken into custody*," corrected Theodosia. "Versus being arrested."

"There's a difference?" asked Delaine.

"It's slight, but there is a difference," replied Theodosia.

"As you might guess, Bobby Wayne is *beside* himself," confided Delaine. She clearly did not want to drop the subject. "He's hoping Loveday and Luxor can keep a tight lid on this. That there isn't too much fallout."

"My hope is that Angie's name is promptly cleared," said Theodosia.

"Oh, that, too, honey," agreed Delaine. "It's just that an investment firm doesn't want to be connected to any sort of scandal."

"Is Bobby Wayne here tonight?" asked Drayton. He was growing a little bored with Delaine's fixation on Fayne Hamilton.

"On his way," said Delaine. "He's obviously a little spooked by that Fayne character." She gave a little shiver, then glanced around. "I sure do wish we could slide these tables closer."

"I don't see how," said Theodosia. Tables were already jammed together everywhere, orchid club members were elbowing each other for display space, and early arriving guests were standing around, watching the chaos.

"We're not sardines," muttered Drayton.

"We just need to make things *fit*," insisted Delaine. "The guests that are coming tonight have extremely high expectations. We're talking about *society* people. The upper crust."

"You know what the upper crust really is?" laughed Drayton. "A lot of crumbs held together by dough."

"Love it," chortled Haley. She elbowed Theodosia. "Isn't Drayton a card."

"He's a hoot," agreed Theodosia as she began arranging tiny lobster salad sandwiches on a footed glass dish.

But Delaine was not one bit amused. "You people," she said, her long pink earrings swaying as she spoke, "could show a little more respect for our donors!"

"Good heavens," *exclaimed* Drayton, as Charlie struggled toward their table, hauling an aluminum cooler. "You should have waited and let me help with that. Besides getting my orchid out of Theo's Jeep, I was planning on making a couple more trips."

"No big deal," said Charlie. "I'm just happy to be here."

"We're delighted to have you," said Theodosia. She was thrilled that Drayton now seemed to view Charlie as a real asset to their team. "And you look so cute, too." Haley had taken Charlie across the alley and outfitted her in a black silk T-shirt, long gauzy skirt, and cute tie belt.

"Thanks to my stylist here," laughed Charlie. While she wasn't wearing formal attire, she certainly looked dressy enough.

"You know the program?" Haley asked her. "Drayton explained it to you on the way over?"

"Pretty much," said Charlie. "He wants me to be in charge of ice angels tonight."

"Making them or serving them?" asked Haley.

"Both, I think," responded Charlie.

"So what flavor of gelato did he finally settle on?" asked Haley, kicking the cooler with her toe. "And what kind of tea?"

"You two are talking about me like I'm not here," said Drayton.

"Get over it," quipped Haley.

"It's a really good combo," said Charlie. "Lemon gelato topped with jasmine tea. The exact recipe being two small scoops of gelato and about a quarter cup of tea."

Haley dug around under the table. "You're using these little clear plastic glasses?" she asked, pulling out a package.

Drayton made a face. "It just isn't possible to use nice glassware."

"Then what about spoons?" asked Haley, always a stickler for order and planning.

"We're not using spoons," said Drayton. "Charlie's just going to pop colored straws into the glasses so people can walk around sipping them."

"Kind of like snow cones," said Haley. "Outdoorsy and fun."

"Well, not exactly," said Drayton. "Our ice angels are far more elegant."

Just when Theodosia was about to give up hope, Parker Scully finally showed up. He struggled in, muscling a large cardboard box that clanked noisily.

"What have you got in there?" Haley asked him.

Parker dropped the box on his table with a thud, then proceeded to pull out liquor bottles and arrange them on his table. "Rum, curaçao, and grenadine," he told her.

"I thought grenadine was a soldier," said Haley.

"You're thinking of a grenadier," laughed Parker. "Grenadine is a liqueur."

"Don't you think it's strange that your first name is the same as my last name?" asked Haley.

"Parker was my mother's maiden name."

"Whoa. Maybe we're related."

Parker gazed at her deadpan. "Heaven help me."

"Do you need help?" Theodosia asked him.

"Already got some," said Parker. "I ran into your assistant in the parking lot. She's giving me a hand."

The words weren't out of Parker's mouth when Charlie showed up hefting another cardboard box.

"Now whatcha got?" asked Haley.

"Glasses, swizzle sticks, stuff like that," said Parker, taking the box from Charlie.

"You need ice?" asked Haley.

"On its way," said Parker. "I made arrangements with the same vendor that delivers ice to my restaurant."

"Why didn't we think of that?" said Haley.

"Good question," replied Theodosia. "Hey, where did Drayton dash off to?"

"He's registering his orchid," said Charlie. "See?" She pointed across the patio to a small registration table where Drayton was bent over, scribbling away.

"This oughta be good," smiled Haley. "Suffice it to say, Drayton's entry is a bit nontraditional."

Twenty minutes later a string quartet struck their first notes and Orchid Lights was officially under way. White twinkle lights glowed in the palmetto trees, flickering candles floated in the reflecting pool, and guests in elegant evening attire strolled from table to orchid-laden table, admiring the gorgeous plants on view. Overhead, the Charleston sky was a piece of dark blue denim embedded with stars.

"Everything looks so gorgeous and romantic," commented Haley, pulling her butter-yellow pashmina closer around her shoulders.

"Perfect," murmured Theodosia. What had seemed destined for disaster thirty minutes earlier had suddenly morphed into absolute elegance. Cream-colored tapers in a brass candelabra lit their tea table. Serving trays filled with lobster salad, cucumber cream cheese, and chicken chutney tea sandwiches looked most enticing. Haley's three-tiered truffle trays were now strewn with edible flowers. To save space, they'd moved Charlie and the ice angel setup over to Parker Scully's table. That way guests could have their choice of either the alcoholic Black Orchid cocktail or Drayton's nonalcoholic but still delicious tea and gelato mixture.

Haley nudged Theodosia. "Here comes Drayton. Bet he shook things up with that bell jar and moss arrangement."

Drayton's heels hit the flagstones like castanets as he approached.

"You're not going to believe this," he began, eyes rolling upward.

"What now?" asked Haley.

"Harlan Noble is protesting my entry."

"Because . . . why?" asked Theodosia.

"He says it's completely nontraditional."

"Hey, that's what I just said," said Haley, happily.

"But your entry is still an orchid," reasoned Theodosia. "Completely within the boundaries. And this is an amateur orchid show at the Heritage Society. Good heavens, it's not as though you broke convention with an American Orchid Society—sanctioned show or some sort of international orchid event."

Drayton grabbed Theodosia by the hand and pulled her along. "Then kindly come and tell that to the people at the registration table!"

25

❧

It was almost fun, Theodosia decided. All she had to do was mention Timothy Neville's name and she had the instant ability to strike fear in the hearts of almost every volunteer. Obviously, the Orchid Society members had heard about Timothy's famously hot temper and decided it wasn't worth the effort to keep Drayton out of the judging. In fact, they probably figured it was the lesser of two evils. Harlan Noble might glower and fuss, but Timothy would completely blow his cork.

So Drayton's orchid was in. Thank goodness!

And Drayton was breathing easier now, acting almost ebullient.

"Let's go inside and check out the silent auction," he said to Theodosia. "See how that's going."

"Only for a couple minutes," replied Theodosia. "We don't want to leave Haley and Charlie short-handed."

"They'll be fine," expounded Drayton, smiling broadly now, waving to friends and Heritage Society regulars that they passed.

"Two minutes," Theodosia told him as they made their way down the wood-paneled corridor to what the Heritage Society called the gallery room.

"Oh, this is going very well," exclaimed Drayton. A pleasant hum filled the room as at least fifty people actively perused the various auction items and jotted their bids on the bidding sheets.

At the first table, they ran into Delaine and Bobby Wayne Loveday. Delaine looked like she was ready to party all night; Bobby Wayne looked drawn and subdued.

Theodosia reached out and clasped a hand on one of Bobby Wayne's forearms. "Sorry to hear about Fayne," she said in a low whisper.

Bobby Wayne's eyes met hers and he shook his head. "Shocking," he murmured back. "Almost unspeakable."

"Such a sad child," added Delaine. "So misguided." She picked up a pen, thought for a moment, then scratched out her bid. "I certainly hope nobody else bids on this Hilton Head trip. I would simply *adore* spending a long weekend there."

"I'm kind of interested in the fighter jet ride," Theodosia told her.

"Goodness," said Delaine, fanning herself. "Way too much excitement for me!"

At Bobby Wayne's urging, he and Delaine followed Theodosia and Drayton back to their tea table.

"I haven't had a bite to eat all day," Bobby Wayne told them.

"You like lobster salad sandwiches?" Drayton asked.

Bobby Wayne touched a hand to his chest as his eyes fluttered. "Be still my heart." He laughed.

Drayton took a small plate, stacked up a half dozen sandwiches for Bobby Wayne. Usually judicious in doling out tea sandwiches, Drayton was obviously feeling a certain amount of sympathy for Bobby Wayne. After all, there was sure to be some fallout for his company.

"You're a lifesaver," said Bobby Wayne, popping one of the tasty morsels into his mouth.

Delaine raised one quivering eyebrow. "Good?" she asked him.

Bobby Wayne rolled his eyes appreciatively and nodded.

"I bet you'd enjoy one of these chicken salad and chutney sandwiches, too," said Haley.

In answer Bobby Wayne held out his plate.

Delaine's eyebrows rose a little higher. "Perhaps we could also get a refreshing drink," she suggested.

"Sure," agreed Bobby Wayne.

Haley suddenly clapped a hand over her mouth. "You know what?" she exclaimed to Theodosia. "I forgot to tell you something."

"What's that?" asked Theodosia.

"Burt Tidwell called you back. I took the phone call just as we were leaving the tea shop. But in all the fuss and furor of getting everything transported and set up, I forgot to tell you."

Delaine stared at Haley as though she'd just committed an indiscretion. "You're referring to that boorish detective?" she asked.

"I guess you must have called him about something?" continued Haley. "Because he said he was getting back to you. From the Bahamas?"

Maybe Tidwell did check on that Bahamian company for me, thought Theodosia. She gave a casual flip of her hand. "Not to worry," she told Haley. "I'll call Tidwell back tomorrow." Then, feeling good about things, Theodosia added, "I'll tell him the case has already been solved. That his services weren't needed after all."

"Hah." Haley laughed. "That'll just about *kill* him. Tidwell thinks he's smarter than Sherlock Holmes, Kojak, and the whole *CSI* team put together!"

Delaine plucked at Bobby Wayne's sleeve, trying to get him away from the table. "I do believe Timothy Neville is going to make a short speech now," she said in a somewhat strained voice.

"Oh, I don't want to miss that," said Drayton.

"What's the big deal?" asked Haley, who had always been a little fearful of Timothy.

"He's going to talk about the partnership with the Orchid Society," said Drayton. "It's one of Timothy's new initiatives for the Heritage Society. Partnering with other arts organizations or like-minded groups. He's even put out feelers for partnering with the Arts Board on the next Charleston Film Festival."

"Thinking outside the box," murmured Theodosia.

"That's a good thing, huh?" said Haley.

"A very good thing," smiled Theodosia. "Whether you're in business, running a nonprofit organization, or just navigating your life."

Drayton and Delaine began drifting toward the far side of the patio.

"You go, too," Theodosia urged Haley. "Scoot."

"You can handle things okay?"

"No problem. Besides, Parker and Charlie are nearby."

"Okay," said Haley, moving off to join the group.

Theodosia heard the PA system click on, was aware of a spatter of appreciative applause from the crowd. Then she turned her attention to her tea table. They'd been hit with a spurt of guests earlier and she wanted to replenish things. Bending over, she grabbed another tray of sandwiches, plucked a brass tea strainer and a tea thermometer from a wicker basket.

"Theodosia."

Theodosia looked up to see Bobby Wayne staring at her, looking a little bit excited and slightly jittery.

"Theodosia," Bobby Wayne whispered again. "Don't say anything to anyone, okay? Just come see the ring I bought for Delaine."

Bobby Wayne's words suddenly struck a chord with Theodosia. "Ring?" she said.

Bobby Wayne managed a nervous smile. "Yeah. It's an . . . an *engagement* ring!"

A wide smile spread across Theodosia's face. "Are you serious? You're going to ask Delaine to marry you?" This was news! Major news!

Bobby Wayne gave a tight, gleeful nod. "She's the one. I know it in my heart."

Theodosia scurried out from behind the table, sliding the tea strainer into the pocket of her slacks. "Show me, Bobby Wayne."

Bobby Wayne made a furtive gesture. "Come over here. Don't let her see us, though. It's gotta be a surprise."

Theodosia stepped off the patio, following in Bobby Wayne's footsteps. They rounded a giant magnolia bush and were suddenly in shadows. "Nobody saw us," promised Theodosia. "Don't worry."

"I've got it stashed in my car."

Theodosia followed Bobby Wayne another twenty feet to the edge of the parking lot.

"What I need is a woman's opinion on this," said Bobby Wayne. He reached into his jacket pocket, fumbled for his keys. "Delaine's got such impeccable taste, I don't want to screw up and give her anything that could be construed as too gaudy or even old-fashioned." Bobby Wayne popped open the trunk and reached into the darkness. When he withdrew his hand, a purple velvet ring box rested in the center of his palm.

"I'm sure she'll love anything you get her," said Theodosia, plucking the box from his hand. *Oh boy, will she ever.*

"Open it," prompted Bobby Wayne.

Curiosity aglow in her eyes, Theodosia opened the box slowly.

It was empty.

In a single heartbeat, Theodosia's curiosity winked out and stunned bewilderment rushed in to take its place.

"Bobby Wa—" Theodosia began just as she caught the blur of a giant shovel swinging toward her head. Inhaling sharply, she had time to move perhaps an inch before the enormous piece of galvanized metal connected solidly against the side of her skull. Absorbing the bone-jarring thwack, feeling every molar rattle, Theodosia was briefly cognizant that she'd sustained a terrible, crippling blow. And then she was falling. Falling softly into oblivion.

26

There was a whoosh and a dull roar in Theodosia's ears that she couldn't quite place. And a wickedly painful throbbing in her head.

Oh no, she thought, as she entered a sort of limbo stage of wakefulness. *How much did I have to drink last night?*

Trying to will away the pain, feeling completely discombobulated, Theodosia pulled her knees up to her chest and rolled over. It had to be a bad dream.

Or maybe I didn't drink too much last night, maybe I just came down with the flu.

Clearly, this was a morning to sleep in. To let Drayton and Haley open the tea shop. She'd call in later, let them know how sick she was. Because Theodosia knew she was sick. Too sick to even crawl out of bed and manage a glass of water and an aspirin. Rolling sideways, she searched above her head for a pillow.

And her elbow connected with something sharp.

"Ouch," she groaned. *What the . . . ?* She brought her arm down, reached out, and touched a hunk of metal.

She pulled back. Something wasn't right.

"Wait a minute," Theodosia mumbled to herself. "Where am I?"

She opened her eyes to total darkness.

Lifting her head ever so slightly, Theodosia was almost overcome with nausea. Piercing, stabbing pain exploded inside her head. Her shoulders were stiff and sore, and she couldn't seem to straighten her legs. Impassively, almost too sick to care, she wondered why that would be.

As seconds ticked by, Theodosia also became aware of movement. The surface she was laying on seemed to vibrate. That strange whooshing sound still resonated in her ears.

Then slowly, painfully, it started to come back to her.

I was at the orchid show . . . and Bobby Wayne wanted to show me a ring . . . and then, dear lord, the skunk clobbered me with something. What?

Theodosia reached a hand up to where sticky dampness matted her hair. Gently felt a painful bump on the side of her head. It throbbed hard and hot. Then she reached her hand out cautiously, eventually connecting with the sharp metal edge she'd touched a few seconds ago. Her fingers traveled slowly, exploring that flat plane, touching briefly on some plastic bottles just beyond.

"He hit me with a shovel," she moaned to herself. "And threw me in the trunk of his car!"

Paralyzing fear grabbed hold of Theodosia and held her in its grasp. Hot tears streamed down her cheeks.

Balling up her fists, she fought to regain control of her emotions. Tried to force herself to think rationally, knew she couldn't afford the luxury of panic. She had to formulate a plan. This wasn't the first time she'd been in a tight spot, but she knew she had to think hard, had to push through the pain and fear, no matter what.

Got to get out of here, got to get out, was her mantra.

Theodosia's head was pounding and spinning wildly now, her respiration felt shallow and labored. Her agonizing, viselike headache seemed to be getting worse.

She knew there was something in that dark trunk that was prickling her eyes and making it harder and harder to breathe. Something that carried a sickly sweet familiar smell like . . . what? She gave a hesitant sniff. Gasoline?

Or acetone.

Like a drowning person who's suddenly been thrown a life preserver, Theodosia grasped on to that single thought.

Acetone. The same compound the art directors at my old ad agency used to peel layouts and storyboards off pieces of foam core. The same stuff that was found in Fayne Hamilton's garage and allegedly used as a fire accelerant.

And on the heels of that realization . . .

Bobby Wayne set Fayne Hamilton up for Mark's murder.

Because Bobby Wayne killed Mark Congdon.

And Bobby Wayne set fire to the Featherbed House.

Theodosia knew she was in terrible trouble. Knew she had to find a way out. But how? What could she use to free herself?

Her mind spun back to the shovel. If she could punch out a taillight, or wield it as a weapon against Bobby Wayne once he opened the trunk . . . *if* he opened the trunk.

Could she do that? Could she pull herself together and go on the attack? She knew she had to try.

Then Theodosia's restless, frantic mind circled back

again and she thought, *Why did Bobby Wayne hit me with a shovel? Why a shovel?*

The answer, when it finally came, rushed at her like a pack of snarling wolves.

Because shovels are for digging graves.

Theodosia lost track of time. Curled up in the dark, nausea increasing by the minute, she had no idea how long she'd been unconscious. Wasn't even sure how long ago it was that she'd woken up.

And then, suddenly, she felt an imperceptible shift as Bobby Wayne's car slowed down. She was jounced and thrown off balance, causing more twinges to erupt in her head, as he negotiated a turn. Then they were bumping along over an uneven surface. She steeled herself, knowing she'd have only one chance to make her stand.

Theodosia wrapped her hands tightly around the handle of the shovel as they rocked to a stop.

She waited, hunched in the darkness, poised to attack. But when the trunk was finally sprung open and cool night air rushed in to greet her, Bobby Wayne Loveday was standing a good ten feet back from the car, a snub-nosed revolver clutched in his hand.

"Get out," he told her.

Cramped muscles protesting, Theodosia gingerly began to uncoil herself and put one foot on grassy ground.

"Drop the shovel."

She touched the business end of the shovel to the ground, then released it. It fell forward and hit the earth with a loud clang.

"Get over here," ordered Bobby Wayne.

Mustering her courage, Theodosia climbed the rest of the way out of the trunk and peered at Bobby Wayne through the darkness. "What do you think you're doing?" she asked.

That seemed to confound him.

"Taking care of loose ends," he finally replied. The gun moved slightly in his hands. "Now get over here."

Standing upright, inhaling fresh air, Theodosia finally gained the presence of mind to look around. And was stunned at what she saw. A silver penny of a moon shone down, illuminating the ancient tumbledown rice mill at Carthage Place Plantation.

Theodosia's first thought was, *Back to the scene of the crime.*

What did Bobby Wayne mean to do? Drag her kicking and screaming into the nightshade garden and force black nightshade and poison rhubarb down her throat?

But no, he had stealthily circled around her, was fumbling one-handed in the trunk of the car.

Fumbling for what? Theodosia wondered.

Bobby Wayne pulled out the bottle of acetone.

The acetone. Whoa.

"You don't want to do that, Bobby Wayne." Theodosia's voice came across far more forceful than she felt.

"Get inside," he barked. He walked briskly up to her, emboldened by the gun in his hand. "Turn. Walk."

Theodosia complied. She turned slowly and walked the ten steps to the rickety door of the rice mill.

"Inside, girlie," muttered Bobby Wayne.

That single order, phrased the way it was, incensed Theodosia. Finally helped clear her head and shoved back the pinpricks of fear. Strengthened her resolve.

Walking through the front door into the dilapidated mill, Theodosia was forced to duck her head. Inside, the ceiling was almost as low. Huge fallen beams were spilled everywhere like Lincoln Logs. Rotting leather belts hung from the ceiling. In the low light Theodosia could see the hulking remnants of the rice mill's giant gears.

Theodosia remembered this old rice mill at Carthage Place Plantation was dry as tinder. The old wood was ancient, well over a hundred years old. One small spark and it would surely explode in a giant, roaring, conflagration.

"Keep moving," said Bobby Wayne.

Stepping carefully, aware the floor was completely rotted through in several places, Theodosia picked her way farther into the old mill.

"Good enough," growled Bobby Wayne.

Theodosia's back rubbed up against a wooden beam as thick as a man's torso.

"This is such a bad idea," Theodosia told him.

Bobby Wayne stared at her in the darkness. "I think this is one of my better ideas, actually." He sounded calm and rational, unlike his mad-dog, frothing-at-the-mouth inner self.

"You're not going to get away with this," spat out Theodosia. "The police will come . . ."

"The police will be looking at other suspects," chortled Bobby Wayne. "Leah Shalimar and Harlan Noble. They'll go looking for them. Because I know how to set a trail."

"Like the one you set to Fayne Hamilton's back door?" said Theodosia.

The lower half of Bobby Wayne's face split open in a mirthless grin. "That was good, wasn't it. I'm good."

"No, you're probably insane," replied Theodosia.

"And you're really quite boring," snapped Bobby Wayne.

He held out his bottle of acetone, sloshed the sickly sweet–smelling liquid all around.

Theodosia lifted her hands from her sides. One of them found its way to a rough railing and she gripped it tight. Her heart was hammering away inside her chest and she wasn't sure what to do. She had to make a stand. But rushing Bobby Wayne when he had a gun pointed at her chest. Not smart.

Bobby Wayne sloshed more of the fire accelerant around. The intensity on his face made him look scared, happy, and giddy all at the same time.

"Why don't you just walk away from this," began Theodosia. "Leave the country. Today. Right now. After all, people are going to find out that your FOREX scheme is a fraud." *Is it a fraud?* she wondered. *It has to be. That's why he panicked when he found out Tidwell called from the Bahamas. That's why he killed Mark and burned down the Featherbed House.*

But Bobby Wayne was not to be deterred, was surely not to be reasoned with.

"Fire is better," he told her. "Fire is . . ." He gazed at her and his eyes seemed to gleam. ". . . cleansing." Digging into his jacket pocket, Bobby Wayne pulled out a lighter, flicked it on, watched the flame jump high.

Somewhere, in the back of her brain, Theodosia remembered Delaine talking about how she and Bobby Wayne had smoked cigars together. Theodosia wondered if this was the same lighter Bobby Wayne had used to light those cigars. Back pressed tight against the rough-hewn beam, Theodosia clutched the railing like a lifeline and also wondered if she'd get out of this alive.

Holding the lighter above his head, Bobby Wayne's

pudgy face looked almost satanic in the dancing light of the flame. "Bye-bye," he called as he pitched the lighter toward her.

Flames immediately shot upward, illuminating the back end of the rice mill where she was crouched. As light flickered and bloomed, Theodosia spotted a gaping hole in the floor just to her left. And did the only thing she could do. Slipped under the railing and tumbled downward.

Plunging down into that dark hole, Theodosia prayed for a soft landing.

And whatever was in that basement, old gunny sacks, moldering pile of rice husks, manure from animals that had once been housed there, it did provide a slightly soft landing spot for Theodosia.

But it didn't afford a moment's respite.

Intense flames hissed and danced just ten feet above her, causing her cheeks to burn. Tiny sparks floated down and Theodosia feared her hair might catch fire. Worst of all, Theodosia could hear Bobby Wayne's voice calling to her, "You can't get away!" But his voice sounded far away, like he was probably outside by now.

Down in the bowels of the rice mill, Theodosia's head whipped left to right, looking for an exit, any place that would lead her out of what would soon become a roaring inferno.

And as flames above grew in intensity, crackling and licking at the ancient roof above, Theodosia suddenly spotted an exit out of this maw of hell.

A tunnel. Approximately three feet high, three feet wide, constructed entirely of brick.

A *tunnel*? She could barely believe her eyes!

Taking a deep breath, Theodosia dove into that dark crawl space just as the floor above collapsed and flames licked at her heels.

27

❧

Skittering along on her hands and knees, Theodosia found herself inches deep in mud and slime. Thick, musty cobwebs brushed at her face.

A tunnel, a tunnel, Theodosia kept telling herself. *Yes, now I remember the quickie history lesson Drayton gave me. Rice was pounded in the mill, and fire to run the steam engine was generated in the nearby chimney. And those two components were connected by a tunnel! A tunnel exactly like the one I'm crawling through!*

She breathed a silent thank-you to Drayton. An even bigger thank-you to the highly inventive rice producers of the Carolinas.

And Theodosia kept crawling in the pitch black. Struggling along, wondering how far the tunnel extended, hoping it wasn't blocked at the other end.

When her fingertips finally hit a pile of broken bricks, she had a few bad moments fumbling around in the dark. But luck was with Theodosia, and when she inched upward and tilted her head back she saw giant streams of smoke and, in between, the faint glimmer of stars overhead!

The brick chimney, which had once soared twenty-five feet into the sky, had crumbled to a mere stub over the years. And now Theodosia was struggling to slowly pull herself up, trying to extricate herself from its archaeological remains. Clawing at broken brick and stone, she pushed and squirmed. Her silk top was in shreds, she had lost both sandals. But, finally, like a wary gopher emerging from its den, Theodosia pushed her head up slowly.

And saw . . . the old rice mill still burning. But no Bobby Wayne.

Is he gone? Did Bobby Wayne take off?

Theodosia swiveled her head around, mindful of the pain that filled her head. No, there was Bobby Wayne's car, parked right where he'd left it. So now the question remained. Where was Bobby Wayne?

What now? Out of the frying pan into the fire?

No, Theodosia decided. *That isn't going to happen.*

But Theodosia found herself confronted with a new set of problems. First was orientation. She wasn't sure which direction would lead her to the main plantation house. And second, would her legs even carry her?

She was exhausted, hurt, and unnerved. Did she even have the strength and inner reserves to attempt a getaway?

Theodosia knew she had to try.

Wobbling slightly, she pulled herself upright and crept along behind the back of the burning building. She knew if she could keep the burning rice mill directly between her and Bobby Wayne's car, she'd have a better chance of remaining undetected. Plus, sooner or later, someone would see this fire and call it in. Then fire engines would come racing out and Bobby Wayne would be forced to flee, to make his getaway.

When Theodosia felt confident she was in the right spot, she began backing away carefully. But the ground was uneven, causing her to stumble and fall a number of times. And every time she fell, her head throbbed more.

Fearing she'd suffered a concussion, worrying that she didn't have much strength left, Theodosia turned and tried to pick up the pace.

She knew she was wheezing badly, was having difficulty maintaining focus.

If she could just make it to that grove of tamaracks up ahead . . .

Theodosia pressed on, feet sinking in mud, willing herself to keep going.

When she reached the shelter of the tamarack grove, she turned.

And saw Bobby Wayne, backlit by the fire, searching for her.

No!

Spinning in frustration, Theodosia broke into a wobbly dog trot. If she could just put some distance between the two of them!

Plunging into a thicket of horse nettle, Theodosia turned an ankle, fought to maintain her balance, and cartwheeled down a hill.

That's when she heard Bobby Wayne's voice, calling after her.

"You're not going to get away!"

Clambering to her feet, Theodosia forced herself to keep going. Dodging trees, she was hobbling down an incline now, so the going was slightly easier. Then mud squished between her toes and she found herself ankle deep in water, then suddenly almost waist deep in a soggy morass.

She'd somehow stumbled into the water bog garden!

No shelter here, she told herself. Just a big, dangerous trap.

Struggling to pull herself out of the bog, Theodosia grasped at swamp grass and reeds, shredding water lily blooms as she fought to free herself. She felt guilty at pulling the blooms apart, destroying these protected plants, but she knew she had to do anything she could to get herself back on solid ground.

Her feet churned through silt that seemed to have no bottom, then finally hit mud. She kept pumping her legs, felt the mud start to turn slightly more solid. Then she was out of the bog and limping up a hill on the opposite side of the bog.

Splashing sounds behind her told Theodosia that Bobby Wayne had hit the far edge of the water bog garden, too.

Dear lord, he's so close behind me.

She dug deep into her reserves and managed an ungainly sprint up the grassy hillside.

"I see you!" crowed Bobby Wayne. "I see you."

As Theodosia reached the crest of the hill, her breath coming in shallow wheezes now, a loud boom filled the air and a bullet seemed to whiz by her head. She flung herself down, aware of a sharp jab at her left hip. Then she was up and running again, scared out of her mind. Dodging left, Theodosia was suddenly confronted by . . .

The hedge maze.

Without hesitation, Theodosia staggered toward it. Elaborate curlicues of wrought iron arched over the entrance, scrolling out words that Theodosia hadn't noticed a week ago: Take Heed This Wyld Tangle.

Ducking through the archway, Theodosia ran straight ahead, zigged left, then zagged right. Hoping this might be her salvation.

Can I get lost in here? she wondered. *Can I outwit Bobby Wayne? Hide from him then circle back and sneak out? Got to hope I can. Got to try.*

But her overwrought mind kept skittering from one thought to another and Theodosia knew she was just seconds away from a full-blown panic attack.

She slowed her steps, trying to consciously slow her mind as well.

Easy, easy, she told herself. *What can I do? How can I stop him?*

Her mind seemed like it was spinning off in a million different directions at once. She suddenly flashed back to a week ago, when she and Drayton had been caught in here. When they'd . . .

Theodosia came to a dead stop and forced herself to concentrate. She stared up at the sky, noted that a film of clouds had slipped in. Taking a deep breath, she thought harder. Seconds ticked by. A thin line etched itself between her brows as she patted the left pocket of her slacks, then reached in and pulled out her tea strainer.

Theodosia spun on her bare heels and headed back toward the entrance to the maze.

* * *

It didn't take more than ten seconds to find what she was looking for. The old grate, sunk into the ground.

Dropping to her knees, Theodosia labored to work one end of the tea strainer into the sod and under the edge of the grate.

At first it didn't want to go. The earth was packed hard, had probably been that way for some time. Years maybe. Gritting her teeth, Theodosia bent forward, put her entire body into it. Her shoulders ached, her fingers went numb. But slowly, the edge of the tea strainer slid under the grate.

Can I really pry this up? she wondered. The answer came roaring back at her. *I have to try.*

She could hear Bobby Wayne stumbling up the hill, not fifty feet away from her. His angry muttered curses filled the air. Theodosia knew that this time he wouldn't miss. This time he'd shoot to kill.

She'd dug halfway around the grate now and had pressed her fingers underneath, hoping to gain leverage. Straining harder, Theodosia focused every ounce of strength she had on her task. And was rewarded when one corner of the old grate lifted upward.

Got to work faster, Theodosia told herself as she heard Bobby Wayne's footsteps crunch gravel just outside the hedge maze, felt the moon slip beneath the clouds.

She had one end of the grate up now, was laboring to leverage it higher. And then it was starting to heave up out of the soil, the black depths of the old cistern yawning at her.

"There you are," said Bobby Wayne, his voice dripping with menace. "Wait until I get my hands around your throat. I'm going to . . ."

"What?" barked out Theodosia. She was standing no more than ten feet away from him. She could just make out his faint outline in the dark. "You're going to what?"

"Snap your neck like a wishbone," snarled Bobby Wayne.

Theodosia stared at Bobby Wayne, praying the moon stayed behind the clouds. Praying he wouldn't see where he was walking. "Then let's get to it," she dared him in a low, mocking tone.

With an angry, strangled scream, Bobby Wayne rushed at her full tilt. Theodosia could make out the twisted anger on his face, put up a hand as if to ward him off. And then, suddenly, there was a mad skittering of shoe leather against earth and a strangled cry as Bobby Wayne plunged down into the cistern.

A dull slosh sounded. Followed by an abrupt silence.

Theodosia blinked, almost not believing her trap had worked. One minute Bobby Wayne had been a hideous, menacing crazy man, rushing to wrap his fingers around her neck, the next second he'd dropped out of sight. It was like Bobby Wayne had suddenly jumped on an express elevator and dropped straight to the subbasement.

Theodosia's brain wasn't so quick to believe her eyes.

Did the trap work? she asked herself. *Did he really fall in?*

She crept over to the side of the cistern, dropped to her knees, and peered down tentatively.

Bobby Wayne was down there all right, like a tiger who'd fallen through one of those bamboo jungle traps. Only there were no pointed spikes at the bottom of this pit. Only muddy, stinking water.

Bobby Wayne suddenly broke his stunned silence. Began thrashing around wildly, screaming his fool head off.

"Get me outa here!" he shrilled. "You hear me, woman? I'm talkin' to you!"

Theodosia's head spun dizzily. She felt a brief moment of triumph, but she also felt like she was going to faint.

"I know you're up there!" screamed Bobby Wayne. "I can *see* you!"

Theodosia pushed back from the edge as a rotten egg smell wafted up to her. With all the willpower she could muster, she forced herself to get back on her feet. She scanned the ground around her, finally found what she was looking for. A good-sized pebble.

With a flick of the wrist, Theodosia tossed the pebble into the cistern. Then she waited until she heard a faint splash.

Good, she decided. *The darned thing's deep enough to contain Bobby Wayne until I get some help.*

No ghostly arms would reach up to grab hold of her legs.

"What was that?" Bobby Wayne called suddenly, his voice rising in hysteria. "What was that you threw in here? What are you doing?"

Theodosia sighed heavily as she stepped carefully across the gaping hole in the ground.

"Don't leave me!" Bobby Wayne's voice drifted up from below, almost drowned out by the shrill of sirens as fire engines rushed toward Carthage Place.

Theodosia wrapped her arms around herself, trying to quiet her shaking. "Shut up, Bobby Wayne," she called over her shoulder.

Then she trudged slowly across the rolling lawn, damp with evening dew, toward the twinkling lights of Miss Maybelle Chase's plantation house.

28

Miss Maybelle Chase turned out to be a real peach. She wrapped Theodosia in a warm blanket and gave her a pair of cozy terry-cloth slippers to wear. Then she got on the phone and called Sheriff Billings, and located Drayton at the Heritage Society.

One of the firemen who'd come screaming up in a rescue squad, had gently led Theodosia into the kitchen where he'd applied antiseptic to her head wound and put a clean white bandage on it. He'd checked her blood pressure, pronounced it okay.

When she came limping back into Miss Maybelle's antique-filled parlor, Theodosia was surprised to see Sheriff Billings, Drayton, Haley, and Parker peering at her nervously.

And of course they all shouted questions at once.

"Are you hurt?" asked Haley.

"Do you need anything?" Drayton wanted to know.

"How did you get away?" asked Sheriff Billings.

"Sweetheart," moaned Parker Scully.

Theodosia had a few questions of her own.

"Where's Bobby Wayne?" she demanded of the sheriff.

"Don't you worry about him," said Sheriff Billings. "My deputies pulled him out of that cistern and carted him off to jail."

"He tried to kill me," said Theodosia. Her knees were still shaking.

"We know that, ma'am," said Sheriff Billings. "Do you feel well enough to tell us exactly what happened?"

"Shouldn't she go to the hospital first?" asked Drayton. "Get a CAT scan or something?"

"Absolutely she should," agreed Parker.

"Wait a minute," said a still subdued Theodosia. "How did you guys even know I was missing?"

Drayton gave a slight chuckle. "Bill Glass saw you slip away with Bobby Wayne. He assumed you two were romantically involved."

Theodosia rolled her eyes. "I think Glass is the one in need of a CAT scan."

"Then Delaine started hunting around for Bobby Wayne," said Haley. "Acting more and more crazy when she couldn't find him."

"Which is when we all got worried," added Parker.

"And then when Miss Maybelle called the Heritage Society," said Drayton. "Well . . . we weren't sure *what* was going on!"

Theodosia held up a hand. "Please, I'd like to tell you all about the night I've had."

She explained how Bobby Wayne had lured her with his story about the ring. Told how she'd been hit with a shovel and tossed in his trunk. How she'd escaped the fire and crawled through the tunnel. How she'd ended up in the hedge maze.

They were astounded to say the least.

"You're so brave," said Haley, clutching for her hand.

"Amazing story," whispered Drayton while Parker fixed her with an admiring stare.

Sheriff Billings just shook his head.

"Does Delaine know about Bobby Wayne?" asked Theodosia.

"I'll be speaking with her personally," said Sheriff Billings.

"It's just going to *kill* her," said Haley. "Being hoodwinked like that."

"But think what Bobby Wayne did to Theodosia," sputtered Drayton. "Besides, he wasn't really going to ask Delaine to marry him. That was just a ruse to get Theodosia off by herself."

"From what you've told me," said Sheriff Billings addressing Theodosia, "I'm fairly certain Bobby Wayne planted that fire accelerant in Fayne Hamilton's garage. To, you know, implicate her in the fire and supposedly the murder."

"Because Fayne was in love with Mark," mused Theodosia.

"Probably more like infatuated," said Drayton.

"But when Bobby Wayne found out that you'd called Detective Tidwell about the Bahamian company, he obviously panicked," said Haley.

"Right," said Parker. "Because there probably isn't any such company."

"But Mark was going there . . ." protested Theodosia. "He'd bought a plane ticket."

"I just got off the phone with Tidwell no more than ten minutes ago," said Sheriff Billings. "If Mark had actually gone to the Bahamas, he would have found a big fat nothing. According to Tidwell there are no Bahamian futures commission merchants."

"So Bobby Wayne was in a panic because of my call to Tidwell," said Theodosia, gazing at Sheriff Billings. "I didn't mean to step on your toes."

"Step away." He laughed. "By doing so, you forced Bobby Wayne's hand so to speak. Smoked him out."

Drayton shook his head. "Bobby Wayne probably figured that since Harlan Noble and Leah Shalimar were suspects—and both docents at Carthage Place—he could implicate them by bringing you out here and dumping your body."

Theodosia thought for a moment. "But Harlan Noble was at the orchid show."

"Not for long," said Drayton. "Harlan stormed out in protest over my entry."

"Really?" said Theodosia.

"And Leah wasn't there at all," added Haley. "So probably Bobby Wayne figured that since both of them were suspects, either one could have kidnapped and dragged you out here."

"Okay," said Theodosia, still digesting all this. "Did Leah Shalimar know about the bogus company in the Bahamas?"

"Doubtful," said Sheriff Billings.

"Leah knew sales," said Drayton. "She told me herself that she'd sold Jaguars and Mercedes and before that timeshare condos. She bragged that she could sell ice to Eskimos. My guess is, you tell Leah to sell, she'll sell. But no way is she a financial genius."

"But Mark Congdon was," said Theodosia.

"Yes," said Sheriff Billings. "Mark knew his business. Which is why he was suspicious. And had probably launched his own investigation. He must have suspected that Bobby Wayne was involved in something nefarious."

"But Bobby Wayne got to him first," said Theodosia. "Killed him and then burned down the Featherbed House."

"He must have thought Mark Congdon had serious evidence on him," said Sheriff Billings. He sighed, fingered the brim of his Smokey Bear hat. "If there's any upside to this at all, it's that your friend is in the clear and she'll soon have a pile of insurance money to help her rebuild."

"Still," said Drayton, "a very sad state of affairs." He stared at Theodosia with sorrowful eyes.

"Drayton," said Theodosia suddenly. She pulled herself upright, put a hand to her head. "I forgot all about Orchid Lights. Did your monkey-face orchid win a blue ribbon?"

Drayton crossed his arms, tucked in his chin, and shook his head solemnly.

"Oh, I'm sorry . . ." began Theodosia.

Then Drayton's hand dipped inside his jacket pocket and he withdrew a bright purple ribbon that fluttered from a giant purple rosette.

"Drayton!" squealed Theodosia.

A grin split his lined face as he handed the ribbon to Theodosia. "A *purple* ribbon," he told her. "Judge's Special Award of Merit."

"I knew it," said Theodosia, grinning at him.

"It was the moss goobers, as you so aptly named them," said Drayton. "And that marvelous bell jar Charlie came up with. The judges said they were bowled over by the creativity of the display."

"There's that thinking outside the box thing," quipped Haley. "Or is it thinking inside the jar?"

"I'm so happy for you," Theodosia told Drayton.

"We better get you to an emergency room," broke in Parker, looking more than a little concerned. "Get your poor head X-rayed, CAT scanned, and stitched if need be."

"I really am feeling a lot better," said Theodosia. And she was. Surrounded by dear friends, her ordeal over, she felt warm, secure, and much loved.

"Parker is quite correct," said Drayton. "It's off to the hospital for you."

There was the familiar clatter and rattle of china, and then everyone turned as Miss Maybelle set an elaborate tea tray down on the low table in front of them.

"Leaving already?" she asked. "And I just made tea."

"Tea." Theodosia sighed. Just the idea of sipping fresh-brewed tea went a long way to soothe her jangled nerves.

Drayton glanced about nervously. "Is there time?"

Placing one of Miss Maybelle's needlepoint pillows behind her head, Theodosia leaned back against the couch and said, "There's always time for tea."

The Indigo Tea Shop

Sweet Potato Scones

   1 cup all-purpose flour
   ½ tsp salt
   2 tsp baking powder
   1 tsp sugar
   1 cup mashed cooked sweet potatoes
   3 Tbsp melted butter
   1–2 Tbsp milk

SIFT flour, salt, and baking powder into a medium bowl, stir in sugar. In a separate bowl, mix sweet potatoes and 2 Tbsp. butter, then add in dry ingredients. Mix to form a soft dough, adding milk as necessary. Place on floured surface and roll out or pat with hands to form a round that's about

½-inch thick. Using a 2-inch cookie cutter, cut out scones, then place on greased cookie sheet. Brush tops with remaining 1 Tbsp. of melted butter. Bake at 375 degrees for 20 to 25 minutes or until light brown. Serve warm with butter and honey.

Lavender Egg Salad

8 hard-boiled eggs, peeled
2 Tbsp minced green onion
1½ Tbsp. Dijon mustard
⅓ cup mayonnaise
¼ tsp salt
1½ tsp. crushed food-grade lavender
2 cups iceberg lettuce, finely shredded
8 slices chewy bread

CHOP eggs. Stir in onion, mustard, mayonnaise, salt, and lavender. Chill mixture. To prepare sandwiches, butter bread, then spread egg salad on 4 slices of the bread. Gently pile on shredded lettuce, then top with remaining bread slices. Using a sharp knife, carefully trim crusts and cut into quarters or finger sandwiches. Keep covered with plastic wrap until ready to serve. Note: this egg salad can also be served in croissants.

Hot 'n' Cheesy Crab Casserole

    1 lb crab meat
    1½ cups white sauce
    2 eggs, separated and beaten
    ¼ cup green pepper, chopped and lightly sautéed
    ¼ cup onion, chopped and lightly sautéed
    ½ tsp Tabasco sauce
    ¼ cup shredded Cheddar or Jack cheese
    Salt and pepper to taste

ADD beaten egg yolks to white sauce and stir. Mix in crab meat, green pepper, onion, Tabasco sauce, and dash of salt and pepper. Gently fold in beaten egg whites, pour into baking dish, and top with shredded cheese. Bake for 20 minutes in 375-degree oven until golden brown. Yields 4 servings.

Strawberry Slush Tea

    2 cups brewed black tea, chilled
    1½ cups frozen strawberries
    1 (6-ounce) can frozen lemonade concentrate
    ¼ cup powdered sugar
    1 cup ice cubes

PLACE brewed tea, frozen strawberries, lemonade concentrate, powdered sugar, and ice cubes in a blender. Mix until smooth and slushy. Pour into champagne flutes and serve.

Profiteroles

1 cup milk
½ cup butter
1 cup all-purpose flour
4 large eggs

IN heavy saucepan, bring milk and butter to a boil. While
boiling, add flour all at once and stir rapidly until mixture
forms a ball. Remove from heat and beat in eggs thoroughly, one at a time. Place heaping teaspoons of dough on
a greased cookie sheet, two inches apart. Bake for 20 minutes at 425 degrees, then reduce heat to 350 degrees and
continue baking 10 to 15 minutes, until puffs are well risen
and dry. When cool, gently pull off the top and add your favorite filling. Curried chicken salad is great for luncheons,
chocolate ice cream is perfect for dessert!

Mini Pecan Muffins

⅔ cup melted butter
2 large eggs
1 cup brown sugar
½ cup all-purpose flour
1 cup chopped pecans

MIX butter and eggs together well. In separate bowl, mix brown sugar, flour, and pecans. Add the dry mix to the butter and egg mix and beat well. Grease and flour mini muffin tins, then pour batter into tins until about two-thirds full. Bake at 350 degrees for 20 to 25 minutes.

Lemon Jumble Cookies

6 Tbsp butter
½ cup sugar
Grated rind and juice from lemon
1 egg, beaten
3 cups self-rising flour
1–2 Tbsp milk

CREAM butter, then add sugar and grated lemon rind. Mix well and stir in strained lemon juice and beaten egg. Sift the flour and stir in lightly, adding milk as needed to keep dough stiff. Turn dough onto floured board and divide into small pieces. Roll each piece out gently with your hands and form into an S shape. Transfer to greased baking sheet and bake at 350 degrees for 15 to 20 minutes.

Bacon and Red Pepper Quiche

8 slices bacon
½ cup chopped onion
½ cup chopped red pepper
6 eggs
1 cup half-and-half
½ cup sour cream
Salt and pepper to taste

SAUTÉ bacon, onion, and red pepper. In separate bowl, beat eggs with half-and-half, sour cream, and salt and pepper. Pour half of this mixture into a greased 9-inch pie plate. Drain the bacon/onion/red pepper mixture and spread on top. Pour remaining egg mixture over top. Bake at 350 degrees for 35 minutes.

Haley's No-Cook Peanut Butter Truffles

¼ cup powdered sugar
½ cup sweetened condensed milk
1 cup creamy peanut butter
6 oz mini semisweet chocolate morsels
⅓ cup chopped walnuts or pecans

COMBINE powdered sugar, condensed milk, and peanut butter in mixing bowl. Stir until well blended. Stir in mini chocolate chips, then chill until firm. Gently shape into small balls and roll in chopped walnuts or pecans. Chill until firm. Serves one. (Just kidding!)

Key Lime Scones

2½ cups all-purpose flour
2 Tbsp brown sugar
1 Tbsp baking powder
1 tsp salt
1 stick butter
1 cup milk
1 large egg
Finely grated zest from 3 or 4 key limes

WHISK together flour, sugar, baking powder, and salt. Cut in the butter with a fork until crumbly. In a separate bowl combine milk, egg, and key lime zest. Add to the flour mixture and stir with fork until dough is blended yet sticky. Place dough on generously floured board and divide into two balls. Gently flatten each ball until it is about five inches in diameter, then cut into wedges. Place wedges on ungreased cookie sheet, then brush lightly with milk and sprinkle with sugar. Bake at 425 degrees for about 20 minutes.

The Last Straw Cheese Straws

½ cup butter
1 8-oz package shredded cheese
1 cup all-purpose flour
¼ tsp salt
⅛ tsp cayenne pepper

COMBINE cheese and butter in mixing bowl. Blend in flour, salt, and cayenne pepper. Form the mixture into 3 or 4 balls, then roll out each ball until dough is thin. Cut into strips and place on greased baking sheet. Bake at 425 degrees for about ten minutes or until golden brown. (Note: These are a perfect companion to soups and chowders!)

Black Orchid Cocktail

1 part blue curaçao liqueur
1 part dark rum
1 dash grenadine syrup

POUR into cocktail shaker over ice, shake well, strain, and serve.

Drayton's Spine-Tingling Ice Angels

BREW a pot of jasmine or rose hips tea and chill in refrigerator. Fill martini or parfait glasses with a scoop of raspberry or lemon gelato, then pour the chilled tea over it.

TEA TIME TIPS

from Laura Childs

Victorian Tea

Lay out your best china as well as a few choice antique pieces atop a lace tablecloth. Serve Earl Grey or an elegant Darjeeling, maraschino cherry scones with Devonshire cream, shortbread, and roast beef and white cheddar tea sandwiches. Floral nosegays at each place setting and a candelabra in the center of the table add elegance. Invite your guests to wear ruffles, Victorian hats, gloves, and cameos. An invitation using Victorian paper dolls or a fancy, scrolled cardboard frame from a scrapbook store would be perfection.

Blue-and-White Tea

In the eighteenth century, Chinese sailing ships and British clipper ships transported literally thousands of tons of Chinese blue-and-white ceramics to Europe and the Americas. The influence of these beautiful dishes remains with us today and these blue-and-white plates, teapots, and tea ware look stunning set against crisp white tablecloths. When your table looks this good, you don't need to get tricky. Serve cucumber and mint butter tea sandwiches, smoked salmon with cream cheese, raisin and apple scones, and Yunnan or Lapsang souchong tea.

Cottage Tea

Choose a cozy spot in the garden or sunroom and create a relaxed cottage atmosphere. Spread a quilt on the table, fill an old watering can with flowers, and use your vintage ceramic pitchers and mugs. Serve scones in wicker baskets, turn a clay pot upside down and top it with a plate of chicken chutney tea sandwiches. Serve a malty Assam and perhaps a vanilla-flavored tea. Old jars, tins, and one-of-a-kind teacups complete the picture.

Tea Blending Party

Buy a selection of loose teas, then visit your local herb store for dried chamomile, lavender, lemon verbena, rose petals, hibiscus, and cinnamon. Purchase small cotton muslin bags or tea sacks of unbleached mesh paper and allow your guests to concoct their own blends of tea. When it comes to serving food, simplify things by using three-tiered trays. And remember, cakes, shortbreads, and sweets go on top, scones in the middle, and savories (appetizers and small tea sandwiches) belong on the bottom tier.

Spa Tea

Fresh flowers, aromatherapy candles, and relaxation music set the mood. Drape fluffy towels over your chairs and place plump pillows underfoot. Then invite your friends in for a spa tea. Serve Egyptian chamomile and lemon herbal teas, fruit juices, bottled water, fruit kabobs, and shrimp salad tea sandwiches. Favors might include small loofahs, soaps, lip balms, and mini bottles of lotion. If you can hire a professional or coax a friend or relative to give shoulder or hand massages, so much the better.

Bird Lover's Tea

Ancient Chinese scholars used to carry their birds with them to the local teahouse in extravagantly woven bamboo cages. While they wrote poetry and sipped delicate teas, their birds would merrily chirp away. You, too, can have a Bird Lover's Tea. If you sit outside, place your table near a bird bath or feeder. For an inside tea, decorate your table with small birds and woven nests from a craft store, tiny bird houses, or ceramic birds. Use table napkins or dishes with bird motifs and serve your tea (a nice oolong or plum tea, perhaps?) in a traditional clay YiXing teapot. To celebrate

the joys of tea and friendship, try your hand at writing a
poem similar to this Sung dynasty poem by Tu Hsiao-Shan:

> *One winter night*
> *A friend dropped in.*
> *We drank not wine but tea.*
> *The kettle hissed,*
> *The charcoal glowed,*
> *A bright moon shone outside.*
> *The moon itself*
> *Was nothing special—*
> *But, ah, the plum-tree blossom!*

An old-world treat in the
brand-new Tea Shop Mystery from
New York Times bestselling author

LAURA CHILDS

THE TEABERRY STRANGLER

It was the Dickensian evening Thedosia Browning had
been hoping for. Charleston shop owners, dressed in
cloaks of yore, threw open their back doors to shop-
pers, who took advantage of bargains and Theodosia's
delicious teas.

But later, the alleys clear except for one body—which
a horrified Theodosia discovers. It's Daria, the map
store's owner. Locals have shown interest in buying her
shop—but enough to kill? Plus there's been a customer
hell-bent on acquiring a not-for-sale map. Most alarm-
ing of all theories, however, is Detective Tidwell's: The
killer mistook Daria for Theodosia. And if that theory
holds, the killer's work isn't done.

M583T1009

Laura Childs

FRILL KILL

For Carmela Bertrand, a New Orleans shop owner, this Halloween will feature more than the usual scares. On her way home from a ghoulish gathering, Carmela finds the dead body of a model—and is then attacked herself. As the witching hour draws closer, Carmela must find what's lurking in the shadows—or get the fright of her life.

"Delightful...Fascinating."
—*Midwest Book Review*

penguin.com

M485T0509

Introducing the
CACKLEBERRY CLUB MYSTERIES from
New York Times bestselling author
Laura Childs

Eggs in Purgatory

Eggs to go. Murder on the side.

Suzanne, Toni, and Petra lost their husbands
but found independence—and, in each other,
a life raft of support, inspiration, fresh baked
goods, and their own business. But when the
Cackleberry Club café opened its doors in the
town of Kindred, who'd have guessed that the
cozy oasis would become the scene of a crime?

M345T0510

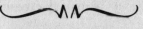
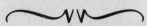